Riaan Marshall published his debut novel in early 2023. Extremely favourable reviews motivated Riaan to translate his first novel from Afrikaans into the English language as *Sucker Punch*. He lives on the Arvert peninsula in southwest France where he writes, does sculpture, surfs Atlantic Ocean waves, plays golf and loves to entertain his five grandchildren. He is a veteran of eleven marathons and a retired electrical engineer, with forty years of corporate career spanning five countries. A certified amateur writer is his second career, though his first love. Born in South Africa, where he lived for forty years, he uses each opportunity to revisit his roots.

To Frank and Thelma, who gave me life.

Riaan Marshall

SUCKER PUNCH

AUSTIN MACAULEY PUBLISHERS
LONDON * CAMBRIDGE * NEW YORK * SHARJAH

Copyright © Riaan Marshall 2025

The right of Riaan Marshall to be identified as author of this work has been asserted by the author in accordance with sections 77 and 78 of the Copyright, Designs and Patents Act 1988.

All rights reserved. No part of this publication may be reproduced, stored in a retrieval system, or transmitted in any form or by any means, electronic, mechanical, photocopying, recording, or otherwise, without the prior permission of the publishers.

Any person who commits any unauthorised act in relation to this publication may be liable to criminal prosecution and civil claims for damages.

This is a work of fiction. Names, characters, businesses, places, events, locales, and incidents are either the products of the author's imagination or used in a fictitious manner. Any resemblance to actual persons, living or dead, or actual events is purely coincidental.

A CIP catalogue record for this title is available from the British Library.

ISBN 9781035898756 (Paperback)
ISBN 9781035898763 (ePub e-book)

www.austinmacauley.com

First Published 2025
Austin Macauley Publishers Ltd®
1 Canada Square
Canary Wharf
London
E14 5AA

Glossary of Culturally Specific Terms, in Alphabetical Order

Afrikaner Brotherhood: A secret, all Protestant, Afrikaner male organisation, founded in 1918, now known as the Afrikaner Bond.

Agtemirrag: Afternoon; see the Cape Flats Dictionary (http://capeafrikaans.blogspot.com/p/cape-flats-dictionary.html)

Antie: Aunt in the sense of respectfully addressing an older woman.

Baas: Usually, a white man in charge of black or coloured workers (now considered offensive).

Beskuit: A rusk that South Africans typically enjoy with their coffee.

Biltong: Dried, cured meat (beef or game).

Boere: Police (see the Cape Flats Dictionary).

Boerewors: Meat sausage.

Boeta: A young male (see the Cape Flats Dictionary).

Boytjie: South African slang for a young man.

Checkers: A retail supermarket chain in South Africa.

Chommie: Friend (see the Cape Flats Dictionary).

Dakskroef: An offensive word for an unattractive, easy female (see the Cape Flats Dictionary).

Djirre: Lord (see the Cape Flats Dictionary).

Dominee: Afrikaans word for 'reverend' in Protestant denominations.

Finfeet: Nickname for fishermen from the Cape Town area.

Fokol: Nothing (see the Cape Flats Dictionary).

Ga-Rankuwa: Part of the former homeland of Bophuthatswana, near Pretoria.

Goudstad: Johannesburg is known as the City of Gold or Goudstad in Afrikaans.

Grasshopper: A famous brand of South African shoes.

Huisgenoot: A weekly South African Afrikaans-language general-interest family magazine sporting the highest circulation figures.

Inna: In the (Cape Flats pronunciation).

Keur: Afrikaans women's magazine.

Kleinbaas: South African term used by farm labourers for the farmer's eldest son.

Kraal: Afrikaans and Dutch word, meaning an enclosure for livestock.

Kurta: Long, loose shirt commonly worn in Asia.

Laaitie: A boy in his pre-teens or teens (see the Cape Flats Dictionary).

Lekka: Nice (see the Cape Flats Dictionary).

Oke: South African slang for a man, guy or bloke.

Oorlat: Because (see the Cape Flats Dictionary).

Matric: In South Africa, the final year of high school.

Milktart: Traditional South African sweet tart.

Moeks: Mother (see the Cape Flats Dictionary).

Mos: Afrikaans word meaning 'after all'.

Motormac: Abbreviation for a motor mechanic.

Naafi: South African military slang acronym for 'No ambition and fuck-all interest'.

Ousie: South African slang for a black woman who is a domestic worker.

Parabats: Parachute Battalion.

Patla-Patla: South African slang meaning to screw.

Reccies: South African Special Military Forces **Reconnaissance Brigade.**

Stoep: Afrikaans word for a small veranda.

Swaer: Afrikaans word for brother-in-law.

Terr: Informal abbreviation for 'terrorist' used in South African military context.

Tickey Box: Informal South African term for a public telephone.

Timothy: Song by Four Jacks and a Jill band.

Tommies: Nickname for British private soldiers in South Africa.

Transvaal: A South African province until 1994.

Tsotsi: Young urban criminal.

Valies: Inhabitants of the former Transvaal province.

Verwoerdburg: Town rebaptised as Centurion in 1995.

Voice of South Africa: The national anthem of South Africa until 1994, also known as The Call of South Africa.

One

Randgate

Figurine

Uncle Ig leads his Randgate Club boxers into the Carletonville City Hall and comes to a halt, "Take a look at that, boys."

Eddie Blignaut stops next to him, thinking, *This tournament is mine and his last chance to win the welterweight provincial champion title as a junior.* In a few months, he turns nineteen and boxes in the senior league according to South African amateur boxing rules. Looking down the town hall aisle, the ring shimmers under spotlights—a centrepiece stage rising amidst the twilight of circles of spectator seats. Sponges against the corner posts in two opposing corners are covered in red or green velvet, and there is a three-legged stool of the same colour next to the steel pan for rosin. Sponges in the neutral corners are covered in white, like the three strands of rope around the ring. A brass gong glimmers on the judges' table next to the ring. Up against one wall, a banner announces the 1975 Western Transvaal Championships.

"Come on, boys. Judging by the smell, they're baking pancakes in the annexe."

Hendrik, the Carletonville Club coach, approaches with a broad smile, "Evening, Ig. Welcome, guys." He introduces them to the host families they'll be staying with during the tournament. "See you all here tomorrow morning at the weigh-in."

*****

Eddie slips off his tracksuit and steps onto the scale. The tournament doctor moves small weights to and fro across the bar; one final tap with the finger suspends the balance lever in horizontal equilibrium and he writes 66kg next to Blignaut on his palette noteboard. Uncle Ig supervises everything through misty glasses across the rim of a polystyrene coffee cup. "Eddie," slurp, "your first fight this morning is against a guy from Rustenburg. If you win, you'll be in the quarter-finals this afternoon. See you in the dressing room in half an hour to strap your hands."

Eddie picks up his sports bag, "I'm going to win today. Now, the time is to go warm up." Following his victory in the Randgate-Venterspos interclub tournament two weeks ago, he kept on training hard and feels in top shape.

In the dressing room, he does a few stretches and shadow boxes in front of the mirror. His supple 1.8m frame dances and dodges—the bounce in his wheat brown curly hair exposing small, protruding ears as left jabs strike out and flurries of punch combinations cut the air. That's enough, his aim is in. He leans backwards and runs his fingers down over his stomach muscle six-pack. Stone hard. At the basin, he splashes cold water over his freckled face and rubs his chin and sunken cheeks where deep wrinkles spread when he smiles—like now. Soft presses on his high cheekbones: his opponents' targets, but Uncle Ig trains him how to protect them.

He appears in the dressing room entrance with a bandage roll in each hand. While carefully bandaging Eddie's hands to protect his knuckles and strengthen his wrists, he says, "Eddie, my boy, I've never seen your first opponent in action, but we mustn't underestimate him. Our plan is to win round by round with more and cleaner punches. It's your first championship fight; you're nervous, but it's his first too. Pace yourself and get the feeling of championship boxing."

Eddie follows Uncle Ig's advice and wins the fight that morning with points over three rounds. "Those three minutes of each round have never felt so short. There's just no time to waste," he remarks, back in the dressing room.

A certain Faf Viljoen from Lichtenburg also qualifies for the quarter-finals.

Uncle Ig step-presses and pulls the ropes open for Eddie to climb into the ring. Viljoen grins from the red corner. Eddie turns his back on him and throws a few determined punches against the green velvet. *Faf, I'm going to knock down your smile this afternoon*, he thinks confidently.

The rosin in the pan crunches under his boots. He bites his mouth guard out of Uncle Ig's hand. "Stay calm, Eddie, hit first. Remember, the ref does the talking. It's championship boxing."

"Right, Uncle Ig." A cold sponge presses behind his neck as the referee positions himself in the centre of the ring—white shirt and bow tie—straightened long-sleeved arms and open hands pointing towards the canvas in front of him. They take up positions there, shake hands and move back to their corners. The referee, as the gong sounds, says, "Box." Between his gloves, the man from the red corner dances closer and delivers a blast of punches into Eddie's defending arms and gloves. *Stay calm. Viljoen's defence has holes*. Eddie stacks up points with lightning-fast counter punches to the face, chest and stomach. The clock puts a stop to his own attack. Another quick three minutes. He hit with more precision than Faf. This round must belong to him.

Uncle Ig waits in his corner—shiny bald head, cauliflower ears, crooked nose, stocky shoulders, and wet sponge in his banana-bunch fingers. The other hand slips a green, three-legged corner stool through under the ropes. "The round is a draw. Eddie, use the entire ring. Hit first and force him to the ropes like you did towards the end."

Gong. He jumps up and jogs to the centre of the ring. Hit first, he remembers. One, two left jabs to the stomach force Viljoen to lower his left arm to cover, which triggers Eddie's right-hand punch to the forehead. A hammer-like blow rattles his own skull and a kaleidoscope explodes in his head—two Viljoens grin complacently. Blinded by pain, Eddie shakes his head to focus. "Stop," the referee points Viljoen to the neutral corner, runs a thumb over Eddie's brow and speaks down to the judges' table behind a cupped hand, "Head butt. Small cut." Faf gets an index finger pointed straight at him, "Red, first warning—another warning for the same foul and you're disqualified. Box."

From the green corner: "Eddie, turn southpaw." He puts his right foot forward and raises his right hand high in front of his injured eye. Punch after punch rams against his glove. *It's my eye you want, you sleaze bag*, Eddie thinks. Faf lowers his right hand for an uppercut—there's a gap: thumping bull's eye left punch to his chest. "Well done, Eddie," coming from the green corner straight left to the forehead. Cross with the right—bang on the heart. Glassy, dazed eyes look for help from the red corner. *Faf, I'll finish you now*. Right, right, block, duck, ouch you shit, right, left. On the gong, the referee dives in to separate them.

Uncle Ig slips the stool through underneath the ropes. Eddie gnashes his teeth with every stroke of the little eye iron over his brow. "Stay southpaw, Eddie.

Chase him anticlockwise. Protect your eye." A quick rub of cold Vaseline over the protruding eye as the loudspeaker crackles: Seconds out, third and last round.

The hammering of punches against his gloves and a blow to his stomach knocked a hiccup out of him. Faf's right cross flashes past his eye, just missing it. His left hook hits the mark. "Bugger you, Faf."

The referee is adamant, "Stop talking, Green. Next time, it's a warning." Knock-knock, his right hook finds Viljoen's forehead.

At the top of his voice, when the gong sounds: *There must be more time.* Faf's glove hits his watch arm, he spits out his mouthguard in the direction of his corner. "Boo, ref! Boo, ref!" the displeasure of the Lichtenburg fans echoes through the city hall—they all give a thumbs down towards the ring.

The referee collects scorecards from the three judges, having each seen the fight from a different angle, and passes it to the main judge. The referee receives a note back and motions the boxers to the centre of the ring, "The winner, on points, is green." Eddie lifts his other arm as well.

Uncle Ig pats him on the shoulder. "Well done, Eddie. You let both your fists do the talking. Viljoen was at a loss when you went southpaw. Let's go nurse your eye," he step-presses and pulls the ropes open.

On Saturday morning, Eddie goes southpaw and picks up speed from the start—he can't afford unnecessary blows to his eye. His straight rights hit the target with great regularity. Deep in the second round, Eddie is throwing punches in bunches when a towel flies into the ring. His opponent's coach decides that his boxer is enduring too much punishment. Eddie wins the semi-final fight with a technical knockout.

In the final, he fights a boxer from Coligny. Gong. "Go get him, Boer," it thunders from the Coligny corner of the hall. Boer is a difficult target. Steel grey eyes glaring over his gloves and with each of Eddie's punches, Boer's face ducks behind his rampart while he instinctively fires counterpunches. How does he break through the guy's defence? Eddie wonders.

He throws body punches as Uncle Ig instructed—having made his detailed study of Boer's style in his semi-final fight. As he sidesteps, a cramp tears through Eddie's calf. Boer's silhouette towers all the way to the spotlights. "It's a slip, no knockdown," the referee concludes, wiping off the rosin on Eddie's gloves against his shirt. Gong.

"The round is a draw. Move, Eddie. Use the whole ring; hook him left-right in the ribs. His hands will drop, you'll see."

"He's tough and I've got cramps in my legs."

"Boer is also hurting. Go get your title," he feels a firm squeeze on his shoulder and a smudge of cold Vaseline over his swollen eye as the gong sounds.

He won't disappoint Uncle Ig. Dance a little closer, head tilted to see past the swelling. Parry. Dodge. Ouch. The crack of a punch below his belt makes him gasp for breath and he hears the referee's pitched voice, "Foul, first warning." *Boer, you bugger, you hit low blows.* Eddie reads his opponent's left, sidesteps and plants a right uppercut that bends him double, leaving his chin exposed for a left cross—the direct hit wipes all expression off Boer's face. Waving ragdoll arms flap across the ring floor.

The referee's pointed index finger motions Eddie to the neutral corner, bends over the ashen face on a sea of rosin crystals and counts, "Nine…ten…Out."

His first knockout. Hopefully, they revive Boer quickly. His legs leap out of the neutral corner with the full understanding, "It's mine! Uncle Ig, I'm the champ! Payback for all my training."

"Congratulations, Eddie, my boy. I'm very proud of you." The referee waves from the middle of the ring.

"In the welterweight division, Western Transvaal champion: Eddie Blignaut from Randgate Boxing Club." He feels the referee lifting his hand. A fast trot as he circles the ring in a victory lap, past Boer's corner, where his camp is helping their man out of the ring.

Eddie jogs out of the dressing room in his Randgate Club tracksuit. Where would a tickey box be?

He finds one further down the street and turns the dial hurriedly. Someone picks up and his five cents piece slips through the slot, "Hallo, Suzette speaking."

"Hey, sis, I'm the champ!"

"Congratulations! You're my hero. I'll call Mom."

"Hi, Mom, I won the championship."

"Congratulations, my boy. I'll make you a large milktart."

Bleep-bleep. Deathly silence from the receiver.

He rubs over his swollen eye. This is what it must have felt like for Mom when Dad split her brow and Eddie could only watch, powerless. What can a young boy do against his father? *If he lifts his paws against Mom ever again, I'll beat him to a pulp.*

Eddie was about ten years old when he stuffed a few toffees into his trouser pocket in the Corner Lounge Cafe and walked out. The owner, Christos, caught up with him on the sidewalk and phoned his parents. Back home, his father's fan belt lashed his back and legs so badly that he wet his pants. Mom intervened, but a nasty backhand slap sent her reeling down the passage. A doctor colleague came to stitch up her brow, where his father's ring had ripped it open. It looked terribly sore, and Eddie's misery knew no bounds while Mom hid in their bedroom for days on end until the black around her eye had disappeared. It was the one time that Mom was assaulted in front of him. His father's usual way was to send the children to their bedrooms with orders that Eddie and Suzette close their doors, saying we have unfinished business, as he gripped Mom's upper arm and forced her into their bedroom. The key turning in the bedroom door clicked like the cocking of a revolver. Every gunshot lash from behind their bedroom door pierced Eddie's heart. He will no longer tolerate that and is also fed up with Dad's Afrikaner way of bringing up children to be seen but not heard, to carry out commands without opposition. Yes, Dad, right, Dad, okay, Dad and so to show respect for your parents—culturally conditioned not to rise up in retaliation.

He gained confidence as Uncle Ig taught him to box. About two years ago, he simply ignored Dawid's orders and did not go to his own bedroom but took up position in theirs', with clenched fists. When Dawid entered with Mom under duress, he loosened his clenched grip on her arm. "You're getting too big for your boots, you little squirt," he hissed at Eddie with contempt as he turned and left the room.

On the way home from Carletonville, his first championship trophy gleams under the small dome light of Uncle Ig's Opel Kadett—a figurine of a boxer. Tomorrow, he'll show it around in Randgate. First to his girlfriend, Charlene. Maybe he'll accept Uncle Ig's suggestion and leave it in his butchery for a few days?

He had hoped Charlene would come along to the boxing championships when he invited her earlier in the week. "Shits, no, I couldn't stand watching them beat up your face." Her thin, cool lips pressed against his ear, "You know what? Girls at my bus stop can't believe you're a boxer. They drop hints about my curly-top boyfriend with his Colgate smile and broad chin. When they get to his chocolate-brown eyes and high cheekbones, I stop them right there," holding up her hand in front of her, tongue sticking out. "Then I say I already know all that. I pretend to be deaf when they talk about the way you swagger when you walk because they look at you too much. You're mine only."

Two

Balance

The December summer holidays arrive just in time. He feels liberation from the yoke of teachers nagging about unfinished homework and snooty remarks like don't know what will become of you. He is not even going to open his standard 9 school report. Over recent months, he had a better idea of what was in every issue of *Ring* boxing magazine than in his textbooks. He never liked going to school, but the past two years were really the last straw. In his first standard nine, Dawid loses his job and starts drinking. Mom begins working the night shift to get a bonus and ensure something in the pantry. Eddie bunks at school to protect her against his father during the day, so she gets a good sleep. He flunks the year and wants to drop out of school—it's humiliating to repeat the year with boys who are younger than him.

His two bosom buddies have his back. Leon's parents get convinced that he must also repeat standard 9. Together, they argue that his birthday is in November and that he was too young when he first went to school. Peet also repeats the year, ostensibly to improve his marks. The three of them have been in the same class from standard 6 and could have been triplets except for differences when it comes to sports and girls. Leon, built like a refrigerator, wears the number eight jersey for their school's first rugby team. Frail Peet is the scrum half for the fourth team, being too much of a clown to get into the better teams. When Peet isn't chosen for the fourth team, he supports his team in a full rugby outfit and waits for his chance in case of a maul on the sideline. Then he dives in and joins in the game, hoping that when the referee notices the surplus player, he will send off someone else rather than him. Eddie, with his slender build, doesn't feel at home on the rugby field.

Leon is an Adonis with the girls, while Peet avoids them, and Eddie is going steady for the first time. Earlier in the year, the three of them came back from the Inter-High School Athletics event at Rob van Reenen stadium in Krugersdorp. In the crowded train, Eddie happened to stand across from Charlene—blond ponytails, slender nose, powder blue eyes, and thin lips. She greets him with a smile and flutters her eyelashes self-consciously. Suddenly his legs become shaky. Once or twice, their eyes meet. At Randfontein Station, he doesn't lose sight of her. On the municipal bus, he goes and sits across from her.

"What are you doing after matric?" She asks.

"Matric will never see me."

Her eyes widen, "But…I thought you were in matric?"

"Standard 9, for the second time." His face blushes with embarrassment. "Feel like a milkshake?" He tries changing the subject.

"Wow, sounds nice."

A few weeks later, he asks her to be his girlfriend. He cannot believe that they have been going steady for a full eight months.

With his swimming towel around his neck, Eddie taps against Charlene's bedroom window and hoists himself inside. Loose blonde curls, bare shoulders, sundress—a boob tube, as Suzette calls it.

"Hey, what about a swim?"

"Hey," she wrinkles her nose. "I want to wrap Christmas presents and…" Her words disappear into his mouth.

Her slim shoulders feel satin soft under his fingertips. It is not difficult to pull down the boob tube elastic. Hard nipples in his palms. She rubs his sex, and unbuttons his jeans—he senses the zip opening k-r-r-rts. What the heck is happening now after she put up a defence for months? Is she just proving her feelings before he goes to the army? Her breathing is racing and turns into a groan when he touches her. Soft hands peel the jeans from his buttocks. Quick—the Durex in his back pocket. He takes it out and tears it open.

His arms keep her wriggling body and hungry mouth in an ever-tighter grip. Fingers press rhythmically and with increasing urgency on the split below his tailbone. Thousands of ants storm out of his groin, tingle down his legs, stream up his back, branch into his arms and run down to his fingertips. Legs intertwine with his own, increasing pressure pushing down below his tailbone.

"Shits, Eddie," she heaves into him and something drops to the floor with a thump.

Five minutes, ten, maybe? His moment of ecstasy in a world enclosed by four walls. Now he knows what it feels like. What would she be thinking?

"That was nice, wasn't it?"

Her shallow hurried breath in his ear, "Terribly."

"I'm thirsty…"

"If we untangle our legs, I'll pour you a Coke."

"And then a swim?"

"First a Milky Bar. Help me straighten the bed. My mom has eyes like a detective."

He leans back on his elbows. "She doesn't like me, anyway."

"What do you mean?"

"Once she said you deserved better than a street fighter boyfriend."

"Oh, don't let it get to you. She's just making things up."

He rolls off the dishevelled bedspread and bends down to the floor. "What's this? The Happy Hooker by Xaviera Hollander."

She snatches the book out of his hand and shoves the prostitute's autobiography under the mattress. "It's nothing; it belongs to my elder sister, Gerda."

At the municipal pool, they share his swimming towel. She wriggles her nose against his. "Your army is coming and it's like a nightmare. A lot of things are going through my mind."

"I've heard recruits get a seven-day pass after three months."

"That's very long. There's shepherd's pie in our fridge. Lunch is on me."

They walk home hand in hand, sharing kisses. Every shared wink brings a blush to her light complexion.

She unlocks their front door, "Put on some music while I put the pie in the oven."

The shepherd's pie disappears from his plate. She picks at her food and pushes away her plate, "Come and look for me when you've finished."

It's the last few lyrics from Bridge Over Troubled Water. The bedroom door is slightly ajar; her arms are thrown back and one leg is pulled up over the other on the bedspread.

She is on fire, like the afternoon sun. Sweat trickles down his sides, her body glued to his. "This is how I will remember you, for every one of your army days."

She slides off him. Simon and Garfunkel start scratching again under the needle of her portable record player. She turns around, wide-eyed, lips pouting, "You didn't wear one of your thingies, but it's nice to think there's a bit of you on me. I'm yours now, anyway."

His shy girlfriend of the past eight months is completely out of control—or what? He now knows that Leon was not just bragging with, 'My girl almost makes me lose my balance when she comes.'

He holds Charlene tightly against him. "That was really awesome."

The day's events have turned his head into a melting pot. What does she mean by I'm yours now?

Three

In Confidence

On the way home, he jogs into the Corner Lounge Cafe. The latest *Ring* has pride of place on the magazine shelf.

"Hello, Christos, how are you?"

He looks up from the horse-racing columns in the newspaper. "Ah, Eddie. I'm very lonely. Angeliki and our children are in Greece for Christmas. I miss them."

"Can I take a *Ring* and pay you for everything on Saturday?" He discretely shows Christos a toffee sign. His thumb protrudes between the index and middle finger.

Christos returns his wink and fidgets a foil packet from the counter drawer. It changes ownership in their handshake. Christos finds the pencil behind his ear and scribbles in his account book. "It's OK for Saturday."

"Thanks, Christos," Eddie slips the foil packet into his trouser pocket. Next time, his Durex medal—Leon's word for condom packaging—will be readily at hand.

"Hey, neighbour," a squeaky voice pipes up behind Eddie, "feel like a game of pinball?"

"Hi, Bertus, but I don't really have time." To tell the truth, he never has time for this blabbermouth and his funny mannerisms.

"Come on. One last time? I hear you're off to boot camp one of these days?"

"OK," Eddie lifts an inquisitive eyebrow at the reins around Bertus's neck. "Where do you go horse riding?"

"At the Gerbers—I broke in their new Arabian saddle horse." A five-cent piece shoots into the air. "Heads or tails? Heads goes first."

"Heads. How did you get to go horse riding at the Gerbers?"

Bertus snaps the spinning coin between his hands. In the palm of his right hand, heads show. "My dad and Uncle Piet Gerber have known each other for years, even before he became mayor of Randfontein." The coin slips into the slot. "You go."

The spring-loaded metal arm shoots Eddie's glimmering chromed ball into play. "Nice when your dad can organise things for you." Click-clickety-click-clack. TILT-TILT-TILT the panel flickers. Damn, he shook the machine too hard, totally obsessed with Charlene's wide eyes and pouting lips.

Bertus releases his chromed ball into play. Above the metallic knocking, "Your teacher was almost in deep shit."

"Which one?"

"Olwagen."

"How so?"

"My dad says Olwagen testified in court that another car bumped into his from behind, and that landed them on the railway line in front of the oncoming train. There's no sign of another car's paint on the wreckage. My dad's constables crawled on their knees along the railway line but couldn't even find the licence or third-party discs—everything crushed with the windscreen. My dad figures the car's brakes didn't work—that Olwagen miscalculated."

"So what?"

Through tightly pursed lips, "My dad reckons Olwagen is guilty of culpable homicide. There are no other witnesses. The engine driver was on the other side of the locomotive, and the stoker was busy stoking. The court only has Olwagen's version about his wife's death."

"Culpable what?"

Between broadly pursed lips, from the corner of Bertus's mouth, "Guilty of murder by negligence, that Olwagen oke."

"Your dad is a whizz. He should be police station commander."

"Oh jeez, never," the giggle pops out like a duckling quack. With a shallow covert look, his chin almost on his chest, "He mos beat a black man to death."

"When? I haven't heard anything about it."

"Ag, it's long ago, but it's on his file forever."

"Beat him to death with a pickaxe, or—"

Nonchalantly, "With his fists."

"How can he then still be in the police force?"

"Case was thrown out of court when the witnesses didn't pitch," a squeaky giggle behind the index finger on his lips. "My dad's pals reduced them to silence." The panel flickers RECORD. Bertus lifts his chin with a self-satisfied smile and runs his fingers through his flame-red hair.

Eddie feels shaken. Sargeant Bert, as everyone in Randgate knows him, a murderer? Mom calls him Sarge Bert—what will she say when she hears that the friendly, pot-bellied giant neighbour across the street killed someone with his bare hands? It won't bother Dad—he can't stand blacks anyway.

By now, Eddie has had his fill of Bertus. "There you go, Bertus. Thanks." The *Ring* under his arm, "Cheers, Christos."

Apart from stories he'd heard at school, nobody had ever spoken to him about sex. What does it mean when you and your girlfriend have sex? What has gotten into Charlene, why is she suddenly his, now? It sounds flipping serious—is she thinking of something like marriage, maybe, or what, because he certainly isn't?

Who can he speak to in confidence?

With his dad, he won't get far. The single time Eddie tried to speak to him, man to man, his father condescendingly called him lovesick, looked away and told him to go and do something useful, like sweeping the pigeon loft. Bosom buddies won't have a clue—Leon is already sleeping with the third girlfriend and Peet is too frivolous; he keeps well away from girls.

Uncle Ig takes an interest in the things that bother Eddie and always has answers. Sometimes, he talks about his own youth, even though Eddie struggles with the idea that a wise man like Uncle Ig was once young and full of doubt. But the problem is his wife, Antie Annette. She's a gossip, according to Mom. "I should never have taken off my sunglasses in their butchery, because straight afterwards, the whole Randgate knew that Dad had cut open my eye." No, if he talks to Uncle Ig, stories would soon be going that Charlene is sleeping around and it won't be true, because until recently, she still joked that Eddie could take her virginity in exchange for a Milky Bar—her favourite chocolate.

He is stretched out on his bed. Magazine pages flip over, but his troubled mind doesn't even let in any photograph image from the *Ring* other than Carlos Monzon's upcoming fight against Rodrigo Valdez. He even gives Monzon's $50,000 prize money a second glance—you can earn good money from pro-boxing. Dust whirls up from the bedspread as he hits it with the magazine. His familiar pillow brings some consolation, but the answers won't fall from the ceiling.

He has to speak to Uncle Ig about him and Charlene.

Four

Babsie

"Hello, kids."

Like a spring, Mom's greeting lifts him straight off his bed.

In the lounge, leaning across the ball-and-claw coach armrest, he gives her a kiss on the forehead, "Still in uniform?"

Not a hair out of place. Pencilled eyebrows are as clearly drawn as when she said goodbye early this morning. Crisp white uniform. The blue name pin reads Babsie Blignaut—her pride and joy: the rank of a nursing assistant. "Hallo, my son. I'm clapped. Twelve hours on my feet—my hip is killing me."

"Why don't you go and see a doctor, Mom? It's already long since the accident."

Two summers ago, as usual, after work, she stopped to buy cigarettes at the Corner Lounge Cafe. Halfway across the street, a drunkard turned the corner and rammed into her. She believes her broken hip was God's punishment for her sinful smoking habit. She quit smoking there and then and no longer needed to listen to Dawid's reproach that she was just another holier-than-thou member of the Apostolic Faith Mission Church. The Blignauts used to be members of the Dutch Reformed Church. Shortly after their arrival in Randgate, a deacon came to introduce himself and enquire what Dad's monthly contribution to the congregation was going to be. He was out of his chair like greased lightning, running fingers through his auburn, Brylcreem-styled ducktail haircut and rolling up his sleeves, "Sonny Boy, I work for myself. I'm a building contractor with a wife and two kids to support. Where would I get money for the church?" The deacon was still reading Leviticus aloud about the tithe when he was helped out through the front door with the Bible and all, Dawid's freckled face a grimace of contempt from Eddie's viewpoint on the coach where Mom made he and Suzette sit, awaiting the churchman. Mom remained in the Dutch Reformed Church until

Eddie and Suzette had finished their catechism. Then she started attending the AFM services.

"No, Eduard. Last time, the doctor wanted to board me on the spot. I've got to keep working to pay for Suzette—it's her dream to go to a secretary's college. Your father says he's got a building contract the one day and I find out it's a pie in the sky the next. He's totally unreliable."

"No worries, Mom. I'm going to turn boxing-pro. There's a lot of money in that. Want some tea?"

"Please, and a beskuit. Lunchtime feels like years ago."

He puts on the kettle and arranges a few rusks on a small plate. He stretches out his arms to find the kitchen table behind him. Mom is right; he tries to remember…Father's first pie-in-the-sky project was at the beginning of his first standard 9 year. His biggest project tender yet, and he brags that he's going to get it: a housing complex for the aged in Randfontein. His story soon changes: he accuses the municipality of being pally-pally when awarding the tender because they apparently get kickbacks from other building contractors. Father's castle in the air does not materialise and he is jobless. Home alone, he starts drinking. This leads to new, disagreeable experiences in the Blignaut household: Eddie finds it disgusting to see his father drunk day after day.

The kettle spout blows a cloud of steam.

On a tin tray, he carries a glass of Coke, tea, and rusks into the lounge. There is room for it on the coach between them.

"Thanks." Mom blows on her tea and sips, "You make a nice cup of tea."

Now, he must choose his words carefully, "I want to ask you a favour, Mom."

"Ask away?"

Sitting on the edge of the coach, he pulls back his shoulders. "Three rand for Christmas presents and a few things for the army please, Mom." He needs five, but how can he ask her for more? Tomorrow he'll find out from Uncle Ig if he can lend a hand in his butchery, The Meat Cauldron, for a few rands.

"Tomorrow is payday. Come and see me at the hospital over lunchtime, then I'll have your three rand."

"Jeez, thanks, Mom." Another kiss on the forehead. "I'm going to read my *Ring* again. You should hear what Monzon is getting for his fight against Valdez."

"How much?"

"Fifty thousand dollars." The last of the Coke disappears from his glass. "The day I get that kind of money, you won't have to work anymore. Promise."

A brave smile unfurls under the beehive hairstyle; her right eyelid limp because of the scar where father's knuckle-duster ring dug in, "You shouldn't make promises just like that. Please give me my storybook—right there, on the radiogram."

He presses the Mills & Boon down on his heart, "Mom, I promise. Night."

"Goodnight, my son."

Five

Antie Annette

The Meat Cauldron's clients are queuing out the door.

"Sorry, excuse me, sorry." He shuffles in, circling carefully around the long neck fan drying out the biltong, and goes behind the counter.

"Afternoon, Uncle Ig looks busy. Can I help?"

"Hello, Eddie. I've got half a cow carcass to dress. Come tonight at six, just before closing time."

"I'll be here."

Heat waves are dancing on Charlene's corrugated iron roof. The stained-glass front door is ajar. He walks in after a soft knock, floorboards creaking under his feet.

A shadow from the passage falls across the hallway. He whistles softly, "Prettiest girl in the entire Randfontein."

Riebeeck High School's Carnival Queen in high heels, hot pants, and sports vest.

She's making her mark on the town. Nothing good ever comes out of Randgate, the story goes—Randfontein's rich live in the Greenhills or Homelake neighbourhoods, but you can't buy beauty, Eddie feels. Charlene says they have the same backstreet roots and when they walk down Randfontein's main street together on a Saturday morning, she notices how both get looks from rich boys and girls with their hands full of shopping bags.

Arms lock around his neck, her tongue furrows into his mouth.

"You alone?"

"Everyone's working. Gerda's coming to fetch me for Christmas shopping just now." With his hand in hers, he follows her down the passage into her room.

*****

"I've never stripped off my clothes this quickly. Gerda will add two plus two when she sees wrinkled clothes and—"

"Get one on one as a result."

Her body arches upwards one more time. Arms open wide, eyes shut, pink, blushing cheeks, "So nice."

In the kitchen, between sips of Coke, "Your hair looks stunning, how do you get it like that?"

"Sleep with curlers."

"How can you sleep with such things in your hair?"

"I fold the pillow double. Remember, not everyone is blessed with natural curls like you."

He flattens his hair with his hands to the back of his head, "Will you still like me with short-back and sides? I heard that in the army, they stick in the hair clipper in front and then lift it up when they get to your neck."

"Oh, you're too cute with your clear face and little jug ears. Your chin looks even broader. Do you really have to go away from me?"

His anguish gets the better of him, "How are you feeling? I mean, you're not pregnant or…?"

"I don't feel nauseous. Gerda says that's the sign. So, I'm not." A car engine roars outside in the driveway. "That's her. I'm already wearing her shoes—so I suppose I can quickly pinch some lipstick?"

*****

Cash box in hand, Antie Annette battles to open the mesh screen door, "Glad you're coming to help, Eddie Otherwise, my dear husband will be busy with that carcass till midnight. I'll bring supper just now."

He gets handed a butcher's apron as he walks in. "Give your hands a good scrub, Eddie."

The refrigerating chamber causes goosebumps on his arms. Uncle Ig sharpens his butcher's knife, zert-zarts-zert. "You take hold of the hind leg."

The half carcass waddles between them out of the refrigerating room. Under the bandsaw, it becomes a forequarter and a hindquarter. Back to the refrigerating room. First cuts.

"What can I do, Uncle Ig?"

"Put the pieces of side flank into the dish right at the end, then come and hold on here."

Get a firm grip. Stand strong. Zeep-zip-zeep, the handsaw works its way. How should he put the question? Four T-bones go into the next dish. With his back to Uncle Ig. "What does Uncle think about girls?"

"Like women, you mean?"

"Well, yes. Girls are also women, aren't they? Do they all think the same?"

A sly smile mixes with the zeep-zip-zeep. "Eddie, I find it difficult to understand a woman from one day to the next."

"What does a girl mean when she says she's yours now…Is it like being married?"

"No, Eddie. When a man marries, you become hers. For life…or at least for a very long time." The zeep-zip-zeep picks up speed.

Another heap of T-bones arrives. "You see, Uncle since the first time we …" If he comes out with that now, Randgate tongues will be wagging tomorrow.

The shining, bald head appears above the beef leg, followed by the cauliflower ears and thick-rimmed glasses, with the tip of a butcher's knife between thumb and index, "Careful, my boy, a drop of that stuff can make you a father. But you young guys know that. Don't you?" A father? No, damn it. His legs have suddenly turned to jelly. He shuffles towards Uncle Ig and props up the carcass with his shoulder, his knuckles white around the heel tendon. "You see, Uncle Ig …" More meat arrives and pieces of short fillet to put on the table. "I know. But I mean…things happen fast."

"Eddie, in my young days in the back of a 1941 Ford, I pulled off her panty." Grrrts-grrrts as the knife point tracks down the cartilage between the carcass knuckles. "She tried to stop me. Then I tore the panty, and she kicked out the car window. Thank God, otherwise, I could have been married to an alcoholic today. That's according to old Theuns, of Randgate Liquor. These are rump steaks."

Why didn't he jump out of Charlene's window? He could have quickly gone to Christos for a Durex medal. Whatever happens, Uncle Ig will understand. And he'll help.

"You and Charlene look very much in love when you stroll past the butchery." A deep red blush starts spreading behind the thick-rimmed glasses.

Should he tell Charlene that he spoke to Uncle Ig about the two of them? He feels better now, but she'd be upset because her mother might hear their story. When it comes to such serious subjects between them, his own words just dry up. He is comfortable chatting to her about school subjects such as friends, teachers or the ongoing archrivalry on the rugby field between his technical school, Jan Viljoen, and Riebeeck High, the posh academic school on the other side of the railway track. Like one Saturday morning after the last winter holiday, over a milkshake at the Corner Lounge café. "What's the news from Riebeeck?"

She pulls her hands out of his and makes circles next to her temples. "Rugby and netball—the place is obsessed with sport. If you don't play sport, you're just nothing. That's how the teachers pass their time. Can you imagine me on the netball court with that bunch of broad-beamed girls?"

"The netball girls don't look so big to me."

"I mean, when they talk, I hear them bragging how they bum the girls of the other teams," she giggles. "They bump one another. Apparently, you're not allowed to touch the opponent with your hands."

"Oh." Eddie laughs. "So, a bum in netball is like a tackle in rugby? In Jan Viljoen, guys are picked for team matches because their dads invite the schoolmaster on hunting safaris and because together, they serve on the church council. Probably as well in cahoots inside that clandestine Afrikaner Brotherhood, my father reckons. I rather box. You get out what you put in. That's what I call fair."

"Aren't you scared?"

"Scared of what?"

"Of getting hurt; the guys hit hard." She reaches across the table and gently strokes his forehead, temples and down his cheeks.

"In the ring, I don't feel a thing." He gets up and comes back with a Keur magazine. The two of them page through it, look at what readers have written in the Lonely-Hearts Column and check their horoscopes.

"Capricorn: Your hard work will be rewarded," she reads. "You see, it's for your Western Transvaal champs, one of these days."

Charlene's acknowledgement of his training and her encouragement boosts his confidence; if only she knew how much guts it takes inside the ring to win.

The telephone starts ringing in the customer section of the butchery.

"Eddie, get the phone, please. It's Annette who's telling us she's coming over with supper—you can already open the Yale lock for her."

He pushes open the butchery door, "Antie, let me take the tray." A curry smell gives a hint about what is hiding under the gauze cloth. Eddie can hear his tummy rumbling.

"Thanks, the stuff is damn heavy. Put it down on my cashier's table over there and tell Ig that supper is ready."

They rinse their hands and come into the butchery. "This looks delicious, Antie Annette." Three bowls of curry and rice, a polystyrene cup with sliced banana, another with desiccated coconut and three more filled with milk. The cash register has been shifted to one side, with the drawer open, as Eddie can see through the window in the evening when he comes out of Uncle Ig's gym across the street. The butchery looks different now from the inside than it does in the afternoons when he sometimes slips inside hoping for a piece of dried sausage. Then, she stands guard over the cash register, behind a layer of plastered make-up and glasses with purple rims and corners like butterfly wings. The same colour of hair, lipstick, and nail polish.

"Let me spoil you while I can, 'cos very soon, Uncle's boxing boy is going away to the army. You can leave your Western Transvaal Championship trophy here with me again, next to the cash register. It is so nice when people ask who the champion is, but Ig always answers from behind the counter before I can get a word in. So, now I already tell our clients when they walk into the butchery; I don't think there's anyone in Randgate who doesn't know we have a boxing champion."

Past a cheek stuffed with food, "That's right, Antie. The trophy is on its way."

When all three bowls are empty, she strokes her purple hair, "You two want to work, and my Dallas television series is about to start."

The clock on the wall shows 10 pm when Ig's key turns in the Yale lock, "Come and get three rand from the Antie tomorrow."

"Thanks, I will. Good night, Uncle Ig."

What a relief, with Mom's three rand, he now has six. It should be enough for Christmas gifts and a few things for the army.

Six

Sammy

"Nursing assistant Blignaut, please. I'm her son."

The receptionist at the Robinson Hospital dials a number.

"Now, I also know the Eddie you're always bragging about," she comments when Mom comes in.

"Thanks, Mom." Three bank notes disappear into his trouser pocket as he hurries to the door. A shudder ripples through his shoulders. So many sick and dying people in this place.

A group of commuters are already waiting at the bus stop; that means the next bus into town is on its way.

A little more than an hour later, he is back at the Randfontein Station bus stop. Just in time, or he will have to wait a full thirty minutes for the next bus—time he can spend with Charlene. He boards—there is a seat free behind a stout woman and a little boy with a home-shaven short-back-and-sides head. Eddie's shopping bags from CNA and Checkers fit in underneath their seat. A metallic scratching noise fills the bus as the driver pulls away and tries to find second gear. Roller coaster tummy across the train bridge to the stop in front of Riebeeck High School, where a few passengers get off. The bus heads back to the road, then screeches to a standstill. The driver's head is halfway out the window, "Fuck you, you think it's your road?" Two fingers lift in the direction of the black driver's overcrowded Valiant taxi: his eyes popped like two big white balls.

From the seat in front of Eddie. "Mister, mind your language." Her shoulder jerks indignantly, sending a ripple through her thickset neck. "There are children on the bus," followed by, "Bloody arsehole…" under her breath, as she pulls the little boy into the warmth of his grandmother's protection.

When the Randgate bus stop comes into sight, the youngster escapes from his seat and stands ready at the door, Pep Store parcels in each hand. The busman gets a friendly smile.

Eddie jogs the steps down out of the bus. Home quickly, now, then go and buy his dad's present. He gets a foothold and hops in through his bedroom window. He shoves the parcels under his bed and is out through the window again. Where in the yard did he keep his bicycle the last time? Aha, in the garage.

The chain creaks down their driveway as he leaves the garage behind him. It sings down Lazar Avenue in the direction of Wheatlands, to Patel General Dealer located just outside the white residential area. Randgate is a working-class neighbourhood on the outskirts of Randfontein. The streets here are narrow and the plots are small, with houses built almost within an inch of the street. From the sidewalk, you take the few steps leading directly onto the red polished porch and through the front door into the hallway, with the vestibule on the left and the first bedroom on the right. Sometimes, it's the other way around. The steel cottage-style windowpanes have all been painted the same colour as the gutters of the house. Here and there is a house with painted walls—mostly white—the rest sport walls of yellow clay brick. Some houses date from the forties and still have a coal stove in the kitchen, like that of his friend, Peet.

He leans his bicycle carefully against the row of shiny new Humber thick-wheel bicycles, strung together with a piece of string, on the veranda of Sammy Patel's shop.

"Afternoon, Antie Amelia."

"Hallo, Eddie. Almost time for boot camp, hey?" Long, pink nails drum leisurely rhythms on the counter.

There was a real hullabaloo in Randgate when she started working for Sammy. Mom was protective of her neighbour. "It's not that Amelia wants to work for a coolie, but when she tried to get work as a cashier at Checkers, they asked for her qualification papers. She couldn't find her standard seven school certificate anywhere."

Sammy comes into his shop from the backyard, "Hello, how can I help Mistel Eddie today, you want some pigeon feed?"

"Hello, Sammy. A pipe please."

Sammy steadies a ladder against shelves overflowing with tinned foods and condensed milk, milk powder, boxes of jelly, oats porridge, bags of cornmeal and a colourful shelf containing canned fruit bottles filled with spices. Two horse saddles hang high up above Sammy's head, tied to the rafters with rope. Something is taken from a box between bags of tobacco, "I've got these thlee pipes left, Mistel Eddie."

The first time Eddie came through Sammy's shop was when he went into the backyard with his dad to go and scoop pigeon feed from a 44-gallon drum, next to bags of cement, car tyres, cans of Castrol engine oil, boxes of Champion spark plugs, a shelf full of flower seed and bulbs and tins of cooking oil. "The coolie's pigeon feed is expensive, but his mix is better than the pet shops' and he's open till six o'clock in the evening." Dad justified himself as he filled his own cooking oil tin and trouser pockets while glancing enviously at where Sammy's Mercedes Benz was parked under a canopy.

Eddie swallows a giggle, "The pipe on the left, please." It never ceases to amuse him when Sammy's round, pouty lips replace the R in a word with an L.

Black slip-on leather sandals feel their way down the ladder steps.

A cream-coloured kurta floats past Eddie towards the cash register. He pays and says goodbye.

"Melly Chlistmas, Mistel Eddie," his wrinkled cheeks pucker behind half-moon spectacles perching on the tip of his nose, above the overbite of his gold-plated front teeth. "And as well, to Mistel Dawid."

"I'll tell my father."

With the pipe safely in his trouser pocket, he walks towards his thick-wheel bicycle.

"Oh, hello, Eddie."

Standing at the entrance to the fabric shop, Sammy's wife tugs self-consciously at the shoulder piece of her pink sari, "Merry Christmas and also to Madam Babsie. Please tell her that my New Year sale starts on January 2. Lay-by is OK."

Rashida's Scratch Patch is Mom's idea of heaven. "Merry Christmas, Rashida. I'll tell my mom. Bye." Lay-by—that's how Dad bought his thick-wheel bicycle from Sammy when he still won building contracts. Nowadays, being at home during the day, from his drunkard's point of view, Mom gets accused that she works in the front garden just to attract the attention of men walking past and so he forbids her to do any gardening. She began doing needlework as a pastime and discovered Rashida's shop when Antie Amelia started working for Sammy. Now that Eddie's got something for Mom, Dad,

Suzette and Charlene, he feels ready for Christmas. He'll ask Suzette to help him with the wrapping.

There's something obstinate in his gait as he pedals home, stroking the rimmed bulge in his back pocket. He still wants to stop at Charlene's. For the past school year, military service felt like a godsend. Now he catches himself counting the days left and trying to make them last forever until he must report for army duty.

How could he have become so attached to Charlene?

Seven

Suzette

"Merry Christmas," Mom's voice calls out, as she knocks for each syllable on his bedroom door.

In the lounge, wisps of steam curl out of the coffee mugs. Mom opens the curtains, and the morning sun reflects on the varnished slate floor. Dad's handiwork—one of the few resolutions that he could keep after he and Mom were able to buy this house from an insolvent estate. Dawid knocked out the cement floor and laid the slate. The radiogram's loudspeakers scratch incessantly as he turns the knob, hesitates a moment as he finds a Christmas devotional message, then turn-turn again and settle with Afrikaans folk music tunes. Suzette rubs her eyes as she yawns and goes to sit down on the pouffe, the toes of her one foot folding over the other, ponytail askew to one side. Mom straightens her dressing gown and takes her seat on the ball-and-claw coach. The burgundy material was bought in Rashida's shop and the upholstery itself was her first major needlework project.

The morning breeze makes the lace curtain billow and the Christmas decorations rustle. "Merry Christmas, Sis, for Dad…and for Mom." Suzette gets a kiss on the forehead, Dad a handshake and Mom a kiss as well.

Her fingers wiggle through his hair. "Will you play Father Christmas?" A small mound of presents is waiting under the Christmas tree.

The crackling and tearing of paper sound with the decorations' rustling: he gets a Swiss jack-knife from Mom and Dad, Suzette, a make-up set. She gives Mom the latest Mills & Boon and Dad gets a cigarette lighter. From Eddie, he gets a pipe and Mom, a small bottle of Charlie perfume, chosen on Suzette's recommendation.

Yesterday, she couldn't help crying while helping to wrap presents. "You're letting me down, big brother. Dad is just waiting for you to go off to the army, and then it's me and his wandering fingers again. After a few tots of brandy, he turns into a pig." Hunched shoulders, arms crossed protectively over her breasts, fountain-like ponytails quivering on the sides of her head. The pitch of her voice became hysterical and her freckled face flushed red, "Why are you leaving me alone with him, and what about Mom?" But what is he supposed to say? He is not just running off; compulsory military service for white men of eighteen or older is law, and that includes him. Guys who do not accept an assault weapon forced into their hands are jailed, or worse, declared crazy. Schizophrenic and unfit for military service, like old Wynand Pretorius whom Eddie thought crazy for a long time—vroom-vroom-vroom scooting around Randgate on his thick-wheeled Humber bicycle. Eddie is not crazy, and he is not going to jail. He'll ask Sergeant Bert from across the street for help during his absence. One can mos trust a policeman.

"I'll think of a plan, Sis." Then he wrapped the last present on his own.

Her eyes sparkle when she opens it. The Parker pen rolls between her fingers.

"It's for writing matric, Sis."

She leans over. "Thanks, traitor." He gets a wallet from her.

Mom blows on the coffee in her mug, "I'm going to church, who's coming with me?" There is such expectation in her voice that Eddie nods in agreement, even though he feels confused about her Apostolic Faith Mission Church with all its new sins like drinking strong liquor and dancing. Smoking too. But didn't Jesus drink wine, and didn't King David dance? He did, and it was quite a wild dance too, because people could see his balls. So, when did such pleasures turn into sins, then? Still confuses Eddie.

Suzette looks half asleep. "I'm also going. At what time are we leaving? I still have a dress to iron."

"Quarter to nine. I'll quickly put the leg of mutton in the oven."

After Christmas lunch, Eddie's feet rush him to Charlene's porch. He knocks softly on the stained-glass door. She emerges from the passage with a finger on her lips and nods her head in the direction of their kitchen.

"Merry Christmas, Charlene," he pulls a seven-single record from behind his back.

"Oh, The Hollies…The Air that I Breathe—that's what you are to me. This is for you."

She takes a present out of one of the kitchen cupboards. "Merry Christmas and congratulations."

"With what?"

Her voice in his ear gives him goosebumps, "You're not going to become a father."

"How do you know?"

"Gerda showed me in her old biology textbook—the workings of the twenty-eight-day female cycle."

"You flippin' sure?"

Her eyelashes flutter, "My twenty-eight-day cycle started just days before we did."

"Okay." One thing less to worry about in the army. Now, he's got to find a way to protect Mom and Suzette from Dawid during the year that he'll be away.

Eight

Sergeant Du Plessis

Eddie is almost breaking into a run as he lengthens his stride on the way to the police station. "Good morning," as he enters. Constable Marais on the police officer's brass name pin. On the concrete slab counter, he opens a book that reminds of a school exercise book.

"Hello. How can I help you?" With an orange-coloured Bic pen, he writes 30 December 1975 on the first faint blue line of a clean page and tops it with a South African Police stamp.

"I'm Eddie Blignaut. I'm looking for Sergeant du Plessis?"

"He's in the back, in the mortuary. I'll call him for you." He writes Eddie Blignaut on the next line of the page, "Before I forget your name."

Bertus's father fills the door frame with feigned fright: he has widened his eyes, his shiny, round cheeks are puffed up, his chin is lowered on his chest and his hands are cradling his potbelly, prepared to hear the worst. "Good day, Eddie. What's the matter?" A brass name pin glistens just above his stomach against the dark blue, safari suit uniform: Sergeant Du Plessis.

"Nothing serious is the matter. Can I see you, Sergeant, quickly?"

"Come in here, the captain is at John Vorster Square today."

Eddie follows. How the hell should he begin? "You see, Sergeant, I'm leaving for the army very soon…"

"Bertus told me. Have you come to say goodbye?"

"That too, but you see, Sergeant…It's my father, Sergeant. He hits my mom."

"Slow down, I'm trying to understand. If something like that happens, you phone the police station. Then a constable goes out and takes down a charge of assault."

"But you live just across the street…"

"Eddie, at home, I'm off duty. Then I have no jurisdiction."

"Even in uniform?"

"Even in uniform."

"Oh. But, while I'm away in the army, can you go and say hello now and then? Like neighbours do. Suzette will make tea and tell you if there's a problem. Please."

"OK, I'll walk across now and then. Bertus can chat with your sister."

Oh, damn. Then the entire Randgate will get to know what's happening behind the Blignaut's front door. But it's the best he can do for now.

"Thanks, Sergeant. I'll tell my mom and Suzette. Goodbye."

"Good day, Eddie. Good luck in the army."

With the Bic pen in his hand, "What must I write down in the charge book, Sergeant?"

"Nothing, Constable. Tear out the page."

Through the bus windscreen, the Randgate bus stop comes into view. Eddie jumps out and jogs in the direction of the Meat Cauldron.

He says goodbye in a hurry, but Uncle Ig doesn't let go of his hand. "Carry your gloves high, Eddie, my boy. You're fighting seniors now."

"Will do. See you, Uncle, on my seven days. Bye Antie Annette."

A last visit to Charlene now. How is he going to get through the army without her? He'll just have to work the gears himself, as Leon puts it.

There's a tickly sensation in his crotch as her house comes into sight.

Nine

Bloemfontein

Goodbye

Dusk suddenly fills the train.

Charlene's head lifts from his shoulder, "Where are we?"

"Johannesburg Station," he reads the signage. The ride from Randfontein felt so short.

A wave of commuters breaks onto the platform and washes up the staircase.

He hesitates on the last step. Charlene's hand clutches his even tighter. He has never seen such a big station building. A huge wall clock shows a quarter past eight. The air is humming with voices, heels click-clacking across the marble floor.

He nods his head to the right, "We must follow that poster."

"Infantry Battalion intake: Platform 13. Is that you?"

"Yup." He ducks left and right, steering her deftly through the mass of people.

"I'm not going to wait around. I won't embarrass you with my crying."

"I'm going to miss you terribly. Study hard at school so you can become a teacher." Her tears have a salty taste. "It's better than being a mechanic. Think of me, wait for me."

She motions to dry his mouth and he backs away from her hand. "Now, there's also a bit of you on me."

Their intimate moments flash through his mind, quickly followed by shadows of doubt, "You will still be mine, won't you?"

"Yours only."

That's all he wanted to hear.

Platform 13 is swarming with crying mothers, aspiring military servicemen and broad-chested fathers: their sons are going to defend the country.

Charlene's hand still clings to his. A poster announcing B comes into sight. Men in uniform everywhere. He shuffles forwards.

"Good day, private. Your call-up papers, please?" Black eyes glare below the beret, dart over the call-up instructions, short cut frizzy hair, barely visible. A muscle twitches in the man's cheek. Is he smiling or grimacing, like John Wayne in Rio Lobo? This is definitely a different story from his favourite movie. The muscled arm shoots past below his nose, three stripes on the short sleeve, the hand open, thumb retracted, and fingers straight, "That carriage over there is yours, Private Blignaut. The little lady can say her goodbyes right here."

"OK, bye. Write to me, will you?" A peck barely touches his cheek.

He clambers into the train coach, turns to look back and wants to return the tiny kiss she blows him, but is pushed inside by the shoving in his back.

"Howzit? I'm Eddie." Danie…Hannes…Rob.. Wilfried…Dirk…Michael Carlo…the compartment of faces answer in a round of handshakes. Two sound English; the one with the long hair must be Italian or German—pinkish red cheeks that remind him of Suzette's plastic doll.

Claustrophobia drives him to where Wilfried is sitting. "I can't breathe. Could we swap seats?"

"I smoke. It's better if I'm seated at the window.'

"Sorry, my English is not good 'cos it's only for own use. I mean, I can't breathe."

"O-n-n your hind legs, fucking civvies! Forget that pussy that clung to you like a clam on the platform," it roars from just outside the compartment. Three stripes appear in the doorway. "You're state property now, soldier."

A cheek muscle twitches. The grimace again. "Woolly Head, pull down that screen in front of the window, don't want the enemy counting my troops."

What enemy, except you? Eddie feels less claustrophobic with his eyes closed.

The snoring wakes him up. Platform 13 feels like hours ago. Charlene must be back in Randgate by now. A tiny flame lights up the sleeping faces. The glow of the cigarette cherry turns from yellow to red. A flash of light cleaves the wisps of smoke and strikes the window seat: "You fucking cunt, you're a fire hazard to my troops. Fall in right here, in the corridor. Go down for push-ups 'til I say stop. You."

Eddie bats his eyelids against the flashlight.

"Count your little friend's push-ups."

"Twenty, twenty-one…" Push-ups are easy. So, what's Wilfried's problem?

The lighting flashes over his back. "Push-ups, you smoker. You look as though you're screwing a mouse. Now what?"

Wilfried is panting—white as a sheet, pinkish cheeks stained a deep red.

Three Stripes prevents Eddie's attempt to help. "Get up," growls from behind the flashlight. The straw-coloured head of shoulder-length hair rises up from the linoleum. A drop of blood lingers at the tip of Wilfried's sharp nose. It splashes down on the floor and another one.

"Your next smoke break is on your seven days if you're still breathing by then."

A crisp white handkerchief folds open in Wilfried's hands. He wipes his nose and stares dumbfounded at the red smudge. Dabs under his nose with the handkerchief again.

Eddie relaxes his fists. Stay calm; even though he could floor Three Stripes on the spot.

"Soldiers, here's a trunk with rat packs. Come, get one, and a bottle of Coke. Then go sit on your arse and eat."

The fizzy taste of dry cookies and Coke reminds of brown bread lunches with Suzette. She's eating alone now. A Traitor. How can his sis think that of him?

The train shudders to a halt.

"Fall in a file where the Bedfords are," booms down the corridor.

Red dust rises where men pile out of the carriage and land, bunching together before scurrying away to the lorries. Eddie scrambles onto the back of one indicated to him with an open hand, straight fingers and retracted thumb—Rex, he reads at a glance on the name tag, a short, burly soldier with sturdy thick neck and two stripes on his upper sleeve. Beret plastered down the right side of his angular head.

The Bedford comes to a standstill. From under the tarpaulin, Eddie makes out the silhouette of a warehouse. The lorry's back flap is thrown open. Poor lighting shines on the officer with the two stripes, creating shaded facial features of a pug dog, "Get out." When the order comes, they all line up for bread and sweet, black coffee. A rumble from deep down in his tummy reminds him of suppertime in Randgate. It feels so far away.

He queues along with all the others for a blanket, sheet and pillow.

Corporal Rex marches the lot of them out of the warehouse, "I'm taking you to the barracks." An asbestos building looms ever closer. Eddie is greeted by stuffy, warm air. He quickly picks a bed in front of a window—here, he could breathe. Wilfried and Hannes have landed up with him in the same platoon.

The guys introduce themselves. "See you men at six tomorrow morning," their corporal yells as he marches out of the barracks, again raising the image in Eddie's mind of Sergeant Bert's pet pug dog: wrinkly, short-muzzled face as if it ran into a wall.

Later, the barracks are dark and silent. The coir blanket has a stuffy, musty smell. It's that time of day when he used to think about everything they did together and look forward to seeing Charlene the next day. Often, he couldn't wait till the next day and would jog by her house on his way back from boxing practice to give her a goodnight kiss. When she took her bath at night, she locked the bathroom door and opened the window for him to climb through. What could she be doing now?

Nothing as nice as that will happen in a place like this, where you are told when to eat or sleep or get up—and this is only his first day here. No personal choices. The realisation sticks in Eddie's gizzard; he never felt himself to be a rebel, but now it is affecting his humanity. It's beyond humiliating.

Ten

Longing

The fearsome howl of a siren pierces the barracks as though coming from right outside the window above Eddie's head.

"What the fuck…" mutters from underneath Wilfried's blanket in the bed next to his.

Six o'clock is barely visible on Eddie's wristwatch, "Sounds like the war has started." Daylight bursts into the barracks.

Corporal Rex stands etched in the door frame, "Soldiers, out of your pissing skins. I'll be back in half an hour. Shitting and shaving done, you'll be standing next to your bed for inspection. I'm not mobilising a bunch of dirtbags." After breakfast, Rex's halt order brings Platoon Bravo to a standstill in front of the gymnasium. "Go in, take a conscription mobilisation form on the table and go sit on your butt."

Eddie can't believe what he sees: a boxing ring like in Randgate—where Charlene is now on her way to school. Is she also thinking of him?

Rex yanks him back to reality, "In de square at de top, you write January 1976."

Eddie works through the mobilisation form and hears that the tickey box is out of bounds and that after a month, he'll be allowed to send his first letter home. How is he going to survive without news from Charlene? And from Suzette—is father behaving himself with her and Mom? Yesterday morning, when he said his goodbyes, she was all tears, "Oh, Eduard, I am so sorry, I couldn't get leave today." His peck on her forehead felt like the kiss of Judas—deserting home and leaving her and Suzette behind; Sis already considers him a traitor. But, the army is law and was he not branded for compulsory military service now, it would definitely have been for the next intake in July. Sergeant Bert is keeping an eye; he assured Mom. Or was he just trying to excuse himself? Damn, why should he be forced to defend his country when he just wants to protect Mom and Suzette against Dawid?

Rex drills them all the way to the barber. Eddie catches a glimpse of three men in white barber jackets outside a small asbestos building, each with one stripe on the upper sleeve. "Atterbury, Blignaut…' Rex reads from a list of names, "Climb up for a cut."

The three One Stripes put out their cigarettes and walk into the building with Eddie on their heels. He gets onto the first chair. The hair clipper vibrates through his skull. Minutes later, the One Striper lifts the white cloth off his shoulders. What a relief that Charlene won't see the guy in the mirror with his bald head and jug ears. Ouch, he misses her so much. He jumps off the barber's chair.

"Next lady for a shave," rings out from the door behind him.

"Bucholz," something between a bark and a howl cleaves the air—Rex makes a tick on his clipboard. Wilfried steps out of the platoon. Wheat brown hair bounces on his shoulders as he marches past. He appears in the door minutes later, unrecognisable.

That afternoon, during the drill exercise on the parade ground, Rex catches Eddie looking around. "That troopie with the Dumbo ears looking around like an ousie searching for firewood in the veld, your pals are getting running exercise because of you. Fuckoff around the camp, on the double." Eddie feels blistering hot under the collar, "Damn sorry, guys." He shoots a sidelong glare towards Rex: right hand stroking down his beret, protruding marble eyes, spiteful grin revealing the tip of his tongue, bloody pug.

Even though, it's Eddie's chance to get to know the camp. Leading his platoon from the parade ground to the left of the camp gate, coming in, the mess hall follows—huge galvanised chimneys protruding through the corrugated iron roof. Onwards past the quartermaster general's warehouse where he had bread and coffee last night. Further on, sawtooth-like roofs come into sight that remind him of the apprentice workshops at Jan Viljoen Technical High School. Save for learning the motor mechanic trade, he detested school. All that now feels idyllic compared to this.

Double pace into a right turn, he leads his platoon all along the hedge. Outside the barber's, the three lance corporals stand in a cloud of cigarette smoke. The medical station where they were vaccinated this morning looks deserted. He takes the group of panting breaths past asbestos-walled offices: Lieutenant, Regiment Sergeant Major (RSM), Staff Sergeant, Sergeant,

Corporals, he reads the descending ranks on the door nameplates. They turn for the last time around the guardhouse and the tickey box. Rex obviously felt like smoking. On the parade ground, he is just busy putting out his cigarette butt.

Shortly before five that afternoon, the order to halt sounds in front of their barracks. At half past five, Rex marches his Platoon Bravo to the mess hall.

Lights have already been out for a long time. Above Eddie's bed, stars come and go as the curtain tangoes with the evening breeze. His body is asking for Charlene's. What would she be doing now?

*****

The longing devours him. Memories of their intimate moments drag his thoughts down a whirlpool of bloody jealousy and overwhelming possessiveness. It feels like weeks since he posted Charlene's letter with Mom's and Suzette's. He didn't write anything that could be considered treason, did he? So, they wouldn't have burnt his letters like Corporal Rex is always threatening to do. Why doesn't she write? And why not Mom and Suzette?

In the mornings after drill practice, they hand out mail. Blignaut lets him step out of his platoon and march eagerly to the front of the podium.

"Get down for fifty."

He does his push-ups…forty-nine, fifty; he takes his letter from Rex, presses it against his left side and marches back. In the platoon, he dares to look down: Charlene's handwriting causes a tingling in his loins.

At last, he gets time to read, back in the barracks.

Dear Eddie,

I miss you, the days without you are long. How are things with you in the army? Randgate is not the same without you here. I miss you terribly. It feels as though you could jump in through my bedroom window any minute. I wish you would, even though it would give me a fright. It's going well at school. Matric is a lot of work. You must be a good soldier.

Hugs and kisses. All my love, Charlene xxx.

She feels like he does. "I can't wait to see my girlfriend."

"Hang in there, Eddie. Seven days are coming up," says Wilfried without looking up from his letter.

Eddie folds Charlene's letter back into its envelope.

One morning, even before the siren sounds outside the barracks, Rex's voice reaches the octaves of Uncle Ig's bandsaw in the Meat Cauldron, "Halt. Half past six, you can expect inspection for you and your little buddies."

"Fuck, guys, never AWOL," Jan stammers as he walks into the barracks. "They beat you up in the detention barracks. You stand the whole day. Only get bread and water. They force you to crush big rocks into stones and stones into gravel. If you speak, you do push-ups until you vomit. The corporal locks up your cell at eight at night. It's just you, your blanket and your plank bed for the night. At four in the morning, they rattle the cell gates. Inspections are never good, and you get fucked up before having dry bread for breakfast. Then you're drunk from the corporal's hangover breath. Everyone in DB is fucking looney."

Eddie catches a sideways glimpse of the two Awollers. "When you didn't come back that night, we thought the Naval Hill girls were in love with you and were keeping you there."

"Yeah, we figured they had screwed you to the hill," Hannes' words drown in a laugh, "…they say when girls come back from Naval Hill, they've got a hill on their navel."

Willie shakes his head categorically. "I'm waiting for my girlfriend now; seven days is in two weeks." His fist wiggles a thumb and a straight pinkie.

Eddie, surprised, "Couldn't you wait another two weeks for a screw?"

"Chum, basics have been going on for ten weeks. My lust was dripping. In bed at night, my body jerks like that of a poisoned dog."

"We're all waiting for our seven days."

Jan, reclining on his bed, "I couldn't wait anymore; couldn't think of anything else."

Wilfried: "Rumour has it that the girls on the hill are coloured. Couldn't you see in the dark?"

Jan jumps up and grabs Wilfried by the shirt, "Listen, you Salty Dick, what the fuck has colour got to do with it? It's the white man's right."

His natural blush turns to a bloody stain under his straw-coloured stubs. "W- was a joke, man."

Eddie is up and ready—fists balled.

Jan retreats and lies down on his bed again. "Willie, what do we answer that pommie?"

"Black pussy is pudding," Willie grabs his penis and thrusts suggestively in Wilfried's direction. "Once you've tasted it, you forget about white pussy."

Hannes presses his wrists together, "If the police catch you smooching with non-white girls, you'll do jail time for sure."

Jan: "Then it'll be war behind bars with all the Parabats we saw on Naval Hill—will look like the border war has come to Bloemfontein. Shit, a mattress under my back feels wonderful."

"Inspection in five minutes, guys. Focus now," Eddie squares his blanket a few more times, chopping it with the sides of his hands.

"My bed is already square. I haven't slept here for three nights."

"Listen, Jan, we're the ones who made your bed square after Rex turned it upside down every evening." Eddie steps forward defiantly.

"Thanks, guys," as Jan hops off his bed.

Eddie takes position next to his and the platoon follows his example. "Attention," he brings them ready for inspection.

That night, the moonlit sky draws white lines between the curtains in the barracks; a few snores are the only sign of life around him. Once again, phantoms are dragging his thoughts down into deep, dark whitchy whirlpools—why doesn't Charlene write anything about her social life?

The times when he bunked school to go and surprise her when she got off the school bus, he saw the lewd looks the Riebeeck boys were giving her. They won't leave her alone. Matric may be a lot of work, but what does she do on weekends?

He fantasises about what they would do during his seven days.

Come quick, seven days, he floats away to dreamland.

Eleven

No Letter

"Get up, guys," Eddie calls out above the wailing siren. "Got to make ourselves pretty for Durex."

After the parade, he goes down for a hundred push-ups. One envelope is from Suzette; the other one is from Charlene. His legs carry him hastily back to his place in Platoon Bravo. During tea break, he quickly reads.

My dear brother,

I am well, but the house is quiet without you. Mabel has left us to go and nurse her brother who is as sick as a dog. She asked if her daughter could work for Mom—you remember little Stephina, don't you? First Dad said no because maids always help themselves to what's in his cupboards. Mom insisted Stephina would be reliable because Mabel raised her in a Christian way. Okay, Dad said, maybe Catholics are not hypocrites like members of the Apostolic Faith Mission.

You won't believe how Stephina has grown. One can see at once that she is Mabel's child. For someone coming out of the bundu, she's a quick learner, Mom figures. I think Stephina is clever and now I have a pal to talk to, so I don't eat lunch alone (Dad mustn't know). She helps me with my English homework. In the evenings, she borrows my Macbeth—says she didn't have that book in her matric year.

Dad drinks a lot.

The other day, I went to buy meat for Mom. Uncle Ig sends his regards. He asks if you are already the army boxing champ.

Some days, I bump into Leon on the school bus. He's looking forward to seeing you on your seven days. (Me too!) Leon says Peet writes that he's doing well in his army basics in Oudtshoorn—he's going to join the Reccies, whatever that means.

It will be the Easter holidays soon; then you'll be here!

Regards
Suzette

PS: Sergeant Bert and Bertus came for tea. I was so surprised.

Peet a future reconnaissance soldier? He didn't even take drill exercises in school seriously. "Check, Eddie, we've got old Bombfucked for drill," Peet giggled one Friday morning during the school cadet parade.

Some distance from the platoon, Mr Kruger comes marching closer. "Halt," his self-command sounded towards the front of the platoon, somewhat to the right. His knees lift slightly, feet making two plodding sounds in quick succession, causing his gallery of Second World War medals to jingle.

"P-l-a-t-o-o-n! Forward, march! Left-right-left-right…"

Somewhere in front of Eddie, Peet sidesteps out of the platoon, falls in behind Mr Kruger and starts acting like a mime artist: waving windmill arms to imitate the WWll veteran, who notices Peet as Kruger swerves his platoon in a sharp left turn. He whirls around and tackles Peet with fists and feet. Ducking low, he looks for refuge between Eddie's legs. Mr Olwagen's flapping tracksuit top advances with long, athletic strides from the gymnasium building—PT teacher and the right wing of Randfontein's first rugby team.

"Run, Ollie, you bloody murderer," someone mutters in the cadet platoon. Everyone in the school has their own opinion about what happened during the train accident in which Olwagen's wife was killed: how come he was outside the car, trying to push it off the railway track level crossing, and why, everyone wonders, couldn't he do it?

Olwagen gently consoles his elderly colleague, Kruger, to the side of the school square. Halfway there, over his shoulder, "Seeing as you know the drill so well, take over the platoon's march."

Peet takes his place in front of the platoon, to the right. "B-o-m-b-f-u-c-k-e-d! F-o-r-ward, march! Left-right-left-right…"

No way, the Reconnaissance Corps is not a place for Peet.

Suzette writes nothing about his father misbehaving. Would Sergeant Bert have told his blabbermouth son Bertus exactly why they were going for tea with their Blignaut neighbours? For sure, he did.

He stuffs the letter into his shirt pocket. Under a shady tree near Platoon Bravo, the tea urn only fills his tin cup halfway—crumbs in the steel pan are the only evidence of dog biscuits from the mess.

"Recruits, form up."

"Who wrote?" Wilfried asks in a whisper as they form the platoon.

"My sister and Charlene, but I'm keeping her letter for later, something to look forward to tonight." In his last letter, he shared with her the dates of his seven days and he's dying to know what Charlene is planning for them.

The barracks are glittering clean—he wants to read before lights out. He reclines on his bed and smells the letter's perfume odour—luckily, Durex didn't, otherwise, he would have had to do fifty extra push-ups.

Dear Eddie,

I miss you so much that I dream about us—also when I'm awake.

I am very excited. I am going on an orientation course for matrics who want to become teachers, from 16 to 19 March at the Goudstad Teachers College in Johannesburg. My mother says I must attend the course, or else I can't continue my studies.

Let me know when you're getting your seven days. I just can't wait anymore.

Hugs and kisses and all my love.

Charlene xxx.

Damn it! The letter gets thrown down on the coir blanket. The door of his steel cabinet opens with a clang.

"What's up, Eddie?"

"Wilfried, something's not right. I'm going to sort it out, right now."

Durex threatens with DB if you get caught in the tickey box, but this is no time for reasoning. The beret of the gate guard becomes visible through the waiting room window—the tickey box somehow between him and Eddie. He leopard-crawls and slithers inside. Damn, the squeaky noise of the hinge rips through the night air. He lies flat amongst the stinking cigarette butts, breathlessly clenching two five-cent pieces in his fist. Back on his knees, the beret is only just visible above the windowsill. He sits on his haunches and dials Charlene's number.

"Hallo, Bettie du Toit."

A coin slips into the slot. He sinks down low, flat on his buttocks with the guard house in sight.

"Hallo, Antie Bettie. Is Charlene home?"

"Hallo, Eddie. Doesn't the army teach you manners?"

"Sorry. How are you, Antie?"

"Fine, it's after ten. Don't you sleep in the army?"

"We do sleep, Antie. Is Charlene ho—"

"I'll call her. Don't chat the whole night, she's got homework." Bleep-bleep-bleep. Another coin.

"Hey, Eddie, surprise. I thought you weren't allowed to phone?"

"Hey, I'm phoning on the sly. Thanks for your letter. I read you're on a course during my seven days?"

"Shits, don't say that."

"I sent the dates for my seven days in my last letter to you."

"What letter?"

Bleep-bleep-bleep. A curse rings out in the phone booth.

He leopard-crawls out until he reaches the back of the lieutenant's office, gets up and walks back to the barracks.

No letter. How could it be possible that Charlene didn't get the letter? He doesn't even know where Goudstad Teachers College is in a place as big as Johannesburg, but he'll think of something—maybe he could see her there? She's the one motivating him through his basics. How will he be able to come back to this hellhole after seven days without having seen her? Or touched her?

Twelve

Stephina

"Halt," Rex's command rips through the air on the parade ground. "Stand at e-a-s-e." The lieutenant leaves his office and answers the sergeant's salute. The two of them come alongside to attention next to the podium and start marching towards platoon Alfa for parade inspection before seven days.

According to Rex, Platoon Bravo's barracks were only just up to standard this morning. He brings his platoon to attention when the two men are a few steps away: thump go the boots, like that of one man.

"This one's good, Bushman." A satisfied grin and a twitching cheek muscle move past Eddie. "Toon Bravo, at ease!" Thump and everyone looks straight ahead, chins lifted, as if they see something coming from afar over the horizon.

One after the other, platoons are commanded to stand at ease and the two men march back to the podium where the sergeant takes up a rest position, as though he sees something coming from afar over the opposite horizon. Lieutenant, from the podium: "Recruits, our RSM is sick today. Of you. Your inspection is up to standard. You may go on a seven-day pass. The sergeant will give you instructions." Leaving the parade ground, he answers Bushman's salute.

Minutes later, the tickey box moves past Eddie and then the guard room. Another few steps to outside the camp gate. Liberation at last. A fleeting backwards glance to the deserted parade ground, then to Wilfried, "Enjoy, Willy." The German's eyes are mere slits as he sucks on a cigarette. The Free State sun has given him a tomato-like complexion which makes his wheat brown hair seem as white as straw.

*****

In Randgate, the front door stands ajar. Eddie nudges the wrought iron gate open with his hip and walks into their yard at a brisk pace: Here he belongs. Who could be home? Suzette is probably sitting and doing her homework.

Nobody at the dining table…But of course, it's school holidays. A vacuum cleaner hums from the passage. Knock-knock on Suzette's bedroom door. No answer.

It's Stephina vacuuming. The bedspread over his bed has been folded back. She bends to reach under the bed and her little skirt moves up—the pink panty stretching. She is certainly not the young playmate from some years ago anymore. He gets a hard-on just thinking about touching her again.

Shortly after the Blignauts' move to Randgate, Stephina comes to live with her mother Mabel in Mohlakeng black township during a Bantu education system school holiday, to do her catechism with the Roman Catholic Church. She comes to work with Mabel a few times. On hot days, Eddie, Suzette and Stephina played in the backyard under the water sprinkler. When Suzette had gone inside, he and Stephina looked, touched and felt one another. Her tiny nipples were hard, like Jelly Tots. What would they taste like? Stephina, when she touched him, "Auh, kleinbaas, Eddie."

Douf, his army bag hits the floor.

The vacuum cleaner handlebar quivers slightly, "Yo, you're here, already." Large, soft eyes peer over her shoulder, her hair plaited in delicate strips close to her head.

In one movement, Eddie is up against her, "Hallo, Stephina."

She anchors herself to the vacuum cleaner, "Hallo, E-e-ddie…auh, you're big now." She stares down at the bedspread. An eyelash blinks.

The cotton t-shirt stretches across her breasts and tightens in the curve above her hips.

"You're a woman, Stephina." Truly desirable. No, Eduard—but why not? He's not the first white man in the country with desires for a non-white woman— Naval Hill is infested with guys like that. So, why not? What's more, he's alone in Randgate for his seven days—maybe this is his only chance.

The vacuum cleaner handlebar jerks to the upright position. "I'm going to wash the kitchen floor."

Eddie takes off his boots and pulls his shirt out of his trousers.

She is pushing the mop across the kitchen floor when he comes in. There is brown bread in the tin and Coke in the fridge. With a thick slice in one hand and a glass of cool drink in the other, he goes and sits askew on the kitchen table—just so nice to be home. With a bulging cheek, "Do you have a boyfriend, Stephina?" Bread washes down with the bubbly soda drink.

"Back in Clocolan, I have. The tsotsi's from this place, I don't trust them." The mop disappears in the bucket of water. She wrings it. Mops the floor under the table.

Her face has not really changed. What about the rest? His hand slips in under her t-shirt. Her breast feels soft and full. "Is your boyfriend a good lover?"

Her back suddenly stiffens, and her voice jumps a few octaves: "Sipho, he is." Water splashes when the mop confusedly lands back in the bucket. "I'm going to finish vacuuming in your room."

He swallows the last of the bread and Coke. In your room is an invitation, isn't it? He has another hard-on. Gliding down the passage on his socks, he rubs his penis in his hand. She bends over to switch on the vacuum cleaner but hesitates when she notices him in the doorway—her look becomes a haggard stare of disbelief at his unbuttoned fly.

Thirteen

Skin Colour

"Are you here?"

Half asleep, he struggles up and buckles his trousers. Reaching for the bedroom door, the knob turns.

Suzette, through the narrow opening, "Can I come in?"

"Of course."

"Just check your tan and short hair, a real soldier in your uniform."

He gets a kiss on the cheek. Her upper arms feel scrawny.

"You OK, sis?"

"I'm fine." Her tone of voice is already a giveaway. "Come, I'll pour us something cool to drink. Have you seen Charlene yet?"

"No, I've only been home for about an hour. Anyway, she's on a course with her school."

"Oh…so when are you seeing her?"

"I'll go and say hello to Antie Bettie tomorrow to hear what she says."

"Now tell me: how are things in the army?" She leans back against the kitchen sink, head to one side, eyebrows raised. Two braids of auburn hair are draped forward over her shoulders, the tips being caressed between her thumbs and fingertips.

He tells her they are thirty recruits living together in an asbestos barracks, stand to inspection at the crack of dawn, drilled after breakfast or run 2,4 kilometres with full kit, then have lectures—then lunch, drill again or learn to shoot with an R1 assault rifle. His corporal, Rex, is a looney and actually, the others are as well, Sergeant Bushman even more so. The guys in his platoon are from all walks of life. Wilfried comes from a fancy neighbourhood in Johannesburg, but Eddie can't remember the name now.

"Hey, we'll talk again later. Krisjan is organising a rugby tournament," she gestures with hands and arms miming as if busying her. "Players from the other schools are staying in our school hostel. He's asked a few matric girls to help him with the preparations." *You murderer Olwagen, what's up your sleeve with my sister?*

"OK, I'll unpack my ball bag."

"Your w-h-a-t?"

"My army bag, that's what we call it."

"What does the thing look like?"

"There it is," he points at it as they enter his room.

"OK, I underst-a-a-nd. Do you vacuum barracks in the army? Then they ought to teach you to put away the vacuum cleaner once you've finished."

He gets a crooked smile under a lifted eyebrow.

Women folk's heads work like detectives. Where would Stephina be now?

"Did Dad behave himself?"

"Apart from his drinking, no other tricks."

Great stuff. It must have something to do with Sergeant Bert coming over to say hello now and then. Eddie feels his plan is working out.

The ball bag is half empty when the Chevrolet Commando engine revs with a roar outside. They meet in the kitchen.

"Hallo, Dad." *Does he even remember that I was coming home today?* "How are you, Dad?"

"I'm well, my boy," one swaying step backwards, bloodshot eyes looking him up and down, "The army ish fixing you good and proper."

"What do you mean, Dad?"

"Y'r she-e-ep's wool is off and y'got sha-ape," in a shaky attempt to pull back shoulders and straighten his arms against his sides, sleeves rolled up two turns, "I'm r-a-cing this weekend. Get the e-n-t-ry formsh ready." A chunky ring shines on the open hand stabilising him on the kitchen table *(that filthy backhand slap, woman beater!).* "Will tell you what pigeonsh I'm flying," as he lurches down the passage.

You think I'm still your bloody skivvy? He unpacks the rest in the ballbag.

"Where's my soldier boy?"

The *Ring* lands on the bedspread with a thud. He finds Mom in the passage, cheeks glistening under the light bulb, "Just look. No wonder I feel so safe back home."

"It's nice to be here again, Mom. It felt like an eternity."

"You've got seven days' leave, haven't you? I swapped shifts at the hospital: not working this weekend, but I suppose, you'll want to see Charlene?"

"I can't."

"But why not?"

The lump in his throat obstructs his swallowing. "She's on an orientation course to become a teacher."

"Oh, dear. How's army food? Who washes and irons your clothes? You don't say in your letters."

"How many letters from me did you get, Mom?"

"Two, why?"

"Just asking."

The conversation moves to the sitting room while Eddie tries to figure out how Mom received both his letters and Charlene only his first. Dawid comes in, pulls up a dining-room chair and, as usual, sits down on it the wrong way round, chin on his arms. "What's with thish sh-i-lent treatment? Put on sh-o-m-e Kimberley Jim." The Brylcreem-ed auburn fringe hangs withered over his forehead; half rolled-up sleeves now pushed above his elbows reveal forearm tattoos: a mermaid on the left and a ship anchor on the right.

By the third Jim Reeves song, he wakes up with a startle from a kick in the shins, "Come on, Dawid, you're not good company. Go snore in bed."

He gets up, mumbles and stumbles, heading for the passage, "Babsh, in my house I sh-l-e-e-p wherever I want to…"

Suzette, staring at her dad and shaking her head in dismay, "I'm saying goodnight as well, must be at the hostel tomorrow at seven to help Mr Olwagen. Mom, will you please drop me off there on your way to work?"

"Yes, my girl, if you'll wake both of us up at six."

"OK. Goodnight, everyone."

Mom cringes. The shining eyes of a few minutes ago have become two teary pools. Her eyelid droops below the scar.

"Eduard, I'm in a living hell. Every payday, your father borrows money from me. Once, when I refused, he threatened to put a stop to my working if he didn't get the benefit. Just to pour it all down his throat." Under a heavy sigh, "I cheat, put away some money in secret, because Suzette so badly wants to go to college to train as a secretary."

"Mom, remember my promise," but a motor mechanic apprenticeship takes time—a full three years. There's only one way to start earning immediately after his army year—pro-box. In *Ring*, he reads about the origins of some of the professional boxers, their rise, and their gutsy courage. Following his win in the Western Transvaal championships, he senses the same feeling inside himself: he can take on a man in the ring and knock him out. Next year, he's climbing through the ropes without a boxing vest, like a true pro.

Mom's look lightens up. "I want to ask you a small favour."

"Ask away, anything."

"Mabel is going home with her brother on Sunday. He wants to die where he was born."

"Hell, what is so bad?"

"TB is eating him up. The Catholic priest is serving a last Mass for him on Sunday morning, at the sanatorium, Mabel sent word through Stephina. The little miss is ill today, apparently. I don't know where the sanatorium is. Will you please go with me on Sunday?"

"Yes, I will. What must you go and do there?"

"Want to give Mabel a little something to take with her to her homeland." In the middle of a yawn, "I suppose we should also get to bed."

"Night, Mom…" Does she notice him blushing? What if Stephina turns up with her mother for communion at the sanatorium on Sunday? How could he look her in the eyes when he feels like a criminal about what happened between them? Does she feel the same way too—South Africa's racial segregation laws and Immorality Act are valid for everyone, both sides of the colour line? Hopefully, she keeps their secret too. When he screws up with other things, he never feels this way: like when he pinched tools from the school workshop and exchanged them at the pawnshop for pocket money. That delinquent behaviour wasn't right either, but it hadn't had an association with someone's face and skin colour.

Fourteen

Father Patrick

"It's half past eight, Eddie. We must go now."

"I'm just brushing my teeth, Mom."

She is busy putting a few Checkers shopping bags into the boot of her Simca when he catches up with her and jumps in on the passenger side.

In Randfontein, the main street is a picture of Sunday morning desolation. His thumb flicks to the left, "Mom, you have to turn at Jan Viljoen High School." Thumb to the right, "Again, just after the Technical College." The road winds on between blue-gum trees and white mining dumps. A road sign comes into view, "Follow that."

"Are you sure?"

"Ollie often sent us this way during PT class for a run to the white sands."

"Sanatorium," she reads the signage aloud.

A red brick building approaches under a shimmering corrugated iron roof. She parks next to a bottle-green 404 Peugeot station wagon.

He has no desire to run into Stephina. "I'll wait here, Mom."

"Come along. What are you afraid of?"

The entrance is closed with a lopsided gate. Inside the courtyard, he feels forced to slow down: to one side, a patient sits on a rickety kitchen chair; a few steps away, two women are huddled together on a wooden bench against the wall, crawled in under one blanket. Over there, another one is sitting in the sun on an empty oil drum. Out of the corner of his mouth, "Creepy place, where's Mabel?" And Stephina—is his face burning because of fear, or guilt?

"Inside there, I suppose. That looks like a church."

"The little building with the pitched roof? How do you know, Mom?"

"There's a statuette of the Virgin Mary above the door. Catholics are known to worship statues."

Blurred figures move around in the chapel. If Stephina should come out of there, he'll quickly escape to the toilet.

"Good morning. Can I help you?"

He turns around; the crisp, white nurses' uniform contrasts sharply with the environment. "Good morning." Mom puts her hand out halfway, "I'm also a nurse. We're looking for Mabel."

"Father Patrick is serving Mass in the chapel. Do you wish to wait in the office?"

"We'll wait here." With so many people at death's door, he's not going in there.

"Please, excuse me; I'm expecting the doctor from Baragwanath Hospital any moment," Eddie shifts his weight from one leg to the other as long seconds tick by.

The Mass, whatever it is, takes an eternity—is it like communion or what?

Mom lifts a hand, "There's someone."

The first people exit under the statuette. "Dead men walking."

"Quiet, Eduard. Those people are very ill. There's Mabel now."

A long, black robe appears behind her. A wooden cross sways on a string of beads around the man's neck. Eddie lets out a giggle, "What a weird bowtie." Can Mom hear that he's nervous? Stephina will appear any moment now. An albino man pushes a wheelchair out of the door, comes to a standstill and pulls a white cloth hat out from his trouser pocket. He positions it down over his golden-yellow hair with both hands.

Mabel walks ahead of the procession. A handkerchief wipes over her cheeks. "M-e-e-s Babsie..." She leans her head on Mom's shoulder and her big body shakes out of control.

The man in the robe says, "Good morning, I'm Father Patrick."

"I'm Eddie," he shakes the hand of the man who sounds as though he talks from heaven.

The priest's other hand rests on the albino man's shoulder, "This lad is Lethabo, my driver ever since I was diagnosed with epilepsy."

Eddie glances rapidly at the pink-red hand reaching towards him from the outstretched African ethnic pattern shirtsleeve. Higher up, the collar is buttoned up around a thick neck and prominent lips, "I'm Lethabo."

Eddie steps backwards, "Hallo, Lethabo."

Mom shakes the priest and Lethabo's hand, "I'm Babsie."

"God bless," Father Patrick lifts his open hand as though saluting Mom and flips it in Mabel's direction. "Come, you've got a long road ahead."

One rear door of the Peugeot station wagon is opened when Eddie passes the lopsided gate. Mabel struggles to get her brother out of the wheelchair. Lethabo points to the brake mechanism, "Mabel, you should first fasten the brake." Eddie's flat hand sends the white cloth hat flying.

"Listen, boytjie, don't think you can give the orders just because you're half white. Help Mabel."

With an arm around Lethabo's neck, the sick man rises out of the chair and collapses into the rear seat of the car, groaning all the way.

"This is for you, Mabel," Mom intervenes. Mabel presses her hands together for the Checkers-bags and Lethabo comes to her assistance like lightning—the station wagon's boot lid jumps open, and the parcels are hastily arranged inside.

"Thanks, madam. Look well after my kids." Big, wet eyes turn towards Eddie.

"Thanks for your nice food. It made me strong." Mabel's hand feels soft in his.

"I can see that." Again, the handkerchief wipes over her eyes, "You must go well." Across her shoulder, Lethabo glares at Eddie from under his hat.

Mom's tone sounds concerned, "Will you see Stephina today? How is she?"

"When we say goodbye to Stephina before we leave for Clocolan, I'll ask if she's still feeling sick."

Father Patrick's hand lifts above the bottle-green roof towards Eddie and his mother, "Peace be with you," as he gets in on the passenger side.

Mom waves at the station wagon departing. A tissue pops out of her dress sleeve and presses down on her eyes as she walks to her Simca.

The car key turns like the last page of one of those Mills & Boon novels which she slams shut at the last page, "That Mabel is a real pearl. Maybe, little Stephina will turn out just like her mother one day."

Cold sweat tickles Eddie's upper lip. Hopefully, Stephina will stay on sick leave until after his seven days.

Fifteen

Peet

A white butcher's apron bursts through the meshed screen door, "Eddie, my boy!" He shakes Ig's hand while a fist pumps in his ribcage.

"Gee, Uncle Ig can still throw a punch. How are you?"

"Well. With you? Come in."

"Boxing's going well. SA champs in September. I want to win. Morning, Antie Annette." Her greeting is accompanied by a fleeting glance as she looks up from the cash register. Straight fingers wiggle purple-painted nails in his direction.

"You're senior now. It's a new game, Eddie."

A piece of dried sausage is pushed across the counter. "Thanks. What does Uncle mean by new game?"

Banana-sized fingers prod a pork rib in the marinade pan. "Seniors are hungry. Some will turn pro—their only way to make a living." There is something serious in the eyes behind the thick-framed glasses.

The screen door slams with a thunderous noise. He nibbles at the dry sausage while Uncle Ig finishes serving a lady customer…"Mom works twelve-hour shifts with her lame hip," Eddie frets. The lady turns to pay at Annette and Eddie's glance meets Uncle Ig's. "I am hungry too; I'm going to make a living out of boxing."

"If ever you turn pro, I'm in your corner." The marinade pan is put down behind the counter glass. There is a moist glimmering behind the thick frame, "Eddie, you can be the champ I could never become."

He throws playful punches across the counter, "Keep your eye on the SA championship results. I'm ready for the seniors," tapping his chin with a clenched fist.

On his way to the door, "Bye, Antie."

"Bye, Eddie."

Behind the screen door, the butcher's apron presses upon Uncle Ig's eyes.

*****

Mom leans through the Simca's window just outside Randfontein early the next morning, "Are you sure you didn't forget anything?"

"I've got everything. Thanks for the rusks. Enjoy your day at work. Bye, Mom."

"Bye. I'll look out for your next letter."

He answers her wave with a salute and takes an at-ease position next to the road: legs apart, shoulders pulled back, straight right-hand fingers folded into his left-hand clutch behind his back, chin lifted at the distant horizon.

After two lifts, one with a travelling representative for cattle feed and the last stretch with two pensioners living in Bloemfontein, he signs the guard's register at the gate late that afternoon. Not a soul in the phone booth. He walks in and dials Charlene's number. It just rings.

In the barracks, recruits and ball bags recline like tombstones. "Howzit, guys?"

"Shitty, thanks." A streak of saliva whips through the air and lands on Wilfried's bed, "Hope they make me a driver, so I can escape from this place for some real-life experience." Eddie packs his boxing boots, trunks, vest, gloves, protective box for his genitals and bandages into his steel cabinet. Toilet bag on the bottom shelf—his Christmas present from Charlene. Nine months before he sees her again. His yearning hurts deeply.

The following day, recruits are placed in operational units. Eddie is posted to the Technical Service Corps of the Orange Free State Command Workshop—those sawtooth-like roofs behind the quartermaster general's warehouse. He moves into double room quarters with Hannes.

On Wednesday afternoon, the recruits must line up on the parade ground. A hefty soldier in a tracksuit and t-shirt climbs onto the podium, "If you're a forward, go to rugby field A. I'll meet you there. If you're a quarterback, rugby field B." Most of the recruits scatter off the parade ground.

"What do you play, the fool?" The soldier mocks those left standing. "If you're too damn pathetic to play rugby, report at the infirmary. Or go and play with yourself in the gym, or in the toilet if you're shy. Just joking, man: tennis players, the courts are over t-h-e-r-e, boxers to the gym. If you don't do sport, you'll work in the camp gardens."

Wilfried walks into the gym next to Eddie, "Definitely no soccer in this place."

Eddie counts about thirty boxers. Some admit they have never been in a boxing ring before—it's just that they don't like gardening.

A man in a tracksuit comes in. "Afternoon. I'm Fritz van der Linde, your coach." He shakes hands and greets some of them by name—they're probably guys in the Permanent Force. "I don't box!" Wilfried retreats, nervously as Fritz asks his weight.

"Can you hold a water bottle and towel?"

"I can."

"Then you're my second. In the back of my pickup, outside, is a ball bag with gloves." Eddie gives Wilfried a thumbs-up.

Fritz rubs his hands together and removes his tracksuit top. It lands on the bottom rope of the ring. "Guys, in three weeks, it's the Annual Tempe Inter-Corps Tournament against the Parachute Battalion. This year, we're bringing the cup back. After the Inter-Corps, I'll be selecting a team for the Defence Force Champs in July at the Reccies' base in Oudtshoorn. Before then we're going to get in shape. You ready?"

Yes, for sure, yup, it echoes through the gym.

He must win in the Inter-Corps, Eddie decides. Then he'll go to Oudtshoorn. Maybe, he'll have the opportunity to see Peet. Doesn't he miss their school buddy comradeship too, or does the Reconnaissance Corps change a person's heart? Here in camp rumour goes that Reccies are cold-blooded soldiers: in the border war, they lead the fight, root out the enemy far beyond the Southwest African border, transgressing deep into Angola, where they kill people in their thousands. Civilians too, who get in their way. Mutilated corpses then get tied to the front of their Casspir armoured troop carrier trucks which are paraded through villages to drive the fear of hell into civilian communities, so they do not secretly help or hide terrorists. Eddie shudders. Is Peet also going that way?

Sixteen

Reminiscing

Before long, the rugby season is in full swing. There's a game every Saturday—sometimes, against one of the town clubs. For players and supporters alike, a chance to escape from the camp.

Eddie pulls tight his military jacket—it's freezing in the back of the Bedford. After the rugby match, there was a barbecue and time for all to relax around the bonfire. Now a hot shower, after which he'll watch tonight's episode of the Columbo television series.

"Blikkies, Blikkies," echoes through the steam clouded bathrooms.

"What's up?"

"Telegram. For you."

The gate guard appears behind the shower curtain. He stands to attention, the envelope held out in his open right hand. Eddie takes it. Tears it open. Water splashes on the paper. Ink letters start flowing: Oh my God, no.

His half-dry body has turned to stone; the piece of soaked paper still in his hand makes him light-headed: Peet died yesterday. Landmine accident. Funeral Friday in Randgate. Leon.

On Wednesday, the sergeant major receives the signal in the mechanics' workshop and calls Eddie to his office, reads out the text from the camp officer in command: Two-day pass granted to Private Blignaut. Humanitarian reasons.

Shall he say *Thank you*? No way, for what—this rotten military mentality? Shall he be grateful? Perhaps for the chance to maybe see Charlene.

Thursday at dawn, on his way out of the camp, he phones.

No answer at Charlene's house. The gate guard looks at his pass and nods. Long strides to the highway, the thudding of boots drives like nails into his sad heart. "Fuck you, PW Botha, and your whole ministry of defence," he mutters. "How can you take away my friend? A harmless clown, Peet, defends his country, but you don't protect him? Who gave you the godly right to extradite my friend to mortal danger for your bloody political ideals of white racial superiority? Have you ever held a R1 rifle in your hands? Flat on your belly at the shooting range with cardboard figures as targets and the corporal's boot up your arse, 'Aim for the heart area, troop. Else the terr will shoot the shit out of you.' Do you know, PW, that Peet was all his mother had left after his father died in a mining accident?"

Following that, a wave of scandal washed over Randgate—Peet's mother lost her mind when the mine management made public the cause of the accident: The mine lift went down the shaft when the cage caught on a wooden beam which had detached from the shaft wall. The cable continued to uncoil into a heap on top of the cage until the weight broke the beam and sent the lift full of workers into free fall down the shaft. The cable jerked tight like a gallows rope and broke, which once again let the lift accelerate towards the dark mass of water at the bottom of the shaft.

Divers from the mine's proto team worked for days on end. Above ground, at the mouth of the shaft, in a refrigerator container, it was impossible for the mine's doctors to determine which limbs from the watery grave belonged to who, Peet's mother told everyone, whether they wanted to know or not. In Randgate, everyone wanted to know; Eddie could testify to that. In the course of their standard six, Peet gave him the latest news, every day, about the mine management's progress on funeral arrangements. Two separate memorial services would be held: one for the white victims and one for the blacks. That sounded right, though Eddie had no answers for Peet's questions about the meaning of life, his father's sudden disappearance and his mother's instability: her eyes don't miss a man in the street. Her comments disgusted him, Peet confided to Eddie.

The highway running past Bloemfontein comes into view—he takes longer strides. Eddie's last lift takes him to Randfontein in a state of macabre excitement—on his way to Peet, but Peet will not be there and his body throbs for Charlene.

He spends the evening with Leon; the visit—reminiscing about times with Peet—goes on past midnight. About his uncontrollable desire to be a hero, which certainly led to his joining the Reconnaissance Corps. They laugh together heartily about Peet's way of telling a story with his feet when he is upset, like when his mother got married again. "I'm still mourning, and the next thing you know, she's standing in front of the pulpit." He peeled off his t-shirt and draped it over his head, stepping to the left and to the right in his search for words. "And then old Dries lifts my mother's veil and kisses her…" His left hand lifts the t-shirt in the air, and he spits in his right hand.

Eddie shares an anecdote with Leon about their standard seven: Peet bursts into his room, half hysterical: Wessel, that fucking fairy. The previous Friday evening after the Apostolic Faith Mission youth service, Wessel Vermeulen showed Peet his new yellow Volkswagen Beetle. This afternoon, the AFM student pastor knocks on Peet's door and invites him for a drive in his Beetle. It takes them out of town along Lazar Avenue, past the coolie Sammy's shop. "Near the Wheatlands plots." Peet lifts his hand in that direction with a step to the right, which makes his blond fringe bounce on his hooknose, "Wessel turns into the wheatfields, pulls out his dick and stuffs it into my hand—Jerk me off."

Eddie is already halfway to his bedroom window. "I'm going to bash him up."

"No, then the entire Randgate will know about everything." With his hands on Eddie's fists and a step to the left. "The AFM youth service will never see me again, that's for sure." The bottom of the bottle of Klipdrift brandy brings consolation: Nothing will ever upset Peet again.

Eddie phoned Charlene earlier that evening from Leon's house. Tomorrow, she'll play sick. They'll find a way to see one another in between late Peet's funeral arrangements.

"Drop me off at the Corner Lounge Cafe, and pick me up there again, please," he asks Leon on the way back from the cemetery.

"At what time? I'm going to Peet's mother for tea and to sympathise."

"In half an hour's time." He's out almost before Leon brings the car to a standstill.

"Are you back so soon?" Christos' look across the counter is aloof; his eyebrows are bushy under lines of wrinkles from frowning, "Milky bar?"

"Hello, Christos, that was before." He throws him a toffee sign half-covered with his left hand.

Charlene flings open the door before his knuckles can tap on the stained glass. Arms around his neck, tongue in his mouth. A leg moves up between his own, "You're with me now."

"I am. Hell, it's nice."

In a tango of kissing and caressing, touching and undressing, they find her bed. She is all over him as they roll over again and again. She is against him, then on him. Her thighs caress his cheeks. The rhythmic harmony in her body confirms every movement with a soft groan—accelerating to ecstatic fondling.

"You're in my dreams every night. With me in my bed," she whispers.

"I fall asleep at night in a fantasy with you."

"At what time must you go? I have so much to talk about!"

"Two o'clock. I must be back in the camp by midnight."

"Shit, no, it's ten to two already."

"I miss your letters; the camp is a lonesome place."

"I've got a long one for you." She slides off him and opens her dressing table drawer.

"Nice." He can't wait to read it.

"N-o-o, you're not allowed to have a look now; only when you're feeling lonely back in camp."

At the front door, she slips the envelope into his shirt pocket. "Love you," and a peck.

"I love you too." Her buttocks feels soft between his fingers.

Leon is ready waiting in front of the Corner Lounge as Eddie jogs into Republic Road, looks back one last time down Niemand Street and waves. She blows a kiss from their veranda.

The car starts op with a growl. "You didn't just become a father, did you, chum?" Leon bursts his sides with laughter. His flat hand slaps Eddie's chest.

On the outskirts of Randfontein, Leon turns the car about its own axis. He gets a joking V-finger salute thrown by Eddie. That's how their late friend Peet would have saluted.

Privates don't hitchhike. A fellow citizen will not fail to stop; he remembers the lieutenant's instruction on the parade ground at the start of seven days. Standing at ease beside the road, in his mind's eye, the national flag is hoisted before the coffin is lowered. Peet's mom, cringing under a black coat and hat, leans forward to put Peet's Jan Viljoen school blazer on the coffin, and loses her footing. Her brother grabs hold of her, so she doesn't fall into the grave, with its coffin full of maimed bones. How could the AFM pastor say that Peet was now in a better place? Someone who saw so much comedy in the normal things would have wanted to live, rather.

A car, with a Cape Province registration plate, stops. "Where to?"

"Bloemfontein."

"Please get in."

"Thank you, Mister."

What are you going back to, Eddie Blignaut? Do your bit for the fucking fatherland. He was starting to feel proud in uniform; he liked the companionship in Platoon Bravo. But no, these browns he's wearing bring death.

Seventeen

Champion

Trainers crunch-crunch deftly over white, frosted grass. Their group of boxers are doing early morning roadwork to build stamina. Then quick sprint lengths across the rugby field for swift legs.

The Tempe Inter-Corps Tournament presents the opportunity to get into shape and become used to Fritz's coaching style. Even Wilfried has been coached into a first-class corner assistant. He and Eddie now alternate to buy the latest *Ring*. Eddie politely accepts the soccer magazines Wilfried offers; they're all in German.

After his win in the final against a former army champion, Eddie's belief in his own ability is even stronger, and Fritz shows new interest in him. Hardus, a flyweight, and the heavyweight Ben are also chosen for the Defence Force Championships. Fritz organises sparring partners for them from the Bloemfontein Boxing Club—afternoons around five the echo of punches can be heard in the gym.

The Nissan microbus sways to a standstill in front of a boom gate. Fritz's head leans out of the window. "Bloemfontein. We're coming to box." He gets a clipboard under his nose. "Welcome, sir. Please sign in." Outstretched arm, open hand, straight fingers, and retracted thumb, the guard shows the way to a row of asbestos offices, "Someone over there at the RSM's office will help you further." The boom lifts in front of the microbus.

Spurts of adrenalin rush through Eddie: another tournament, one more chance to prove his mettle.

Infantry School Oudtshoorn the nameplate reads on the Little Karoo stone wall. This must be where Peet arrived on his first day. The guard's room and a tickey box glide past on the left-hand side.

He phones after dinner. "Bettie du Toit."

"Hello, Antie. Eddie speaking. How are you?"

"I can hear it's you. I'm well. Shouldn't you be on the parade ground?"

"I'm at the Defence Force boxing champs here in Oudtshoorn. Is Charlene home?" Bleep-bleep. From Bloemfontein, he can speak for longer with five cents? Another coin slips into the slot.

"No, she's at a school function."

"Will you please tell her that I phoned? That I'm boxing in the Champs?"

"I will—"

Bleep-bleep-bleep…What school function could that be?

The championships take place in the Oudtshoorn City Hall where the walls are decorated with embroidered banners bearing the arms codes of every one of the army corps present. The judges are in uniform, the referee in tracksuit pants and a white t-shirt. On the first afternoon, Fritz and the medical service corps lieutenant struggle to bring Ben round—his championship does not even last three full rounds. A private from Pretoria, one Kallie Knoetze, knocks him down with a nasty short left hook.

Hardus and Eddie perform better and become army champions, qualifying for the South African Amateur Boxing Championships in Port Elizabeth in September. Eddie allows himself to dream big—when he is discharged from the army in December, he could go home as the South African Senior Welterweight Boxing Champion. He's going to make them all proud, Mom and Suzette, Uncle Ig, and especially Charlene—the entire Randgate, and make his mark on Randfontein, like Charlene did as a rag queen.

*****

The khaki-brown microbus chugs along downhill. "No wonder the place is called the Windy City," Fritz mumbles behind the steering wheel.

"I've never been to Port Elizabeth…" In the distance, Eddie sees the ocean for the first time. The great blue rising up behind coastal buildings, stretching all the way to the horizon, has an unreal beauty. A ship dots the ocean here and there. Maybe there is a chance after the championships to swim in the sea?

"My aunt will meet us in front of the PE post office." Wilfried sounds proud to have been able to organise their accommodation during the boxing championships with his aunt. "She promised."

Hardus reaches the semi-final, until Fritz throws in the towel, "Well fought, Hardus."

In the dressing room: "Fwitz, why? I was close to dwopping that guy."

"It's my decision when my boxer is taking too much punishment. Wilfried, call the tournament doctor. Eddie, start warming up." First, a quick look at Hardus' bottom lip. It resembles a piece of bloody sausage in Uncle Ig's butchery.

Wilfried comes running back, "Fritz, the doctor is on his way. I'll bandage Eddie's hands."

Another tug at the red ribbon around his waist. "Willy, tighten my glove laces as well." On the opposite side of the ring, a man is shadowboxing in the green corner. In his previous fight, he received a head butt—the half-moon under his puffy left eye is dark blue, almost matching his thick beard. "C'mon, Daniel," a group of fans from Durban Naval Base encouraged him earlier in his semi-final. Eddie sat studying his style in detail: a heavy hitter who rather goes for a knockout than collect points by proper boxing. In round two, Daniel's opponent collapsed to his knees, the wind out of his sails and Daniel through to the final against Eddie. Fritz, as the gong sounds. "Start southpaw, Eddie." He was impressed by Eddie's skill in both orthodox and southpaw boxing styles.

Lightning-fast, straight right punches on the dark half-moon pile up his points. Daniel taunts, gloves at his sides. *Sailor, you don't catch me like your previous opponent.* More leading right-hand stings strike the target, while Eddie retracts his arms in defence equally fast, to block Dan's thunderbolt punches.

The referee's index finger warns Daniel, "You're in the ring to box." Left hand in front of his ringed eye, the right swaying at his side. Rapid combination punches by Eddie exploits his opponent's recklessness—left hooks finding Daniel's chin. Ow, a solid right-hand short rib punch from Daniel stuns Eddie. Must get his breath back. The sailor's got punch. Dance away—anticlockwise with the right foot in front. Gong. Phew.

Fritz drops down to one knee in the red corner, sponge in hand, "Take the orthodox stand, Eddie. Use your speed and reach. Box him with more combinations. The gaps will come." Gong—orthodox stand, left foot in front, clockwise dancing. Duck, block, lean back. Daniel's punches are predictable, except for his pounding torpedoes on Eddie's heart area. Another one. Oof. Breathe deeply, dance back a step. Daniel walks head-on into a left-right salvo.

The beard shakes with contempt—you're pretending, sailor—Eddie feels the firm kick back in his shoulder joints with each hit.

"Stop." The referee keeps a cool head and winks at the tournament doctor to come closer—"Small cut, we'll keep an eye on it."

"Box."

Duck away left and right from Daniel's whirlwind punches. The referee stops his streetfighter attack—"You're punching in the back of the head, first warning." Wide-eyed, sarcastic glance above the dark semi-circle, another whirlwind. Counterpunch, duck, protective gesture, firm foothold and a ripping right uppercut through the sailor's defence that casts a glazed stare from behind the beard, Daniel as white as a sheet. Follow up right crossover chopping punch on the blue bull's eye target. The wound exposes bone and then a fountain of red.

The tournament doctor: "You can lose your eye. I'm stopping you."

Strings of curses prompt the referee to rush forward: "Last warning for swearing at me or I'll have you suspended for a year."

Daniel has already left the ring when Eddie's hand lifts and the floor sinks away under him.

Fritz's hand reaches up, past Wilfried's shoulders: "Take that, champ."

He can't wait to tell his folks. After the medals' presentation ceremony, he jogs around downtown Port Elizabeth and at last finds a tickey box in Albany Street.

"Hello, Babsie Blignaut speaking."

"Hello, Mom, Randgate has a South African boxing champion."

"Congratulations, congratulations, Eduard," she sniffs. "Oh, what did I do with my tissue, now? I'm proud of you."

"You'll see my medal in December, Mom. Please go and tell Uncle Ig. I have to phone Charlene quickly."

Antie Bettie picks up. Another school function tonight—really?

Something's wrong.

Eighteen

Dropped

Days feel endless, and his nights awfully lonely. Sundays are the worst when minutes tick by even slower, aimlessly. This morning, privates were driven by Bedford to attend church service in Bloemfontein-central congregation of the Dutch Reformed Church. Seated adjacent under the tarpaulin cover, Eddie and Wilfried joked about their alternating between Christian denominations to attend each other's service. Wilfried's Evangelical Lutheran Church service takes place on Sunday evenings—a second chance for both to escape the austere military camp ambience. Across them on the back of the Bedford, en route for downtown Bloemfontein, sat three privates who claimed to be Jewish on last Friday night to also join Shabbat meal in town, prompting the sergeant major to threaten that at the next parade ground inspection, he'll have them checked out for being circumcised.

Sunday routines of life in Randgate now seem idyllic, the streets there like highways of freedom on another planet; a normal one. Mom's Sunday lunch around the kitchen table with her, Suzette and Dad; one time in the week, he managed to be sober, careless hours with Charlene at the municipal swimming pool. It's no life to be caged up in an army camp.

After Sunday lunch—differentiated from weekday lunches by the mess hall serving jelly and custard as dessert—some soldiers play cards or darts in the recreation hall. Others queue at the tickey box. Five cents buy almost three minutes of call time to Randgate. Other guys watch the slot with eagle eyes, to make sure no one puts in a second coin. Every conversation with Charlene ends too quickly. He wants to hear more about how she spends her free time and get answers to the questions of suspicion multiplying in his head, but then the receiver dies with a bleep-bleep-bleep.

Memories of their intimate moments become dragons in his head; her school functions warped perceptions as orgies. Beautiful recollections of their intimate moments disintegrate under the weight of a growing possessive jealousy. His fingers touch her last letter in his shirt pocket—the smell of perfume has long since evaporated. His memory is fading. He leans forward and rummages for the writing pad and Bic pen in his steel cabinet. The coir blanket is hard enough to serve as a writing table. The pen rolls between his thumb and index finger…it used to be so easy to talk to her.

Slowly, words turn into sentences. He is looking forward to spending December with her—only another three months to go, that's all. He won the SA Champs in Port Elizabeth. Pity, she was out to (another damn) school function when he phoned with the news. From the beginning of September, he wears one stripe—as a lance-corporal he gets an extra R2, 40 per week. When does her final matric exam start?

The letter shoots into the post-box. He asks the gate guard for mail. It's Suzette's handwriting on the envelope. The queue at the tickey box is short. Charlene was vague during his last telephone call—was old Bettie perhaps eavesdropping?

Back on the coir blanket, the orange pen slashes open the envelope:

Dear Eddie

Congratulations, once again, that you are the SA boxing champ. Uncle Ig says he felt it coming. I'm studying hard for my final exams, but it's difficult at home. Last Friday night, there was a big party going on in Stephina's room in the backyard. I heard Dad swearing outside my bedroom door on his way outside. Through the bathroom window, I saw two black men running out of our driveway. One tripped and then Dad was on him. I heard the blows dropping. The other one fortunately got away. Afterwards, Mom is the one who takes the brunt: she is just lazy and doesn't need a maid.

The next morning, Mom told Stephina to go. Dad shouted from their bedroom that no one was going to turn his backyard into a whorehouse and a shebeen. If Stephina doesn't go immediately, he's going to use his whip. She cried terribly, and later she climbed over the fence with her suitcase to next door, where Motle works. Afterwards, Mom still gave Stephina a Checkers bag with a few things from her trousseau chest—probably to say sorry.

Now, I'm the one who must clean the house. It takes a lot of time.

You must keep your spirits up for your last army days.
Sisterly love, Suzette

He turns onto his other elbow and sighs, relieved—she would have said if Dad was misbehaving towards her.

After three months of basic training, the recruits from the July intake are placed in operational units. Old man Eddie delegates his responsibilities in the mechanical workshop to his successor.

One morning, during tea break, he makes a quick trip to the guard's room and feels his heart racing: it's Charlene's handwriting. Halfway through the workshop, his curiosity gets the better of him. He tears open the envelope.
Hi Eddie

Congratulations on your SA champ title. I couldn't believe it when I read the news. You're the best boxer there is.

It's going well. I'm working hard. The final matric exams are around the corner. My record exam marks got me admission to the Goudstad Teachers College.

Eddie, my feelings have changed. Ten months is a long time—a lot of things are happening here. I don't know if we are still going steady. I don't think so. I am sorry to do this to you. You must be a good soldier.
Regards, Charlene.

The spring in his step lapses into a funeral march and a dazed swerve towards his room. He forces his feet back on course for the workshop because the sergeant major is unrelenting about punctuality. Slatted roofs swim in front of him. The inside of his arm rubs across his face. Deep breath. Go inside, lance-corporal.

"Eddie, we're dropping the Bedford's gearbox today. Loosen the bolts on the prop shaft and the bell housing. I'm leaving for Bloemfontein main station now, to go and fetch a crate of spares from Pretoria."

A quick glance. "Yes, sergeant major," echoes hoarsely through the workshop.

Drop the Bedford's gearbox. Just as well go and do it—you were dropped today as well, a break-up letter? It doesn't fit with the kiss Charlene blew him from their veranda after Peet's funeral.

The next morning, Wilfried is in very high spirits when Platoon Bravo is dismissed on the parade ground. "Hang in there, guys. Fucking counting down the few days till 14 December." The heatwave over the Orange Free State forces the lieutenant to schedule the rehearsals for the passing-out parade in the mornings, before six o'clock.

At eight o'clock on 14 December, Eddie calls Platoon Bravo to attention. Corporal Rex marches them behind Sergeant Bushman. In between the berets, the parade ground comes into view. Mothers with umbrellas and fathers with hats on a pavilion made of wooden boards. A girlfriend here and there. Charlene would have been here if only they were still going steady. For months, Eddie saved money to pay for her return train ticket. The lieutenant's inspection is followed by his speech: The January 1976 intake is the country's pride. A brass band accompanies the Voice of South Africa. One last time, Bushman bellows: 'D-i-i-s-miss.' A platoon choir follows suit: Two-three one-two-three. Berets fly through the air, like Dad's racing pigeons when the cage opens in Randgate.

Wilfried arranges for himself to be in the same train compartment as Eddie. Outside the window a flat, fleeting Free State landscape—maize fields, plains, and sheep. Grim countryside, or is it just his mood? The monotonous, faraway chook-chook of a steam engine is no upbeat tune either.

They shake hands and tightly embrace at Johannesburg Station. "Go well, Willy. In a couple of years, you'll be Doctor Bucholz. That sounds great." He got selected to study medicine at Wits University in Johannesburg.

"Cheers, pal. Keep it up in the ring. I'll see you in the sports pages of the *Sunday Times*." The linoleum smell hits him unexpectedly—it feels like yesterday when he and Charlene travelled in a suburban train carriage to Johannesburg Station.

On the platform signage, the name Randfontein reads like a verdict. Ball bag slung over his shoulder, he gets down from the train and walks to the bus stop. Arms wrap around him from behind, "Hey, soldier boy! Thought you could just like arrive here without anyone noticing?"

"Suzette, nice surprise."

Leon suddenly appears as well, with his handshake grip like a pair of pliers, "This is Sandra," he introduces his girlfriend. "Let me carry this," Leon lifts the ball bag onto his shoulder. "Bloody hell, what's in here?"

Pain, my friend. "Army shit."

"Tonight, all of that is history. There's a barbecue party at my place," Leon gives Eddie a high-five.

Suzette, defiantly in front of Leon's Volkswagen Beetle: "Guess what, Eddie?"

"What?"

"Got my results this morning. An A for typing, and Bs for shorthand writing, Afrikaans, English, cooking. I've been admitted to Secretarial College."

"Congratulations, Sis. Tonight, we celebrate."

He feels admiration for his sister—she is so clever, and she works so hard. But anxiety gets the better of him. Mom can never pay for Suzette's studies—not with her nursing assistant's salary. The thought that Suzette's dream of becoming a secretary could dwindle away and her grabbing any available job she could with her matric certificate, turns his heart to ice.

Professional boxing is the only way for him to help them.

And he will.

Nineteen
Randfontein, 1977-1981

Moving Out

Propped up on his elbow, legs stretched out across his bed, he flips through the pages of *Ring* and lingers on the article Muhammad Ali versus Ken Norton—Yankee Stadium, New York—the third showdown between the two heavyweight bulls. In their first fight, Norton broke Ali's jaw with a short left hook in round one, when the Louisville Lip piped up in the ring again—after twelve rounds Norton won on points. Ali won the second fight. *Ring* creates great expectations in the boxing world about what could happen in a month's time in New York's baseball stadium.

A swim at the municipal pool? No. He doesn't have the heart to see Charlene in someone else's arms.

For breakfast, he had the leg of lamb left over from yesterday's Christmas dinner, mixed with putu porridge. He's thirsty now. The *Ring* is closed with a flutter. Maybe there is Coke in the fridge?

Dad is busy fumbling in a kitchen cupboard. He takes out a piece of paper, "I'm racing in the New Year'sh race. Here'sh the entry form. On New Year'sh eve, you musht get the bashket…"

"Dad, go stick your bloody racing pigeons in a basket yourself."

"Little Mister, hey? If you live in my houshe, you do what I shay."

He ducks as his father's flat hand whistles through his hair. A fanbelt whip curls out from behind the kitchen door and draws blood from his upper arm. The kitchen table is a battering ram in his scrotum and shoves his back against the wall.

"Ow, Dad. Damn."

More pressure from the table scrum, "And then you shwear at me, too."

The second whip strike flicks across his cheek and neck. He wipes his hand over the burning sensation. It is all covered in blood.

Suzette, through the open crack of the kitchen door, "Dad! Please stop it."

"Go to your room, nothing here for you women." He utters a deep growl, "I should have beaten the living daylights out of you when you were little, but it'sh not too late."

The whip draws an S in the air. Grab, tug, aim and crack it. He jumps across the kitchen table and rushes down the passage. Knocks and turns the door handle. The bedroom door is locked. "Suzette, open up."

Cl-i-ck. "I was scared he was going to come in."

"He won't believe me. Sis, I'm moving out."

With eyes like saucers. "What? Again, leaving me and Mom alone with him?"

"Suzette, it's not like when I had to go to the army. I'll be around here. Nearby."

Sobs and sniffs. "Don't decide too quickly."

"I'm not a child anymore and for him, nothing has changed. I'm going to talk to Uncle Ig." Halfway out through her bedroom window, "Keep your door locked and close this window."

"My God, Eddie, are you dating a wildcat?" Uncle Ig's arm motions him to come inside the house. A kitchen pot clangs from somewhere in the house. So, Antie Annette is home—Eddie flicks his thumb to the right, "To the gym, please, Uncle Ig."

In the backyard, the door bleats and creaks under Uncle Ig's hand. The neon light flickers on. Smells of leather, Dubbin and wintergreen fill the air. "It's…my father's whip."

Uncle Ig's head juts out a few centimetres, his jaw drops and eyebrows like exclamation marks jump out from behind his thick-framed glasses. "It's assault. I have never seen anything as bad in the ring. What about?"

"He's drunk again. I'm not staying in his house a moment longer. Do you have a place for me to stay?"

He leans back against the ring, hands to the back on the canvas floor, "Family business is private. I'm not luring you away from your parents' house. In our neighbourhood, nobody will ever believe it was your own choice, as a grown man. Everybody makes up their own story and then they just add bits as they please—I know them."

"Then I'll talk to Leon's parents to rent his room—he's going to the army in a few days." In a soft whisper, in case Antie Annette is eavesdropping, "I punched…my father. I'm moving out, no question." He tries to swallow again. The surge, as bitter as gall, burns his throat.

"You can rent our maid's room in the backyard. The Antie has a single bed and a cupboard if you're interested. Six rand a month."

"Deal, Uncle Ig."

Back home, he taps against her window. A slit appears in the curtain. "Open up, Suzette."

"What happened?"

"I'm renting the outside room from Uncle Ig."

"I was so scared while you were away."

"If you need me, just phone. I'll be here in no time."

Later on, Mom's Simca whirs in the driveway.

She is locking the door of her car, a smoking cigarette pressed between her lips when he comes out of the kitchen back door, "Hello, Mom, I'm sorry…"

"Hello, Eduard. I heard everything. Fred from the racing pigeon club brought your dad to Emergencies this afternoon. He's lying there to sober up for anaesthetics, so the surgeon can set his jaw."

"I had no choice."

"I saw it coming. Now, it's happened. Make me some tea, please."

What a disappointment. Mom was so proud when she quit smoking two years ago. Now, she'll judge herself again for giving in to the habit. Apart from this, it's a definite reminder of Dad's accusation that she's just another hypocritical member of the Apostolic Faith Mission, hiding her sins.

Maybe he could fix his mistake, if he helped Mom with money for Suzette to study at college. But then he must get things in place urgently to start earning.

Professional boxing, that is what he will do.

Twenty

Chris

He wants to get fighting fit again. After the SA championships in Port Elizabeth, he kept on exercising and sparring, but with no goal as his next milestone in mind. His aim now is to box professionally—to earn a living with his fists, like Uncle Ig did as a young man. Didn't he say that when Eddie turns professional, he'll be in his corner? That's a big vote of confidence.

Early morning, when Eddie comes into the gymnasium, back from roadwork, Ig is already waiting in the ring—a mug of coffee clutched in his bunch-of-bananas fingers.

Eddie's practice schedule is prescribed on the blackboard nailed to the wall: 300 sit-ups, push-ups and leg-ups and five times three-minute sessions of rope skipping. Every second day, half a dozen rounds against the speedball and punchbag, or shadow boxing under watchful eyes behind the thick-framed glasses—building muscle memory for salvos of punch combinations, like his heroes Mohammad Ali and Carlos Monzon. Eddie works hard to float and swing his upper body, just like they do, always in balance on his front foot, planting firm punches and retracting his arms lightning fast, in defence. Already during school days, when he heard that SA Mirror was screening a fight of heavyweight Ali or middleweight Monzon before the main movie, he would climb over the fence of Randfontein drive-in theatre to see him in action. He often went back a second and a third time, and then shadowboxed against himself in a mirror, mimicking their every move, believing that if he is that good at home, he could be that good anywhere.

After the gymnasium practice schedule, it's a quick shower, getting dressed and on his way to Bertz Automobiles. He passed the N1 Automotive Mechanics exams by the skin of his teeth. "Fifty per cent is a pass, Mister Bertz, please." Eddie follows the example of other professional boxers to get qualified in a trade as an alternative career—in *Ring*, he reads that Gerrie Coetzee's first profession is a dental technician.

On weekday mornings, he keeps a lookout from his backyard room for when Sandra, Uncle Ig and Antie Annette's afterthought daughter, leaves the house to catch her bus to Riebeeck High School. Walking with her provides a few agreeable minutes of talking, but his heart protests. The bus stop is his and Charlene's special place. Here, he waited after he had slipped away early from his own school to surprise her and carry her school bag all the way home. Everything of that is lost now.

In mid-February, Uncle Ig parks his Opel Kadett in front of a red brick building in Booysens on the western outskirts of Johannesburg. He did not stop talking for a minute since they left Randgate. A business-like Uncle Ig: contracts with promoters, coaches, managers, and the royalties paid to each out of a boxer's winnings. "To make a living with your fists is tough. Professionals don't ask for mercy, and don't give any." Then silence fills the Kadett, with an affectionate look through the thick-framed glasses.

Is this his gap, in case, he wanted to turn around and quit his dream?

"Uncle Ig, I don't expect any mercy."

Thick fingers clutch his thigh with a hard squeeze. "With Chris Rossouw, we've got one of the best managers in the country; the others are money-grubbers."

"I take your word, Uncle Ig."

A late afternoon ray of sunlight reflects on the sign above the entrance: Booysens Boxing Academy, Home of Champions. Eddie feels curious to see what it looks like inside.

Resolutely, he makes his way to the wooden doors, ascending the few stairs two by two. His future starts here.

One hefty pull on the shaft of the polished bronze door handle and he follows Uncle Ig inside. The entrance hall is hung with photographs and framed newspaper covers. John McGregor, triumphant over a bloody Kurt Weinstock on the ring floor—in the army, he listened in on the fight on Hannes' portable radio. Excitement carries him further in.

An array of neon tubes lights up the ring in the middle of the hall. On the left, three punch bags in the semi-dusk. He dance-steps closer—thump-thump. Adrenaline rushes through his veins—everything feels so unreal. Thump-thump, the pain in his bare knuckles confirms that he is not dreaming.

"Here, Eddie," someone pipes up from the opposite side of the hall. The light from a table lamp shines faintly on someone seated next to Uncle Ig. "Eddie, meet Chris Rossouw, the owner of BBA."

An open hand appears under the lamplight, "Hello, Eddie." The other hand offers a sheaf of paper. "Standard terms for my boxers."

"What is this, Uncle Ig?"

"Your contract; you must sign before you are allowed to spar in the BBA. It safeguards Chris against any injury you sustain here, while he negotiates your fights and earnings, organises sparring partners, travel and accommodation—that kind of thing. He gets ten per cent of your prize money, like me. I know the contract. If you're OK with it, you can sign."

A three-legged stool sticks out from under the table. He sits askew on one buttock and reads.

The language of the contract sounds like something from the Tower of Babel. Mom's voice resonates with more clarity in his mind. "Eduard, I'm paying Suzette's college fees with a loan. I've pawned my sewing machine to buy her a typewriter. The thirty rand must be paid back in three monthly instalments. If not, the pawn shop will sell my machine." He takes the pen that Chris holds out to him. He knows zilch about contracts, but if he doesn't sign, he can't even start sparring. He signs his initials on every page and his full name on the last one, just like Chris. Uncle Ig does the same as a witness—which is reassuring.

"Welcome on board. You spar on Monday and Wednesday evenings at six. Don't be late." Can't he expect a warmer welcome from his manager? Or is Chris living proof of the rumours in Randgate? Jo'burg people are upstairs—even more than those from the Greenhills or Homelake neighbourhoods of Randfontein.

Well, Eddie could only be himself and will impress him with his fists.

Twenty-One

Second Chance

In his first appearance without a boxing vest, he fights for the vacant Transvaal middleweight title—since his army days, he gained muscle weight and now tips the scale at just over 70 kilograms. Champion Geerts' wrist was broken in a motorcycle accident the previous weekend. Uncle Ig says, "Eddie, my boy, I'm not pressuring you for a title fight, but Mulder's experience is only one fight more than yours."

Outside Ellis Park tennis stadium the banners still proclaim: 'Ben Geerts vs Rudolf Mulder'.

Mulder remains standing for three of the scheduled four rounds. Eddie becomes the new Transvaal middleweight boxing champion, "Rudolf hasn't made any progress since I knocked him out during our amateur days."

Chris contracts Eddie against John Roberts for his second fight.

A week before the fight, the daily newspaper, *Beeld*, reports:

John the Jab is back

Our former welterweight national champion, John Roberts, is back in the ring as a middleweight. Next Saturday, at 39, he will be the oldest professional boxer in South Africa to climb through the ropes. In the post-war years, Ignatius Bester, the trainer of Roberts's opponent, defended his title at 38. Roberts will be up against newcomer Eddie Blignaut. He can prepare himself for fireworks—Sybrand Goosen, Sports Editorial.

Thousands of Hillbrow city lights are framed by the windscreen of the Opel Kadett. The streets are teaming with people. It's so different from quiet Friday nights in Randgate.

"Wow, Uncle Ig, now I'll find out what a hotel room sleeps like."

Keys are pushed towards them across the reception counter at the Stages Hotel—rooms twelve and thirteen.

"You take room twelve, Eddie; thirteen is bad luck. Sleep well. You weigh in tomorrow morning at eight."

"I'm going to read my new *Ring*. There's an article on Carlos Monzon in it."

"Night, Eddie. Oh, yes, I asked Manny Perreira to second me tomorrow night."

"Manny who?"

"Manny boxed at my club five years ago, he was about your age then—also a middleweight. Could have become SA champ but has absolutely no discipline."

"OK, I understand. Night, see you tomorrow." He turns around and then turns back again. The number thirteen door is half open. He knocks and pushes it. "Uncle Ig? Can I come in?"

The toilet flushes and he emerges from the bathroom. "Now what?"

"I…well, I want to say thank you. You know about my troubles back home. This is my golden opportunity."

Two taps on his shoulder are worth more than words. He unlocks room number twelve. What? Double bed and sofa on a thick cream-coloured carpet. One step over the threshold, the lily-white bathroom to the right. His sports bag and small suitcase fit neatly into the wardrobe. The smooth nylon bedspread puffs up with a whooshing sound when his back hits it, arms and legs outstretched across the bed. What would Charlene say about such luxury? Does she know he's boxing tomorrow night?

After a long shower and reading *Ring*, he is suddenly preoccupied by John Roberts. The man is as old as Dad.

He swings his legs out from under the bedclothes.

His pair of new white sneakers trot down the stairs.

At reception, "Good evening, does the hotel have a tickey box?"

"It's broken. Go to Fontana, up the road on the left. They're open twenty-four-seven."

"Thanks," he says halfway to the door across his shoulder.

He dials Charlene's number but slams down the receiver when it starts ringing on the other side. He doesn't want to hear from old Bettie that Charlene is at yet another school function. The alarm clock says one o'clock when he gets into bed again. In his normal routine, he would be in dreamland by now, but his mood did not feel normal tonight. He rolls over and over into the night.

*****

Who's breaking down his door?

Oh hell, that's right; he's in the Stages Hotel.

Uncle Ig's sneakers dance impatiently outside room number twelve.

"It's seven o'clock." The baseball cap in his hand bounces with every word. "Didn't you set your alarm?"

"Must have hit it mute—sorry, Uncle Ig. I'm coming." Hands full of cold water. Tracksuit? There, draped across the sofa, sneakers on the floor. Somewhere in his sports bag are his socks. In the suitcase, his toilet bag: last Christmas present from Charlene—wish you were here so badly.

Moments later, he pulls open his bedroom door. "Here I am."

"Come."

Uncle Ig turns around in a determined way and marches down the passage and then bobs in front of him down the stairs, through reception and out along the pavement.

His Opel Kadett bounces out of the parking space. "That was the last time, Eddie. Next time, I'll leave you to finish your beauty sleep, you'll miss your weigh-in and you'll be a motormac for the rest of your life. You fuckin' understand me?"

"I do, Uncle Ig."

"The boxing game has a few golden rules. One is time management: how long you sleep—and how long you train for. Every minute counts. In the ring, it's seconds: ten on the canvas and your career is over. The ring forgives no one—and that includes you. It's every boxer's moment of truth. Don't expect special treatment. Grow respect for yourself by how you treat yourself…and discipline yourself."

His name appears at the bottom of the banners tied to the Rand Stadium fence, opposite that of John Roberts—the opening fight of the evening. The gate guard nods at Uncle Ig's BBA ticket and the boom to the parking lot lifts. The Kadett comes to a halt under the grandstand, across from a notice which reads Press, Boxers & Trainers.

"If you make eye contact with John this morning, pin him with your eyes." Uncle Ig's right hand lifts off the steering wheel, pointing the index and middle fingers at Eddie, "Then stalk him visually—every time he looks at you, he gets your stone-cold emotionless glare. Let's go. Once inside, present your boxing licence to the tournament doctor."

Eddie answers with a thumbs-up.

The air is humming with voices. Cameras are flashing. In the middle of the venue, a doctor is busy examining a boxer with his stethoscope and a small flashlight.

"Hello. I'm Eddie Blignaut. Here's my licence."

"You can't use your driver's licence here," someone calls out. "If you're old enough to have one." Ha-ha-ha.

"It's Roberts and his English troops, Eddie. Give me your tracksuit."

The doctor listens to his heartbeat, takes his blood pressure and shines a torch light in his eyes and down his throat. "You're fit. Please get onto the scale."

The cold foot plate sends a shiver up his back. Small iron weights shift to and fro on the balancing bar Eyes take aim over semi-rimless glasses. "Seventy kilos. Within the limit. Good luck to you as well." the tournament doctor says and hands back his licence.

That English accent, again, "Eat Weetbix for breakfast, or are you still on Rice Krispies?" Ha-ha-ha.

Uncle Ig pushes a cameraman to one side. "Come on, Eddie. I'm hungry."

A man in a t-shirt, jeans and a leather jacket walks up to them in the reception area of the Stages Hotel.

"Hello, Uncle Ig."

"Hello, Manny. Meet Eddie."

"Hi, Manny."

Manny greets with a high-five, "Howzit." Shiny teeth. Sallow complexion. A scar across his right cheek. Knife? Knuckle-duster, maybe? Wavelets of hair, like the steel wool pot scourers mom uses in her kitchen. Tufts of beard here and there. "Uncle Ig, I went by the BBA this morning. Picked up a couple of boxing movies and the projector from Chris. Also brought a pack of cards and dominos so Eddie's not too preoccupied with Mister Roberts."

"Thanks, Manny. The dining room is through that door, guys."

A sugar bowl with a spout sprinkles sugar over Eddie's maize-meal porridge. Manny seats himself opposite him. He didn't miss one course on the buffet table.

"Figure, I'm getting a second chance, together with Eddie?"

Uncle Ig bites a forkload of bacon and eggs and chews heartily, "Not everyone in the boxing game gets a second chance." Sprinkling sugar into his cup of coffee, he says, "I was Commonwealth Games champ, and then I turned pro. After a few fights, I was the South African light heavyweight champ. Square Ring Promotions offered me a contract in London—a cold, wet place. I knocked out Kevin Naylor, the British champion, in the third round. I won against a Yank, a Spaniard, and a Frenchman in a row. I was the first contender to fight the International Boxing Union champion when the bloody Jerries started making war—within a week, I was on a ship heading home. The prize money for my last fight is still somewhere in an English bank. Probably landed up in some Tommy's pocket." Business-like, "I'm going to the Rand Stadium to finish some admin and should be back at the hotel around four."

"I'll go get some grilled chicken at Fontana for lunch. Protein's good, and light to digest."

"Manny, so you know Fontana?"

"Eddie, look at the Hillbrow Hit. Ain't no joint in Hillbrow this guy doesn't know."

"I wish you would hit the men in the ring like you hit the Hillbrow streets. Tell Eddie about the potholes in the road of pro-boxing."

"Too much sex and booze make you lose." He blushes a deep red and darts an oblique glance at Uncle Ig, "Appreciate this second chance."

Twenty-Two

This Far

Banana-sized fingers press tension knots out of his neck and shoulder muscles.

"Roberts is a broke has-been. Rookie Blignaut stands between him and his next pay cheque. Tonight, he will try to trick and cheat you. I know him from his heyday, Eddie."

A panting Manny appears at the cloakroom entrance. "Uncle Ig, the judges are seated. We must go. C'mon, Eddie." His boxing gown is already hanging from Manny's hands.

Uncle Ig leads the three-man squad from under the grandstand, with Mannie on Eddie's heels. Across Ig's chunky shoulders, Eddie gets a view of the brightly lit ring. Suzette's silhouette appears in front of them in the aisle, her arms motioning to the left, "We're sitting there with Leon. Mom stayed at home; says she can't see you getting hurt—she's praying for you. A guy called Wilfried phoned—and said good luck for tonight."

Wilfried follows his career. Why doesn't Charlene phone? Underneath his boxing gown hood, he shifts his focus back to his name on the back of Uncle Ig's tracksuit jacket.

Manny step-presses down and pulls open the ropes. Eddie ducks and slips through into the spotlight. Suddenly, nobody is visible in the half-light outside the ring.

Uncle Ig, this afternoon, on the way to the Rand Stadium, "You're also an entertainer, Eddie, the crowd has come to see you perform. Acknowledge it—take a bow in front of them." He does, in all four directions. Back in his corner, he grinds his boots in rosin. A loud roar fills the night: Roberts, a real show-off, with swaying shoulders, gloves triumphantly above his head, and dances ever closer to Eddie.

From behind his neck, fingers tighten comforting. "Eddie, take your crowd-roar at the end of the fight. Now remember, pin him and stalk him from first eye contact."

The loudspeaker crackles from above, "In the red corner, fighting out of Vereeniging and back from retirement after fi-i-ive years...welcome, John the Jab, R-o-o-berts. The half-light answers: John, John...In the green corner, the young hopeful from Randfontein, Eddie Blign-a-u-t."

The referee nods them to the centre of the ring. His prescriptions end with...protect yourself at all times. I want a clean fight. Shake hands.

Manny has vacated the corner. Uncle Ig, leaning over the ropes, "Box him, Eddie, you can."

The loudspeakers crackle again. Seconds out. R-o-u-nd number one. Eddie pounds his corner sponge with a salvo of quick punches and turns around—his body like the pebble in the tightly pulled elastic of a catapult.

Gong. Between his gloves, he sees John coming for him. Contact. Duck. Left-right. Cover-up—punches hammer against his armour, graze his face. Roberts clinches him and burrows his chin into Eddie's shoulder, a crunching k-r-rts sound from his ear shell. *You're head-butting*, John. The referee scrambles in between. "Break." Roberts' incessant left jabs leave a gap in his defence. Eddie fires a lightning-fast punch. Rotate hips to slingshot his right hook with his full weight, "Take that, old man." His mouth moving inaudibly above the crowd's chanting, Roberts again comes looking for a place to curl up against Eddie. He tears himself loose and ducks down, a left punch flying over his head. Gap—a right punch thuds into Roberts' heart. Follow-up left-right-left drives him in reverse towards the ropes, head ratcheting backwards. His gloves once more burrow under Eddie's arms. K-r-rts goes his ear, on the clock.

"Dirtbag," Eddie growls through his mouthguard. Manny pushes the little green stool through the ropes. Uncle Ig climbs over.

"The round is yours, Eddie. He's lost speed, but not his tricks." In between strokes of wet, cold sponge, "Attack sooner. Open a path for your right with some left jabs." He feels a smirch of Vaseline on each ear.

Seconds out, r-o-u-nd number two.

The minute was short. He gets up, bites his mouthguard out of Uncle Ig's hand and dances forward. "Is that your best, Grandpa?" When John locks arms again. The referee separates them. Uncle Ig, a sponge in his fist, throws left punches in the air outside the ring. "Move, Eddie. Left jabs."

It works. John is on the back foot when the gong chimes. Eddie grows in self-confidence, feels in good physical shape and the butterflies have left his tummy. He makes a light-footed dash for his corner.

"Well done, you're using the entire ring and the ropes. Let your fists do the talking, not you. Rather bite your mouthguard firmly, otherwise, John can break your jaw." Seconds out, r-o-u-nd number three.

Eddie's lightning-fast left punches keep Roberts off balance. He locks arms. Break. His swing shot yanks Eddie's jaw to one side as they break, sending his mouthguard flying and bouncing across the floor. In amateur boxing, the referee would right away interrupt the fight to have the boxer put it back. "You hit after I said break. Next time, it's a warning." Roberts's left immediately strikes the target. "Stop," he gets ordered to a neutral corner. Eddie wipes across his mouth. A broad, bloody stripe stains his glove.

He swallows the salty taste, bites the mouthguard out of the referee's hand and dances forward. Duck. Roberts' left misses the target. Sidestep. He feels his right fist sinking away into John's stomach and another uppercut. Hips twisting, he fires a left-right-left salvo. Glassy eyes glance back at Eddie. Bull's eye right on John's chin. A desperate left swing shot from him finds only empty Rand Stadium evening air. At the sound of the gong, the referee rushes in between fighters.

The little green, three-legged stool is waiting. "It's burning like fire under my arms."

"You're chafed raw, Manny, rub Vaseline. It's your round, Eddie. Shit, your lower lip is split. Turn southpaw. Jab him with straight, right punches. Move quickly, anticlockwise, and keep him off balance."

"Uncle Ig, ask the ref to look at John's gloves. I'm sure he made them rough at the laces."

"Manny, I'll decide what we do. Give Eddie some water."

Seconds out, r-o-u-nd number four.

Roberts shows blind spots for Eddie's attack. Right foot in front, two-three-four right-hand punches flash into John's face and stack up points. A left hook sends his sweat spraying from under the spotlights. John comes forward like a collapsing wall. Another frantic left swing shot misses. Arms lock. "You've never gone this far, sonny boy. Will you make it?" Out of the green corner, "Move, Eddie, move and jab. Use the entire ring."

Take a deep breath and focus. Jab-jab, his southpaw right stops John's advance. He half stands, half collapses, feet flat, jaw hanging, and breathing heavily in Eddie's neck. He rips himself loose and his right leads; his follow-up left cross also hits the mark. Cling-cling-cling, resonates through the air.

"Sponge me down under my arms, it's burning like hell." As Eddie reaches his corner.

"Like raw liver," Manny works fervently, rubbing Vaseline on the sides of Eddie's upper ribcage.

"Your round, Eddie. Stay southpaw. Jab him. Punish him with body punches if he clinches and treads water."

Seconds out, r-o-u-nd number five.

Roberts glares from under a swollen left brow. With rolling fists, he dances just out of Eddie's reach, "C'mon, chicken, where's your punch?"

Don't start the street fight now that John is provoking. Box clean—whip him with straight punches and arms pulled back lighting fast in defence against John's windmill swings. Gap—left hook, punch to the chin. John half stumbles to the red corner on the gong.

"Well done, Eddie, move, you're becoming static. Stay within reach and beware of headbutts."

Seconds out, sixth and final…f-i-n-a-l round.

The referee motions that they must shake hands. They tap gloves. Box. John throws his back to the referee and spits on Eddie's chest. Instinctively, he wipes clean. Boom cracks the swing punch; zing goes his ear. Forward bounce from the ropes, aim, punch. John's brow bursts open like an overripe tomato.

Stop, a white shirt flashes in between them. "To the neutral corner," the referee orders Eddie.

The tournament doctor touches and prods around Roberts' eye. "Cut's away from the eye, no danger to his sight," He speaks down to the main judge. Box.

Arms locked, "Grandpa John, I'm going to bleed you before I knock you out." Tear away. John blocks with crossed arms to protect his eyes and jaw. Dances victoriously with lifted hands when the gong saves him.

From the green corner. "Well done, Eddie. Damn good work."

"Thanks, Uncle Ig. Was the fastest half hour of my life."

Manny dives halfway through the ropes, "Hi five, Eddie."

The referee collects the scorecards from three judges, each seated on different sides of the ring for an all-around vantage point of the fight. He hands it to the main judge, who compares and hands one note back with a nod of his head. The microphone crackles: The winner, on a unanimous points decision…Eddie Blign-a-u-t and the referee lifts his hand high. Eddie waves his other hand to the crowd. Roberts peers at him askance from under his swollen brow, "Your punches look easy, land like bricks."

Manny helps him put on his boxing gown. Again, he waves to the crowd—longer in the direction where he figures his tribe must be sitting and then through the ropes and down the steps. Suzette sparkles, "Congratulations."

Leon pulls him in amongst the spectators, "Randgate is proud of you."

Hey, Eddie! Well done. Eddie! Nice fight! Can be heard from the seats around him. His first public supporters—it feels unreal, but strangers are calling him by his first name, the same way people talk about Mohammad Ali or Carlos Monzon. His joyful mood feels dampened. There is a void in the fullness of his heart. If Charlene had been here, his evening would have been just perfect.

Twenty-Three

#1

Sunday morning, his courage fails him. If he saw Charlene again, he would fall back into depression. It would be even worse if she was with another boyfriend. He would rather phone with the news about his win last night.

In the cream-coloured red-top phone booth across the street from Corner Lounge Café, he hears her father's voice in the receiver: Charlene is not home. Antie Bettie has just taken her back to the hostel at the Teachers' College.

Wilfried's number turns on the dial. "Eddie, congrats. Read all about you in the *Sunday Times* Sports pages this morning."

"Thanks, Willy. How are you doing?"

"Lots of study work. Girls are fun. We should meet up sometime."

"I'll come over for a beer one evening. I'm training in Booysens."

"Cool. That's real close to the Braamfontein campus. See you soon, pal."

"Goodbye, Willy." As true as Bob, you could just as well have been an Afrikaner. Eddie feels satisfied that his money plans are working out. With his four hundred rand winnings from his fight against Roberts, he pays the thirty rand to buy back his mom's sewing machine from the pawn shop; just in time before they sell it. He also gives her Suzette's college fees for the second term, as well as the fees for the first term, to pay back whoever Mom borrowed it from. For a while already, he's had his eye on the pair of golden-yellow Adidas boxing boots in All-Sports' display window in Randfontein's main street. They feel as light as a feather on his feet—three silver stripes on the sides remind him of lightning bolts. Now he can return Manny's worn-out pair of boxing boots. He could also not resist a pair of Ray-Ban sunglasses. He doesn't replace his diamond-black boxing trunks—it's Mom's sewing pride.

*****

After eight victories in a row, including five knockouts, Sybrand Goosen reports in *Beeld's* Saturday, 24 May 1980 issue on The Crown Prince of South African Boxing. A middleweight sensation. In his strong-headed, conservative way, Uncle Ig shapes and hones Eddie's fitness and improves his fist technique and psychological preparedness. He listens to advice in different octaves and decibels on how to prepare for every fight as though it is going to go the full distance—Don't count on a knockout; you discover the right moment for that in the ring, Eddie boy.

While sparring at the BBA, he learns how to work through a fight round by round. At the start of every round, each boxer has ten points. If there are no knockdowns and one fighter has dominated, the opponent loses one of his ten points. When a fighter knocks his opponent down and he takes eight counts, the opponent loses an additional point—if he gets back to his feet immediately without taking the count, he does not lose the additional point. If a fighter is thoroughly outclassed in a round but does not take a knockdown, he may lose two points. A fighter may lose a point in a round for committing a major foul and being warned by the referee for that. Serious fouls include butting with his head, punching below the belt, hold-and-hitting. Those are the rules, Ig said the day when he had finished writing it up on the black board in his Randgate gymnasium, Eddie, you will respect it.

Uncle Ig reminds repetitively, "It is damn tough enough retaining your ten points in a round, don't lose even one in a stupid way. Strike only clean blows in the target areas—face and upper body. If you score with the cleanest blows, you may be allowed a point in deciding that round—remember that judges are also people with emotions. But, do not mess around; taps do not count. And, for each fight, we will have a game plan, which I will adapt as your fight progresses. If your opponent wins a round; you must come back immediately and win the next to retain an equal say in the fight. When your opponent shows signs of fatigue, his concentration also wanes. Keep eye contact and be on the lookout for any sign of wandering eyes, then strike immediately. Always remain positive in the ring—even when defending. That too, makes a subjective impression on the judges."

"I can be better managed. I'm going to change managers," he announces one morning after roadwork.

From inside the ring, across the ropes, a frown deepens above thick-framed glasses, "What do you mean?" An index finger points nonchalantly to the training schedule, "That's your menu."

After six rounds of speedball, he tries again, "I'm only sixth in the rankings. I can give any contender above me a hiding. With Chris, I would never get a shot at the title."

A spanner gives a tightening turn to every screw behind each corner post. Uncle Ig leans back and assesses the tension in the ropes. On his way out of the ring, "Your opponents are not Chris' decision on his own." Fingers are pressing down on a rolled-up bandage, "Left hand." One time around Eddie's hand, then between two fingers and around again, the bandage plaits his hand and wrist into a weaver's nest. "Chris and I plan your fights together. Eddie, if you want to make a living out of boxing, you must feel at home between those ropes, like me with a cow carcass in my butchery. You must know every square inch and how to use it. You're not there yet. Take the punchbag for six rounds and work on your counter punches from the back foot. It discourages an opponent who still gets the daylights punched out of him when he attacks."

Like every Saturday morning, when Sandra does not have school, he walks to work alone, but today, he is hot under the collar. As Eddie's winnings increase, so do Chris' demands for even higher fees with every future fight, above and beyond his percentage share. High-flown references accentuate yet another fine print clause in their contract, of which Eddie doesn't understand a word. Chris is just making money out of him. Damn, money-grubber.

*****

The streets of Randgate and Randfontein are now no-go areas for him. He underestimated Hitboy Malinga and disappointed his supporters—just can't look them in the eye. His house has become a prison. The dormant bitter taste of a tied result against Hitboy makes the days unbearable. At night, sleep evades him—nightmares of Wolwehoek, with delusions of Hitboy in between.

Wolwehoek near Fochville, where farmers from the region come to listen in on rugby commentary on Saturday afternoons at mom's Uncle Andries' farm. One afternoon, Western Transvaal beat Western Province in Potchefstroom. The bottle of Klipdrift brandy is taken down from its place on the rock-built kraal wall and glasses are refilled: Here's to the maize farmers! You fucked up those finfeet really good. Soon after, Uncle Andries is on Satan's back. Roughshod. Neck pulled to one side, saliva foaming from its mouth with pearls of sweat on its back, the black horse prances. Glasses raised, again.

Now everyone gets a chance on Satan.

The boys are arguing about whose father is the best rider when Dad slides off the horse's back and cups his hands, "Get on, Eduard—time that I make a man out of you."

The beast's skin is smooth and slippery wet. "Dad, what about the saddle?" His legs grip tightly around the animal's thick body. From far down below, "Your belt, Andries." Drumbeats thundering in Eddie's ears. A whack behind him, across Satan's buttocks. Trees flash past, winter grassland rocking back and forth. Barbed wire fence. Swerve. Nosedive. Humiliation right in front of all the other boys, mouth full of sand, his cheek a ball of fire. He better get up quickly before Dad helps him up straight with that belt.

There were maybe half a dozen ten-twelve-year-old other boys at Wolwehoek, that humiliating Saturday afternoon. But Hitboy knocked him down in front of thousands of people. From the first round, he found Hitboy's style annoying—his left hand, always pawing towards Eddie, limiting his vision for the exploding bombs delivered with his right hand. Having become known for that, Hitboy gets his nickname from journalists. He must have observed the moment when Eddie's concentration wavered, just a whisker because he didn't see the punch coming. Instinctively, he is off the floor and up on his feet. The mandatory eight count echoes in his head, which feels filled with cotton wool. A hazy Hitboy-silhouette pushes and pushes his long left in Eddie's direction and tries to limit his sight for a knockout punch. Block, clinch, pray for the end. After the last gong: We have a draw.

How humiliating. His unbeaten record, his pride, in shatters. He was ready to notch up his next victory. Now, his record bears the scar of a draw. Was he careless, and if so, where? Inside or outside the ring, or in his head? His fight now is against low self-esteem. A few months ago, he bought a townhouse in Greenhills, for cash. He hired a caterer for the housewarming and invited his tribe: Leon and his girlfriend, Mom, Uncle Ig, Antie Annette and their afterthought daughter Sandra, Suzette, and her fiancée Krisjan Ollewagen, Sybrand Goosen, Chris and a few other of his BBA friends. Their attitude towards him, especially, is not the same anymore—it's as though he has gone down the rankings in their esteem. Luckily, his motor mechanic apprenticeship is almost at an end—the N3 national apprentice exam is around the corner. Maybe he deserves nothing better than being a motormac—Mister Bertz is already talking about a permanent appointment. The winnings in his savings account are a source of comfort; in case, Mom's hip collapses and she can't work anymore, he can help her. No way, Blignaut. There is just one way forward: go fight Malinga again and win, like Ali against Norton. You must become Hitboy's superior, in mind, body and soul—Uncle Ig's new slogan in the gym.

He is already there when Eddie jogs in from road work, the next morning at 6 am, "Eddie, my boy, if there's someone who believes in you, it's me. Here in my gym, as in the BBA, I'm at your side; I'm in your corner when you fight. But in the ring, it's just you and your body. That's your first step: a top-fit body will give you self-confidence whether you throw punches or take them—you must feel good about both." He rewrites Eddie's training schedule. More hours on the road, around and around the local rugby field with a car tyre in tow until his thigh muscles glow—a sore muscle means nothing; it's when a muscle burns that you build it up, according to Uncle Ig. Chopping stacks of wood, until his upper arms and shoulder blades contract in a spasm, and then carrying on chopping to regain control over his body. Sparring at the BBA against lightning-fast featherweights who strike like a swarm of wasps and against heavyweights with cannon fists whose punches knock him back a step. Stand up wrestling against champion wrestlers to learn grips and how to break free from theirs.

Chris organised an interview with the press in the BBA. According to Sybrand Goosen in *Beeld*, a few days before the fight, Eddie Blignaut's aim is to win back the trust of his supporters. He is preparing extremely hard for his rematch against Hitboy Malinga. This afternoon, in Chris Rossouw's BBA gymnasium, Eddie let the sparks fly during his sparring rounds—he has new fire in him, for sure.

*****

Uncle Ig, as the gong rings: "It's your moment of truth, Eddie. Box him the way you know how."

It soon becomes clear that Hitboy also wants to restore the honour of his tarnished, previously unbeaten record. Like in their first fight, his right hook is relentless in seeking Eddie's jaw but finds the defensive left-hand glove and a counterpunch right followed by Eddie's firm left in the short rib, to where Hitboy doesn't bring back his right hand in defence fast enough—a salvo of combination punches practised over and over until Uncle Ig was satisfied with the accuracy and intensity.

"I score this first round to you. Come sit. Take the fight to him and get him on the back foot," he listens in the one-minute break.

Seconds out…ro-o-o-und number two.

Eddie hops off his little chair and trots towards Hitboy. Left, left, right, left, duck before the right-hander. With his short rib unprotected, Hitboy is driven back against the ropes. Shrewdly, he closes his defence, floats, waves like a cypress tree in the wind in front of Eddie and then launches a counterattack. His right hook shakes Eddie's jaw in its seams. He rides the punch with backward momentum and swings an uppercut into the pit of the onrushing Hitboy's stomach, sails out from under another right hook and plants one more short rib left followed by his own right hook which snaps the cypress-like figure. The referee has counted an entire handful when the gong rings and Hitboy pulls himself up against the ropes.

Halfway through round three, a right uppercut knocks the wind out of Hitboy. Facing Eddie, he tries to escape from the corner under the murderous attack, to the left and right, covers up, tries to tread water and in his clumsiness, leaves an opening for a ripping overhand chopping right punch which lunges him through the ropes and out of the ring. Ten seconds later, he still lies there.

Uncle Ig, in the cloakroom: "Today your weeks of training paid off."

"Recently, I couldn't understand. You were sort of different."

"I wouldn't have left you in the hole where you were after your tied result. You had to change, Eddie—your way of training, thinking, everything. We had to make a plan." The thick fingers feel firm in his hand.

"Thanks, Uncle."

"Tonight, you completed your apprenticeship."

Ring's December 1980 edition ranks him the #1 contender for Jerry McIntosh's South African middleweight title. As he reads it, it's like a song—he buys a stack of copies and everyone he knows gets one. He can probably find Charlene's address and send hers by post. But, it may rock the boat of her life: she may be in a relationship. Why would she be getting posts from a stranger out of the blue?

Twenty-Four

Champion

This morning, *Beeld's* headlines bannered to street lampposts predicting snow around Johannesburg. On the Highveld in September? Blowing over his fingertips, he calculates the last few metres of his roadwork. The gym's door handle presses open under his elbow. Inside, quickly, choke the hinge's bleating creak with his heel. "Morning, Uncle Ig."

Tracksuit top zipped up, worn slippers, steaming coffee in his hand. Sparse little grey hairs, soaking wet, plastered back, "Morning, Eddie. Take one-pound weights and shadow box fast. Six rounds of three minutes."

"Why?" Uncle Ig once said that weights slow you down.

"If your title fight goes full distance, you'll have to use your arms in the last round, the same way as in the first. I'm not getting Hitboy nightmares next to the ring again."

After six rounds, with one minute's rest in between, the gym clock shows half past six.

"I'm going to open. Come around to the butchery after work. Chris is expecting news from Square Ring Promotions."

*****

Eddie washes his hands, takes off his overalls and gives long strides towards his Ford Escort.

Bought from Mister Bertz, below book value—a concession to staff.

He gets parking right in front of the Meat Cauldron.

From behind the counter, "Just heard from Chris." Above the clients' heads Uncle Ig's hand motions to the cold-room. "Twenty-two February is your chance at the title. Tomorrow night, we're meeting the Turner Brothers and Jerry McIntosh's camp at the BBA to sign."

Has he ever seen Uncle Ig this radiant? "I'm going to take that title. Ring's 1981 Fight of the Year—promise."

*****

Manny step-presses and pulls open the ropes. Eddie slips through. The February night air echoes his arrival in the ring. A cacophony of applause and jeering—his draw against Hitboy clearly not forgotten yet. Tonight, he'll fix all of that.

McIntosh's experience and ring-sense put him in the lead at the end of round nine. "Eddie, the Lord is my witness: Box. If you lose tonight, I lose as well. Mac is tired. Turn southpaw and hunt him out with straight right jabs. You've got three rounds, use every second and every inch of the ring."

"Right, Uncle Ig."

Seconds out, ro-o-und number ten.

Jerry! Jerry! The arena doesn't stop talking. Shoulders pulled back. Jog up to him.

"Com'on, kid, you've never gone ten roun—" is silenced by a right fist. Half-rotate hips for a full-weight left hook that sends McIntosh's mouth guard shooting out in a saliva squirt from under the lights. Fake left. Half-hearted counter, gaping midriff exposed. The uppercut sends him swaying to the ropes. Right chop punch against the temple and Mac topples like a cricket wicket.

His momentum carries him to a neutral corner, past McIntosh lying on his face halfway under the ropes.

Eddie! Eddie! He focuses on the referee's fingers. One hand shows five and waves sideways over McIntosh. On the count of eight, he grabs a rope, tries to get up, and sinks back into a pool of blood. The referee waves his hands in crossover movements above McIntosh.

"Mac, you has-been! I'm the champ!" Manny sails over the ropes—with Uncle Ig coming through in between.

Blinding camera flashes. He slides from Manny's shoulders and embraces Uncle Ig. Behind him, Suzette makes her way through the milling crowd, "Hey, you champion. I am so proud of you."

"You're putting Randgate on the map, chum." He can feel Leon's vice-grip handshake through the boxing glove.

In the cloakroom, he rubs over the copper work on the champion's belt. Tonight, he'll show it to Mom. And Charlene? Maybe he'll phone her—perhaps Suzette has her number.

Body of steel, fists of stone, *Beeld's* front page proclaims the next morning. Eddie Blignaut surprised everyone by outwitting McIntosh with punch combinations and inexhaustible stamina. Under the leadership of coach Ig Bester's conservative approach, Eddie went from friendly iron boy of the West Rand to South African middleweight champion.

Twenty-Five
Buenos Aires, 1982-1985

Trudy

After a third successful defence of his title, he is seen on billboards, jogging in Adidas trainers with a group of schoolboys. His dominance inside the ring and sparkling smile outside of it, become his trademarks.

Chris finalises negotiations with Chevrolet. On their billboards, Eddie gives personality to their Braaivleis, rugby, sunny skies, and Chevrolet advertisements.

"Morning," echoes from the head guard. "I'm almost done. Warm up your upper body so long." Eddie exchanges running shoes for boxing boots, the corners of his mouth turned up in a smile: two pink-white legs protrude from Uncle Ig's shorts and disappear lower down in a pair of black socks, punches poof-poof against the punchbag. Sometimes, he relives his lost glory days—other times, he talks about them until his voice wears thin.

While he bandages Eddie's hands, he gives him a straight look over the thick-rimmed glasses, the down feather hair dishevelled by the head guard, "It's your fifth title defence. Elijah Ndlovo has been waiting for two years to fight you. He was highly ranked when you became champ and then he got a panga chop on the head in a Zulu tribal fight. At thirty, he has nothing to lose. With McIntosh in his corner, we're fighting against two."

"I'm ready for both."

"You focus on Ndlovo. Imagine that you're seeing his face on the punchbag—six rounds." He throws on his tracksuit top. "I'm going to shower and open my butchery." Moments later, he is back, "I want to tell you something."

What about? The index finger curved like a banana, and the measured tone of voice paralyses Eddie's legs, far more than the ten kilometres of roadwork earlier this morning. Look busy—he tightens the laces of his gloves with his teeth.

From the corner of his sight, "I don't want to interfere in your private business."

Oh damn. Would Uncle Ig suspect that there is something between him and Sandra?

"Don't let the publicity stuff make you punch-drunk. Keep your head, Eddie. When is that shopping centre thing again?"

"Saturday morning."

"At what time?"

"Ten o'clock."

"See you in my gym at 6 am. After that, you can go and play the showman."

His determined way of turning around and marching off looks pretty military.

*****

Cars are backed up in Ontdekkers Road. "Come on, move." Good thing he trained early this morning; doesn't want to be late for his first public promotional appearance. The Radio Highveld channel belts out over the car radio Check-Checkers just around the corner. New shop in Flora Centre Mall.

Parking, at last. He looks at his image in the rear-view mirror. Combs his hair with his fingers. Trots to the centre's entrance. Jacket collar turned up, Ray-bans on—low profile, no time for signatures now. He pushes through the crowd of people and slips underneath the red ribbon. Where to now? A man with a portable loudspeaker approaches him, "Eddie, good morning. Ben Bezuidenhout, shop manager."

"Pleased to meet you, Mister Bezuidenhout. What are our plans for this morning?"

"My little speech at ten, and then you and Trudy cut the ribbon. A newspaper will come and take photos."

"Trudy who?"

A nonchalant wave of the hand—don't you know? "Trudy Potgieter, Miss South Africa first princess. Here she is now—" fades and swerves with eager steps, voice and all, in her direction.

Thin as a rake. Elegant swaying of the hips. Shoulder-length brown hair rhythmically follows every step and folds around her slim neck. Can a girl be so beautiful?

Get a grip, Eddie, you're staring. He touches his hair, pulls at his leather jacket, and pushes up his sunglasses. Nothing in his wardrobe can compare with her little two-piece suit.

"Eddie—Trudy—Eddie," Ben's hand flaps this way and that.

"Hi, Trudy, nice to meet you." A soft, warm hand, an endearing smile that grows dimples on her cheeks.

"Hi, Eddie." Standing there in her flat shoes, green eyes look straight into his. Be strong, now. But he still peeps at the low-cut blouse.

Ben's voice jerks him back to reality, "After the opening, we'll meet in my office quickly—your cheques are ready. And the newspapers have just arrived."

"Good morning," the female reporter waves her notebook. "Vivienne, *West Rand Times*. Eddie, please take off your sunglasses." She adjusts her camera lens. "Ladies and gentlemen…" the hand-held microphone crackles. Irrelevant—Trudy is beautiful. She looks so much at ease in all of this.

In Ben's office, Eddie accepts the cold drink offered. In between sips, "Do you do this sort of thing regularly?"

"I'd like to do more of it. I also sing in a band." Her thumb and index rub together, "Can always do with a little bit extra."

"Your band?"

"My brother's. I hear you're a boxer?"

"It's my job."

"Painful way to earn a living, if you ask me."

His turn to impress. "Yes, that's pro-boxing."

He swallows the last drop of Coke away quickly. Trudy mustn't leave before he does. She took her envelope but refused the drink, by the way remarking it was not good for the figure. How can he see her again?

On their way out of the centre, "May I…Maybe we could see one another again? I mean, can I phone you?"

She stops. Sparkling white teeth; dimples even more prominent in sunlight. Seconds drag past.

Head askew, one eye tightly shut. "OK, you can phone me if you want to."

"What's your number?"

"678 2088."

"Where's that?" He fumbles in his jacket inside pocket, feels his Parker pen, and scribbles on Ben's envelope.

"I'm staying with my brother and them in Windsor." Her finger lifts towards an olive-green Mercedes Benz, "He's waiting over there in his car."

"OK, I'll phone you. Bye."

"Bye, Eddie."

Twenty-Six

Vulnerable

Tonight, he concluded preparations for the fight against Elijah Ndlovo. He feels in top form and full of confidence. On the way back from the BBA, he stops at Uncle Harry's Roadhouse outside Randfontein for a roasted chicken.

The key turns in his front door, roadhouse paper bag in the other hand. His townhouse smells of Cobra floor polish—Wednesday is Paulina's housecleaning day. He puts the bag on the kitchen table and a pot of water on the stove plate. Inside the pocket of his leather jacket, he reaches for the crumpled envelope…6-7-8-2-0-8-8 turns on the rotary dial.

"Good evening. Petrus Potgieter speaking…"

"Hello, this is Eddie Blignaut. May I speak to Trudy, please?"

"At this time of night? Eddie, you say? Are you from a model agency?"

"No, uhm …" So rude! "I'm a friend."

"Trudy, do you know someone called Eddie?" The voice yells from the receiver.

With his shoulder, he presses the telephone to his ear and empties half a packet of pasta into the boiling pot. Ages go by. Will she come to the phone?

"Hello, Trudy speaking."

"Hi, Trudy, Eddie speaking. How are you?"

"Hi, Eddie, I was starting to imagine you weren't going to call."

"I've been training every night. Sorry, I know it's already a bit late."

They arrange to meet on Sunday afternoon.

"Will you find our house if I give you the address?"

"Go ahead." He smooths the envelope with his hand.

"183 Dukes Avenue, Windsor, townhouse number 7."

His Parker pen scribbles. "Thanks. I'm looking forward."

"Bye, Eddie, and…strongs for Saturday evening."

He puts the receiver back on the stand and performs a few dance moves around the table, more excited about Sunday afternoon than about Saturday evening.

"Ndlovu's camp is trying to win the sympathy of the Highveld public," is Uncle Ig's topic of conversation on Friday evening, on the way to the Milpark Holiday Inn. "According to The Sowetan, Elijah has no gym in Soweto. His manager has appealed to the Johannesburg magistrate's court. Now he's been granted a temporary pass, so he can legally spend the night at a hotel in downtown Johannesburg."

"Bigmouth Eli. Tomorrow evening, he'll be sleeping in Baragwanath Hospital." Eddie drives away the ghost that Ndlovo will shatter his dreams of international fame. He is looking ahead at bigger pay cheques in international boxing, but he is only an interesting opponent for other international pro-boxers if his national record is spotless.

On Saturday morning, just before eight, the Opel Kadett stops close to a Press, Boxers & Trainers notice. A few cars are stationed all over the parking lot of the Milner Park Showgrounds. Has Eli arrived? Their names grace the bottom of the banners, printed in bold—the main card of the evening. Should he share his anxiety with Uncle Ig? If he loses tonight, his dreams about an international career will be in tatters.

He follows the scale weights that move this way and that and balances on seventy-one kilograms. A tribal ngoma comes dancing into view at the entrance to the hall leading the Ndlovo entourage inside. He throws a few whitish cow knuckle bones on the floor, sinks down on his knees and with big, round eyes explains his future insights for Elijah, gained from forefather spirits. He gets rid of his traditional Zulu vestments, down to a pair of underpants with a leopard skin design and onto the scale. Rumour has it that he had trouble making the weight limit. Seventy-two, comma five kilograms, the tournament doctor assents; inside the middleweight limit, with not a gram to spare. The tribal dancer does a traditional riel dance and Ndlovo flexes his muscles.

The showground arena crowd chants. Eddie waves and bows in all four directions.

Cow hides around his calves, an assegai clasped in one glove and a shield in another, Elijah jogs into the spotlight. The roar from the furthest corner of the stadium, where supporters from the Soweto black township are allowed to sit, goes up an octave for his tribal dance in the ring.

Cheering turns into bloodthirsty cries and shouts when Elijah comes to a halt and glares at Eddie from under quavering ostrich feathers.

"Take the fight to him." Uncle Ig's voice instructs from across Eddie's shoulder. Fingers prod his neck muscles and shoulder blades. In the opposite corner, Eli's vestments are stripped off, down to golden-yellow trunks and boots. A scar, like a thick earthworm, curves under pearls of sweat around his shiny, black scalp.

In round six, Eddie gets him against the ropes. Darting left punches drive him to the corner. Uppercuts explode in Ndlovo's midriff and lower his defence. Bull's eye right-hand punch tilts his head to the right—lateral left punch on the chin, a salvo of right cross punches. A towel comes flying in between. The referee follows, waving his hands as though stopping a steam train.

He bends over Ndlovo who is down on one knee, shaking his head.

Eddie's hands shoot skywards; he dances two-step paces all along the ropes.

Elijah gets his feathered headdress from someone in his corner and puts it on Eddie's head, "You're the king."

During the press conference, Chris Rossouw breaks the news: Turner Brothers Promotions have clinched the deal and, minutes ago, Eddie signed the contract to fight Luis Mendez from Columbia in April 1983, the tenth contender for the World Boxing Association middleweight crown. It is unknown territory. His intention to change managers is put on ice for the time being, even though Chris reveals still more of his money-grubbing side as time passes.

In his Milpark hotel room, Eddie watches himself on the late-night television news—he listens to how he thanks his fans and vacates his South African middleweight title.

He is now starting out in the international arena and feels vulnerable. One defeat and his career is over. Uncle Ig will be able to advise him, hasn't he done it himself already? The thought fills Eddie with a certain calm. What a privilege to have a man of world champion calibre at his side when facing the world.

Twenty-Seven

Petrus

He potters round his townhouse, keeping busy with trifles. This Sunday morning must go by quickly.

He leaves shortly before twelve, with his purchase from the Central News Agency on the passenger seat, the Witwatersrand Street Guide, folded open at Windsor, Randburg. Ouch, damn. Every bump in the road pushes the Ray-Ban frame against his puffy marshmallow brow.

The light blue Chevair crawls up Dukes Avenue while he's reading the numbers of the houses. One with a thatched roof becomes visible between high, white columns with wooden beams across the entrance. A signboard suspended from small chains above the entrance: The Ranch.

Hell, there are no two ways about it, he simply has to win internationally, and then he'll build his own thatched roof house and also call it The Ranch.

Number 183 comes into view. A townhouse complex. There is parking space under a jacaranda tree across from it. It's five to two on his watch, a last squinted eye looks in the rear-view mirror and adjusts the sunglasses to hide his marshmallow.

Quick steps along the paved garden path, she's waiting for him. And last night? Was she out? With whom? Get a grip, man. Today she's with him. That's what counts.

He lifts his legs over a child's tricycle standing halfway in the path. Knocks. The door swings open. Fingers comb her hair to the side. "Hello, come in."

"Hello, Trudy. Are we hanging out here? Thought we would go out somewhere."

In high heels, she's a bit taller than he is. "Catch your breath first, after the long trip." Her open hand invites him to enter; the other one stroking coyly across her mouth. "Petrus asked me to sing at a wedding last night; I only heard over the radio this morning that you won. Congratulations. Tell me everything."

"Thanks, it was my last fight as SA champ." The leather creaks under him. From the sofa, his eyes sweep across the open plan ground floor: hi-fi set, chrome-and-glass dining-room set, teak in the kitchen.

In front of the fridge, Trudy turns around towards him, a can of beer in one hand and a carton of fruit juice in the other, "What do you prefer?"

"Beer, please."

She makes herself at home across from him, long legs stretched out in front of her. The jean fits her like a second skin. "Are you going to stop boxing now?"

"No, I'm going to box internationally—earn more. The International Boxing Federation requires that I vacate my national title." He can't very well keep his sunglasses on inside the house, can he?

"Shame, poor you, your eye." A soft rub and fragrant whiff of perfume, "When are you then boxing again?"

"In three months. You model and sing in a band?"

"Just sidelines. My job is a junior clerk in vehicle financing at Barclays Bank."

"So, you sell cars?"

"I don't sell cars," she giggles. "Barclays provides financing. My job is to get the client's details: what they earn, what they owe that kind of thing. My supervisor is the one who decides yes or no." She rolls her eyes. "It sucks—the clients think I'm the one who says no. I actually just want to model." With a light growl, pulled upper lip showing sparkling white teeth, "There are more models than job opportunities. Petrus hates it; says he's my chaperone."

"Chape-what?"

"My guardian." Head tilted, lashes fluttering, "Says he's there to protect me against the wolves of the fashion industry."

"So, what are we doing?" The last of the beer glides out of the glass, leaving a foamy tail.

"What about the Johannesburg Zoo?"

"No clue where that is...was there once on a primary school outing."

"I know the way—did a couple of photo shoots there."

"OK, zoo."

She hands him a small backpack when she comes down the stairs again, in sneakers with a rooster trademark. "There's a blanket inside, and room for cool drinks."

Backpack over one shoulder; he holds the front door open for her.

"Their kids are allowed to mess up the place, but if I don't put something away, all hell breaks loose." With one hand, she slings the child's tricycle into the house.

"Doesn't sound like you have a soft spot for their children?"

"Children irritate me. And you? Children?"

"I want a little guy—to raise him as a pal."

"Sounds to me like you'll be spoiling him into a brat." Her eyes widen when they get to the sidewalk, "So, you like a Chev?"

"The car was part of my contract."

"How do you mean?"

"I've got an advertising contract with Chevrolet."

"Wow, you must tell me more."

A Highveld thunderstorm cuts their outing short.

"How do you get modelling work?" He asks on the way back from the zoo.

"Stars-up! Model agency. I did a course with them—then they groomed me for the Miss SA competition. Petrus calls them the fashion mafia. How do you get fights?"

"In much the same way. I've got a contract with Booysens Boxing Academy—well connected with Turner Brothers Promotions."

She frowns, looking surprised, "Turner Brothers?"

"Every profession has its mafia. In the boxing world, it's them."

He parks under the jacaranda tree again. Wow, what brand of perfume is she using?

"You in a hurry? There's milk tart in the fridge."

"That'll be nice; in no hurry at all." Maybe he gets more than that little peck in the zoo?

No sooner has he finished his milk tart than a racket can be heard at the front door. "Hello, I'm Eddie—I suspect we spoke over the phone?"

"Please to meet you. I'm Petrus. My wife, Sarie."

"Hello." She lifts her carrier bag from her shoulder, thumps it on the dining table and disappears up the stairs.

What a grump! He rummages in his jacket pocket for the Chevair's keys—his visit ends in a draw. He extends a hand to Petrus, "I've got to get going."

Is Trudy going to say goodbye right here?

"I'll walk you outside."

He slackens their pace to the car. "I enjoyed the afternoon with you very much, Trudy. Can we see each other again? I mean, when?"

"Next weekend, we're playing at a wedding in the Magaliesb—"

"What about Wednesday evening?"

"I though you trained during the week?"

"I'm my own boss. I can take an evening off now and then if I want to."

"OK, Wednesday. What time?"

"I'll meet you at the office?"

"The bank closes at 3 pm on Wednesday afternoons."

"Fantastic. Wednesday at 3." Her peck on his cheek gives him goosebumps on his arms. Wednesday must come quickly. For the past three years or so, he's been going out casually with various girls, always hoping that the relationship with Charlene will start up again; meanwhile, he was excited by none of the girls whose paths he crossed, until now. There is something rhythmic to Trudy's personality; she also likes the spotlight, and her body is maddeningly exciting to him.

The girl of his dreams.

Twenty-Eight

Dries

It's three o'clock and his Chevair has already been parked for some time in front of Barclays Bank on DF Malan Avenue. Sunday afternoon on their way back from the zoo, Blackheath seemed a quiet suburb when she showed him where she works. Now dual lanes are packed with traffic in both directions. To his right, from the west bound lane, the land rises from roadside boutiques and restaurants to lush green treetops, turning to shrubs and rocky outcrops before reaching the towering heights of Northcliff mountain. His excitement knows no boundaries. Eventually, Trudy steps out of the door with a few other women, all in light blue two-piece bank uniforms. The prettiest one is mine.

He leans over and pushes the passenger door open for her.

"Come; let me introduce you to my colleagues." He jumps out and swiftly walks around the car.

"Girls, this is Eddie. Eddie, this is Estelle. We work together in vehicle financing. Marleen is my supervisor. Martie and I were at school together…she's a cashier."

"Hello, nice to meet you all."

Marleen says, "Ladies, we're going to miss the bus if we don't go now. Enjoy your evening. What do you have planned?"

"Movies. See you tomorrow," as Trudy slips into the car and Eddie closes her door.

He gets a peck and a pinkie rubbing the lipstick off his cheek.

"You look smart."

"Thanks, but I hate these silly bank uniforms. At least, I don't have to spend my salary on clothes for the office. Stop at Petrus' house quickly, and then I'll change into something nice for the evening."

On their way out of the bioscope, "There's a roadhouse close by, Eddie. I'll stick you for a cool drink."

At Paloma Blanca Roadhouse, he parks way back, in a dusky spot and toggles the headlamp switch. A waist-cut waiter's jacket flaps closer. He orders a Coke and Trudy a milkshake, "That will do as my supper as well."

Fingers rub softly behind his neck. "Tell me how much you earn from advertising contracts?"

"They're yearlong contracts. Chris helps me to negotiate…"

"Chris who?"

"My manager, Chris Rossouw. He owns the gym where I train."

"Maybe I can go there with you, just once?"

"The gym is a tough place, Trudy, it's for men."

She wipes the foam from the glass' inside edge and licks her finger. "Just a thought, maybe I can talk to your Chris about advertising contracts?"

"The way I know him, he'll make an effort only if he can get something out of it." His finger again flicks the headlight switch.

The tray is lifted from the window. "Thanks for the cool drink. When are you coming to visit me—then I'll show you my valley?"

"I have to speak to Petrus first."

"To hear if his band is play —"

"No. My parents have threatened him with the worst if I mess up."

"O-K." His head tilts to one side, like hers. Soft lips press against his and he leans over. "My blouse will crease, when we get home, rather."

On Thursday morning, he drives her to work. From Barclays Bank, he heads for the Flora Centre Mall.

In Sterns' jewellery shop, a saleslady approaches, smiling, "Good morning, sir. Can I be of assistance?"

"I'd like to look at some engagement rings."

*****

For weeks, he drives around with the ring in the Chevair's cubbyhole. At last, he plucks up the courage and invites Mom, Suzette and Krisjan for a Sunday barbecue with him and Trudy. Suzette is late for lunch; apparently, she had to nurse Krisjan's migraine headache. Her aloofness towards Trudy catches Eddie unawares—might it be her way of levelling the playing field for the cold war between him and Krisjan? Mom's reaction is decisive—her chuckle can be heard from the kitchen where she and Trudy are busying themselves. On the way back to Randburg, Eddie feels confident enough to ask for Trudy's hand. But wait. Maybe one more meeting with her father, Dries, to convince him that a good fighter can make a living from boxing? Then he'll ask Trudy. It is easier now to ask her about her impressions of Randfontein.

"Hmm, not like Randburg," she starts, pouting. "All those mine dumps—grey, yellow, and white…and, black, yes, the town is pretty black—much more so than Verwoerdburg, where I grew up. And, Randfontein's roaring cars with their fins, even on the tail, broad tyres on chromed rims and those coloured, furry mats on the dashboard." Her hand stifles a giggle, "Hillbillies, that's what my mother calls such people."

But they are my people? "The grey mine dumps are the granite rock that must be removed before the miners can get to the gold-bearing ore. The yellow dumps are the slime that remains after the gold ore has been crushed and the gold filtered out. The white dumps…well, that's just waste sand from the mine."

A few weekends later, he helps her father to change the oil in his car's engine. "You see, Uncle Dries, guys get huge pay cheques when they box internationally. Enough to…take care of a wife."

The stream of oil misses the funnel and splatters a line over the engine. "What?"

"I mean enough to live well."

"How much would that be?"

"For my fight against Mendez on Saturday, I'm getting four thousand dollars."

"If you lose, it's your last."

"I don't lose."

"Show me." Steel blue eyes, expressionless face under the bonnet, every wrinkle a carved contour. His moustache was trimmed perfectly symmetrical and grey hair combed backwards across his head, starting from the straight line of the side parting. He lifts the can of oil, and the lid gets a determined crank.

This sergeant major is sterner than anyone Eddie had ever met in the army—the old man's shiny-toed air force boots are standing squarely on Eddie's heart.

Nothing else to be done, Uncle Ig must give him advice now. He knows all about marriage and women—then also about fathers-in-law.

For his own part, he will box his way through any barricade old Dries puts around his daughter.

Twenty-Nine

Main Event

Tr-r-r tack-tack tr-r-r tack-tack-tack echoes the speedball-music to every corner in the BBA.

Faster. Faster still—Tr-r-tack-tr-r-tack until Uncle Ig lifts a hand, "Eddie, I know when a man is in shape. On Saturday evening, you'll be drilling old Luis' cheeks like that speedball." A towel is draped around Eddie's upper body.

"Could we meet tomorrow night in your gym?"

"Your preparations are done, Eddie. You now need rest for your first fight over fifteen rounds. Anyway, tomorrow night, I'm dressing a carcass—the young apprentice butcher can't yet cut it up on his own. We'll meet on Friday morning."

"Can I help with the dressing?"

"You want to catch a cold right before your fight?" Uncle Ig puts on his track suit top. Over his shoulder, as he walks away, "I'm driving to Randgate now before peak-hour traffic starts."

Friday is too far away. He has to talk to him today and rid himself of the Uncle Dries phantom.

He comes out of the cloakroom, Adidas bag slung over one shoulder. Chris' office door is ajar. He knocks and enters: How do winnings work in an international fight, exactly? He wants to get a better understanding of the financial side of his contract.

"Turner Brothers Promotions receive the money by cable transfer from the international promoters, immediately after the fight. They take ten per cent commission and pay the rest to the BBA bank account. I pay it into your account, minus the royalties due to Ig and myself, ten per cent each," Chris explains.

He turns the Chevair key with a new fire in his fingers and revs the engine—that's good money he is getting to fight Mendez. Maybe he should get a lawyer to advise him on the financial clauses of his contract with BBA. He can afford one, can't he?

His open hand slaps the steering wheel—why are his guts churning? Maybe he should put his wedding plans on hold and finish off Mendez first. But why wait? There are other married boxers.

In Randgate, he knocks on Uncle Ig's door, "You forgot something?"

Purple-white reflections flash from the parlour. Annette is almost certainly watching some television soap or another.

"Gym, please, Uncle Ig," he whispers and flicks his thumb to the right.

"Just a few minutes." The bunch of keys swings open the Yale door lock, and the hinge gives way with a shrill creak.

"Shit, I've got the chills, Uncle Ig."

"Because of Luis?"

"Because if I lose, then I lose my wife as well."

A frown grows like a rose twig above the thick-framed glasses, "Your wife?"

"I want to ask Trudy to marry me. Her father insists that I beat Mendez and prove that I can look after his daughter."

"One thing at a time, Eddie, my boy. First Luis. Now take a few deep breaths." One calm step backwards, fists in the air, Ig leans back against the ring floor. "On Saturday, you're fighting a man with two arms. The difference being that you know best how to use yours—better than any other middleweight in the world."

"I'm going to win, Uncle Ig."

"I believe you will, Eddie."

How should he say it? "Uncle Ig, Trudy is the woman of my dreams."

"I'm glad for you, Eddie." One step closer, his large, open palm on his chest, "Trust your heart and let her see it. Don't worry too much about her father. A dad throws any spanner in the works to keep his daughter to himself. I've also treated some boys like dogs when they tried to get cosy with Sandra."

His anxious churning disappears. "Thanks, Uncle Ig. Now I feel ready for Saturday evening." He senses achievement when he sees *Beeld's* banners outside the arena of the Johannesburg Showgrounds, reading his name at the bottom of the evening program: Eddie Blignaut vs. Luis Mendez. His fight is the main event, and it's even international. His money plan has worked out well: nowadays, Suzette is a secretary at Randfontein Estates Gold Mining Company. When recently he suggested to Mom that she should stop working, she answered,

"It's my only chance to get out of the house; otherwise, I have to dance to your father's tune the whole day long." At least Mom's not facing a humiliating church mouse existence. Now, Eddie feels he can start building up his own treasury.

Uncle Ig flashes his BBA pass at the gate guard, "We're with the car behind us." Leon drives into the parking area behind them.

The Opel Kadett's engine fades away. "Manny, go and bandage up Eddie's hands. Make sure an official gives the OK when you're finished—WBA rules. Trudy, we're going to see where Chris and they are seated."

"Box well, my love. Carry your gloves high," Trudy whispers in his ear and presses a small piece of paper into his palm.

He blinks against the spotlight swinging above them as they exit the cloakrooms in single file. The night air booms Eddie, Eddie. Closer to the ring, he feels a tap from behind on his shoulder. "Look to the left," Manny gestures.

Suzette is waving her hands above her head. Chris gives a thumbs-up and throws a little punch in his direction. Behind him, Trudy blows a kiss. Manny wrapped her letter in his right fist: You're my champion! I love you!

In round seven, the same right fist sends Mendez to the floor for the first time. He started like a whirlwind and won the first two rounds. "Box him like we've trained, Eddie. Counter punch each of his blows, plus give him one for interest. Break his rhythm and his self-confidence"—Uncle Ig calmly advises before round three. By round six, Mendez is not even a shadow of his former self anymore—Eddie's counterpunches rain down with double interest. Once more in round seven, he lands Mendez on his backside. The third time he only drops down on his knee, which counts as a knockdown—three times on the canvas in one round triggers the referee's arms swinging above Luis' head. "Fight over," he calls to the principal judge.

The last question at the press conference comes from Sybrand Goosen, "Eddie, tonight you proved that you are made of international mettle. Who have you got in your sights now?"

"Any of the other nine contenders. Chris can give a better answer."

"We're talking to the camps of Rudolph Schmidt from Germany and Jeff Porter from England; contenders number six and eight for Gonzalez's world title." Chris' waving hand puts an end to the questions.

"Sybrand, lend me your pen, please." Eddie hurriedly scribbles a few words on a piece of paper and follows the others to the reception hall.

Trudy's bosom presses firmly against him, "Ah, congratulations. You're a fantastic boxer." Suzette appears over Trudy's shoulder and gives him a peck on the cheek.

Leon shakes his hand fervently, "Tonight, I'm chauffeuring an international boxer to Randgate." In the corner of the hall, Mom struggles up out of an easy chair. She limps once before finding her rhythm. A trembling hand reaches for his shoulder, "Eduard, I am proud of you. It's not that I am not interested. I sit here praying while you're boxing."

Her cheek feels humid under his palm. "It was good to know you were here, Mom." Further down the hall, Chris and Trudy are talking.

"Come, I want to show you something." With a mysterious air, Eddie hooks his arm around hers, "Excuse us, Chris."

"Ha-ha. Can't you wait until you get home?"

Halfway up the spectator terraces, he rummages in the coin pocket of his pair of Lee jeans and holds the note out to her.

"What now? Are you giving back my love lette—"

He kisses her words away, "Read it out for us."

"I know what I wrote."

"Look on the back."

The letter is unfolded in the crisp April evening autumn air, under a bright Highveld moon, "You are my princess. Will you marry me?"

"Yes-s-s, I will, even if you haven't even asked me to go steady first." Her lips feel soft and her breath warm in his mouth. The stadium appears celestial when he opens his eyes, or is it just his mood? So calm, compared to earlier in front of the amphitheatre filled with bloodthirsty spectators. He waited, Uncle Dries tried to stop it, but now nothing and nobody will get in his way. He slips the ring on her finger.

"I'm going to brag. Come along."

He follows her trotting down the stairs. There is an extra swing in her hips when she walks into the reception hall. He lifts her left hand into the air. Suzette shrieks. Congratulations coming from all sides. Mom puts her arm around Trudy, "You are like one of my own children to me."

His lips together in a drawn smile: He made the right decision.

The rear end of Leon's Volkswagen Microbus lifts and the rebuilt Ford V6 engine growls and grunts against Eddie's kidneys. Trudy is lying on the back seat, her head on his legs. "My parents, you still have to ask them," she murmurs.

"Tomorrow afternoon, we'll drive to Pretoria."

"OK." Her dimples form and disappear under the glow of the red traffic light on Ontdekkers Avenue.

The gong rings incessantly. He cannot get up from the canvas. A heavyweight boxer stands grinning in the neutral corner and the referee starts counting. He awakens with a fright, jumps up, pulls the bed sheet back over Trudy and jogs to the kitchen where the telephone is ringing. "Hello, Eddie Blignaut." He rubs behind his neck—Mendez really has a kick in his fists.

"Good morning, son. Listen to Rapport's sport page: A step closer to the world title. Last night, Eddie Blignaut proved in his fight against the Central American champion, Luis Mendez, that he has the punching power to stop any opponent. Congratulations," comes her father's voice from the receiver.

"Thanks, Uncle Dries. We would like to come over this afternoon. Will you be home?"

"We're home, yes. Be here by noon for lunch. I'll tell Gerda."

Quickly, before Dries can ask if Trudy is with him, "Thanks, that will be nice. See you later, Uncle." He does not want to lie to his father-in-law-to-be.

She appears in the kitchen door—the bed sheet draped around her. He turns her around gently towards his bedroom, "We leave the sheet here in the kitchen."

Thirty

Wedding Bells

The bridal car makes an elegant turn into Kyalami Ranch resort as he feels Trudy's hand tightening around his, "Look, it's so pretty." Eddie peers past their driver. A lane of jacaranda trees stretches out before them. Pink and white ribbons tied in a bow around every trunk—just like the bows on the pews down the aisle in church.

They decided on a small wedding with family and close friends only. St Saviour's Church in Randjesfontein is love at first sight for them both—a red-brown face brick building amongst towering conifers. The porch with its pitched roof of yellow wood and a mosaic of brick-red, ivory and slate-coloured floor tiles all the way to the cross on the altar under a trinity of vertical stained-glass windows.

Ma Gerda was pleased: it is close to Valhalla for the wedding preparations in St Saviour's and for the reception; Kyalami Ranch is just across the Ben Schoeman Freeway.

The BMW comes to a standstill and Eddie leans across to open the door for Trudy. "Mister Blignaut, the pleasure is all mine," Leon nods across his shoulder.

A cloud of confetti fills the air. Sybrand's camera flashes non-stop. Eddie feels bursting with pride, having Trudy on his arm. At the main table, he pulls out her chair and sits down beside her, "You look lovely, Troedels." Seated next to him are Pa Dries and Ma Gerda, and next to Trudy, Ma Babsie and Pa Dawid.

Congratulations—his father's first word to him in years brings a sense of relief, during the signing of the wedding register in the vestry. It was not a given that his father would attend the wedding. Another scandal threatening the Blignaut household: an accusatory empty chair next to Ma. That would have been a big setback because, for Eddie, it is a challenge just to fit in with Trudy's parents in the Valhalla neighbourhood and to find acceptance in the stiff military domestic atmosphere where everything happens according to set rules. Thanks go to Ma and Suzette for convincing Pa of his responsibility.

The toasts make Pa Dries more talkative. He has been in a sombre mood since the Church Street bomb blast in front of the South African Air Force headquarters in Pretoria during this past week. While knotting his tie in Valhalla this afternoon, "The two ANC members who planted the bomb also died, but that is no compensation for my friend Ben's life. Thirty years ago, in 1953, the two of us joined the Permanent Force together and suddenly this week, he's gone."

Thirty-One

Cinnabar and Musk

Eddie beats Rudolph Schmidt in Germany and Jeff Porter in England.

Fair-haired Rudolph is a well-built jack-in-the-box from Monchengladbach, an industrial city in West Germany. Eddie, Uncle Ig and Manny have their hands and heads full following the announcements and the referee's instructions in German—their first experience of a country where they don't understand a single word. The fight demands more discipline and box sense of Eddie than any of his previous bouts: he needs all the concentration he can muster to hear the referee and make out his explanations like sign language above the crowd's chanting Rassistisch! Rassistisch! Eddie adheres strictly to Uncle Ig's instructions against the orthodox and terribly unimaginative style of his tough-as-nails German opponent's straight left punches alternating with follow-up right-hand punches but attending to his defence more than to his attacks. Uncle Ig, after round five, "The Jerrie is scared of being knocked out. Use your speed and stack up points, round by round."

Eddie is convinced he deserves it when his hand is lifted after ten rounds, under loud protest from the home crowd: Est is Rudolph, Rudolph! The Sporthalle is like a freezer and Uncle Ig is waiting to wrap him in his boxing gown, "The Jerrie just came to a payday, not to box. To become a champion a man needs to win under any circumstances—tonight you did just that. Well done, Eddie boy." In the cloakroom, Manny's teeth chatter as he unrolls the bandages from Eddie's hands, "It was your first German language lesson in that ring. As for me, I actually saw snow for the first time in my life tonight. With the last snowfall in Joburg, I was visiting a girl in Durbs."

In London, against Porter, Eddie feels more in control. Although he takes the individual measure of every opponent, Porter has the same approach as John Roberts—head butts against the ear, getting a punch in before the boxers have broken clean from the clinch when commanded by the referee, and leaning forwards like a collapsing wall to drain Eddie's energy. He is no longer the young, inexperienced boxer he was a few years ago against Roberts. His left uppercut folds Porter in two, beyond the threshold of stability, and the chopping knockout right to his head collapses him between Eddie's feet.

"Thanks, Eddie. Tonight, you won back my prize money from the Tommies that I had to leave behind," Uncle Ig comments back at the hotel. "Now we can go home. More than forty years later, London remains a cold, wet place."

Three fights later, the 1985 edition of *Ring* ranks him as the first contender for the world title of the Argentinian, Roberto Gonzales—one position ahead of America's Floyd Peterson, a contentious ranking, according to American box critics.

*****

He brushes his teeth before going to bed.

Flapping his arms upon entering the bedroom. "We're flying all the way to Argentina, my love."

Trudy always peers out from under the sheet, but tonight, she is sitting up straight. "It's not exciting for me to go to Argentina. Why isn't your title fight in America?"

"America refuses to give me a work visa. There are anti-apartheid demonstrations in front of Madison Square Garden in New York after *Ring* reported that Roberto and I were possibly going to box there. But Troedels, what does it matter in which country I'm boxing? Aren't you there with me in support?"

"I must support you to become world champion. Then everyone will know about you, but what about me?"

Where does such spitefulness come from? Maybe he's just imagining things. "It's my job—our bread and butter…things I can't control, and you get in a tizz about it?"

"I just find the world weird: my dad says that in America, they make a difference between white and black people. Who are they to demonstrate against a white South African boxer when we're doing here just what they're doing over there?"

He explains that, according to Chris, it is Floyd Peterson's camp who are behind the demonstrations: they think Floyd should get the first chance against Gonzales. Under pressure, the Turner Brothers then agreed to Buenos Aires.

"It's unfair; Gonzales will have home crowd advantage."

"Uncle Ig says I will have to knock him out to get a win on points there. That's what I'm going to do."

"OK. Hold me."

Gasps of breath against his cheek, like keeping time with the tick-tock of the pendulum clock in the sitting room.

Twelve beats come and go. What upset her out of the blue like that tonight?

Behind the glass wall of the Departures Hall, a handkerchief pops out of the sleeve of Mom's dress and wipes her eyes. With Trudy's hand in his, he walks towards Babsie and taps the inside of his fist on his heart. Suzette's wave displays her shiny engagement ring. Eddie waves back and grins at Ollie: you two-faced murderer. Leon radiates admiration. Eddie winks back at him.

"It's two weeks before the fight in case you two want to swim to Argentina. Our flight is about to depart," the words reverberate through Jan Smuts Airport. Uncle Ig swings around with a determined air and starts walking—Eddie follows.

Hours later, a vague thumping awakens him. Trudy's head rests against his chest. Her hair feels as soft as satin. "Troedels, wake up. We've landed. Now we must speak Spanish. Hola—if I remember correctly?"

"Hola-a-a," as she yawns. "I could sleep a lot more." Lazily, she stretches her arms above her head.

"My backside is numb from sleeping seated." He peers at Uncle Ig: he is sleeping with his chin on his chest, as though he had swallowed his upper lip. Manny's broad smile appears next to him. Wavy steel wool hair in all directions.

Eddie can't help asking. "How's your head? Last night, you must have emptied the bar." "Strong as a lion. Let's wake up the old lion." He taps on Uncle Ig's leg.

Trudy leans over and straightens out his tracksuit. "Shame, it's a pity to wake Uncle Ig."

"Good heavens, I'm all crumpled," he mutters with a shapeless mouth. A rummaging hand finds the pocket of his trousers. Thick-framed glasses and a set of false teeth appear, "Ah, I see you are all here as well."

After customs control, Eddie slips two shiny passports back into the leather bag hung around his neck. Trudy's fingers burrow deeper into his. The luggage comes closer on the conveyor belt and Manny steps forward, "I'll grab it, Eddie. You have more important things to do with your arms." Suitcases are lifted from the belt onto a trolley.

A man with a slate board is waiting in the Arrivals Hall: Eddy Blignaud. Uncle Ig shakes hands.

"I, Miguel, driver."

Outside, in the parking lot, "You get inside the van."

The luggage lands in the back of the Dodge bus.

Miguel weaves through the Buenos Aires traffic and shares unintelligible snippets illustrated by hand signs.

"Ocean."

Eddie quickly glances in the direction Miguel is pointing at. The sea flashes past in between buildings.

"Fight." Small punches against the steering wheel. A finger motions to the left where a colossal stadium glides past.

Estadio Alberto J Armando, it says on the concrete wall above the entrance.

*****

Roberto Gonzales vs. Eddy Blignaud, the posters read on the lampposts around the Estadio Alberto J Armando—6 April 1985 at the bottom. At last, Eddie sighs, because things are fraying at the edges. The two weeks since they were first introduced to this neighbourhood of Buenos Aires feel like a lifetime gone past. Uncle Ig had trouble finding a gym with facilities at least matching his own in Randgate. Two of the five contracted sparring partners pitch up. The one smells of liquor. The other is an overweight amateur. The cramped hotel room and communal bathroom were getting too much for Trudy—the door did not even have a lock. In the mornings, she waits for Eddie; after his training session, they shower together.

The Dodge van swerves into the parking area behind the stadium. Miguel parks. His sign language indicates that he will wait there while Eddie weighs in. Uncle Ig's head bobs forward an inch, "Miguel, you go with us, and you stay with us."

He and Uncle Ig walk in front. At the entrance, Miguel lifts his hand like a traffic cop and then goes in alone. Eddie closes his hand around Trudy's. Through the narrow door slit, an argument can be heard, a wild gesture now and then. The door is flung open and Miguel motions them inside. A thickset man in a white coat takes his stethoscope and flashlight out from a small suitcase. Stripped down to his underpants Eddie approaches him.

"Tu estas en forma." The doctor points to the scale, 72 kg appears in black ink opposite his name on a form. Manny holds out his tracksuit. Slipping it on, "I'm half a kilogram off my weight in Johannesburg. It's their food here. My stomach was upside down more than once." Uncle Ig gets a carbon copy from the doctor and insists on a stamp by banging his fist on the paper. "Miguel, let's go."

A group of people pour into the little hall. The sight of his face in the crowd gives Eddie a runaway heartbeat—adrenaline spurting through his veins. Since the signing of the contract in Johannesburg, Gonzales has grown a moustache. Fringe combed back, broad forehead, dark eyes, deep scar across his left eyebrow. Their eyes meet. A giant suddenly steps in between the two of them. One step to the right around the bodyguard, Eddie looks Roberto squarely in the eye. Smaller scars are visible on his cheekbones. Tonight's targets.

"Come. Photograph." Miguel presses his index finger and thumb together in front of his eye.

Uncle Ig's hand clasps his upper arm. "No. Miguel, we go."

Outside the stadium, posters flash past, Eddy Blignaud—after tonight, the whole world will know the true spelling of his name.

"Listen, guys, I would like to have breakfast alone with Trudy."

"Why?"

"Uncle Ig, it's our last quiet moment together before this evening."

"OK. Manny and I will be eating at the cafe near the harbour. I like their Spanish omelettes."

"Cafe Mendoza, please Miguel," Uncle Ig requests when Eddie gets off at the hotel.

The metal door handle creaks under his hand. She stands silhouetted in the window frame, loosely-tied hair waving in the sunlight as she turns around.

"I'm scared, Eddie."

"What of, my love?"

"Tonight."

"I'm not; tonight, I'm putting old man Roberto on pension."

"Then you'll be everyone's champion. What will become of me?"

"Troedels, I have one chance. That's tonight. I'm climbing through the ropes for the two of us. All of this is for us."

A light pull is enough to loosen the gown's tie belt. Supple hips. Yesterday's Cinnabar still slumbering in the hollow of her neck. His tracksuit top is unzipped and falls to the floor. Fingers slip around his neck, stroke down his back, slip the tracksuit pants gently over his buttocks and hinge him backwards. The cool sheet sends light shivers over his loins. Her heat wraps around him, her bosom tenderly on his chest.

"Take me, Troedels."

Her panting breath and hair in his mouth. Electric pulses discharge from his nipples with every pinch of her nails. Turn around, maybe? Too late. With a shriek of pleasure, she triumphs above him and sinks back rhythmically into him. Cinnabar and musk mix in the air, her palms against his temples, thighs glued to his hips—ecstatically nestled into him.

"You're mine, even when you're the champion," she breaks the silence.

Trudy's mood is calm. That's all he needs when he climbs through the ropes tonight.

Thirty-Two

The King

Spectators are queuing in front of the entrances to Estadio Alberto J Armando, reaching all the way back and disappearing between houses and apartment blocks. The colossal, armoured concrete, yellow-painted structure dominates the surroundings. It towers above everything—about seven storeys high, Eddie guesses. Walls in the neighbourhood have been decorated by graffiti artists. Miguel rolls down his window and shows his access permit to the guard at the gate. Spectators' voices, like the chirruping of finches in bush reeds, stream into the minibus.

Uncle Ig clears his throat. "Trudy, kiss your husband and get it over and done with."

Giggling, she replies, "I already have, Uncle Ig."

Eddie moves closer to her, whispering, "You're even prettier when you blush." Miguel parks the Dodge behind the stadium grandstand.

Uncle Ig nudges the door open with his shoulder, "Now we must get to work."

At the dressing room's entrance, a man in uniform stops them. "Las mujeres no estan permitidas," a finger pointing at Trudy.

"What now?" Uncle Ig prods Miguel in the back.

"Women not allowed."

"Tell the damn idiot we're all going in here. If he doesn't like it, he can go to hell. Come, everyone." Miguel gives way somewhat as Uncle Ig pushes past the official and into the dressing room.

"Trudy, please unpack Eddie's shorts, gown, shoes, and socks—see if you can get rid of the worst creases. Manny, check our little suitcase: sponge, Vaseline, ironing weight, earbuds, water bottle, towels. Eddie, I need to talk to you," his head nodding towards a warm-up space next door. With an energetic rhythm in his step, the tracksuit top disappears around the corner. Uncle Ig sits bolt upright on a rickety chair, pointing to the wooden bench against the wall, for Eddie. The chair waddles closer and stops in his face.

"Eddie my boy, Gonzales is known for his body punches and crossover hook shots. That makes him predictable, a boxer without imagination, but as tough as leather. He isn't a world champion for nothing. Keep him at a distance with left punches and target his old scars with your right-hand fist. Make your speed count. Tie his arms up and tap his energy when he comes for your body. Don't let your guard down; he's got a reputation for playing dirty."

"No one plays dirty better than ol' John Roberts."

"Forget your previous opponents. Tonight is your entire career. Our strategy is to win the first three rounds—usually, Gonzales's strongest rounds to impress his mark on the fight. You have the reach and speed of hands and feet to grab the first three rounds from him. That will destabilise him—behind on points, he will feel dominated. We'll see how his camp reacts and adapt our fighting strategy every three rounds until the fifteenth. And remember, you're fighting a man, not a god. I believe in you as everyone in South Africa does. Start warming up. I'm going to look for Trudy's seat—apparently, she's sitting with the people from our embassy."

His weaver's nest hands are finding their focus on Manny's fluttering open-hand gloves when she peers around the corner and tiptoes along towards him, as though nobody can see her, "Love you. You're going to win." She disappears just as quietly.

From behind the open-hand gloves, "Rub your cheek, Eddie."

A small smudge of red lipstick on the bandage becomes the only trace of her visit. "Hell, Manny, didn't figure you could blush," as Eddie pat-pats against his fluttering gloves.

In the distance, Gonzales is already parading in the ring. Almost there, Uncle Ig stops, turns around and motions with a wave of his right arm towards the sea of faces in the dusk, "Trudy is sitting about somewhere around there." Eddie waves in that direction and again focuses on his name on the back of Uncle Ig's tracksuit top—tonight, the whole boxing world will know Eddie Blignaut.

Up the small stairs to the ring. Manny step-presses down and pulls open the ropes for him. He ducks through. Announcements rattle on. His name crackles almost unrecognisable through the air. One step forward, right fist in the direction where Trudy is probably sitting. Images in the dusk mock and whistle.

The gong rings as if coming from far away. Black fringe combed backwards, broad forehead, dark life-size eyes approaching between Eddie's gloves. Some instinctive left punches spot on Roberto's nose draw out a war cry from his corner. Behind boxing gloves, he looks shorter than at the weigh-in. Eddie takes his measure by nipping at him with a few more left jabs. Two, three hits hammer Eddie's defence. Clinch. Roberto's arms work like mechanical levers, manipulating the referee by breaking the clinch himself and immediately firing a series of body punches seeking a target behind the harness of Eddie's arms. Gong. Damn, there was little opportunity.

"You've done enough, Eddie. More accurate hits than Roberto. You are both fired up." Uncle Ig after round five, "Eddie, pick up speed. Hit first. I score you the first three rounds, the fourth is his and the last one drawn. The fight is reaching a turning point. You can give him all you've got now."

Eddie stacks up points with shots to the face and chest when Roberto lowers his arms to bombard him with body punches. A stabbing pain shatters his left ribcage for the umpteenth time. A few dance steps backwards, breathe deeply. Again, Roberto targets his heart. What should he do with the wriggling bunch of muscles? Peers askance at Uncle Ig. His forearm wiggles, signalling a thumb over his shoulder. Quick backwards two-step. Gonzales storms towards him. Hips swivel with a bounce—bull's eye right punch on the chin. Left hook. You tough bastard. Another salvo of punches in the ribs. Ouch, damn it. Dance backwards.

Gonzales steams closer—hasty, milling arms. Face open. Take that. The right punch sprays a flurry of sweat from the black fringe. The bell rings.

In his corner, blood streams from Roberto's cheek.

"Your round, Eddie. Manny, pass the chair."

"It's gone, Uncle Ig."

"What have you done with the bloody thing?"

"Put it down there, same as after every round."

"Come on, spray water on Eddie."

"That's also gone. Was on the chair."

World Boxing lays down rules for referees to apply inside the ring. Outside the ring, it's the law of the jungle. Bookmakers make their living out of supporters, which feeds their interest to influence the outcome of a fight over and above raw patriotism for their hero—it's been like that since his time in London, says Uncle Ig.

A half-dry sponge wipes his face and behind his neck. "That man Gonzales is really tough. Think he broke my ribs. Can hardly breathe."

"You're also tough. He was nicely hampered in the last round. Turn southpaw. Lure him towards you and drill him with the right jabs. Protect your ribs tightly with your left arm." Roundabout turn on the gong and trots towards Roberto—a first right-left combination kicks back solidly into Eddie's shoulder. Bewilderment shows in the pair of dark eyes. Blood oozes from above Roberto's eye and he peers at his corner which triggers a lightning-fast straight right punch that whips his head aslant, preventing him from seeing the left uppercut coming. An intuitive counterpunch takes Eddie's breath away. He grinds hard into his mouthguard to silence a scream of pain—Roberto mustn't sense the damage he has done. The ref comes between them, motions Eddie to the neutral corner and winks a hand at someone outside the ring. This morning's thick stuffed white coat struggles through the ropes under intense objection from Roberto's corner. His coach climbs through the ropes to hear for himself what the doctor is saying. The referee orders him out of the ring and the doctor follows.

"Box."

On the bell, Eddie turns around in satisfaction. A nasty punch sends the corner posts flying towards him, a dull booming roar from the crowd. Manny's voice comes to him as someone faintly familiar, "The son-of-a-bitch floored you with a sucker punch after the bell." He must get up from here. His eyes blink as he tries to focus on the hazy image of the referee's shoes, flashbacks of his first fight against Hitboy Malinga. On all fours, he waddles towards Uncle Ig's small suitcase as a makeshift chair in his corner: Here, he gets up for Trudy and the entire South Africa. Biting into his mouthguard gets him to his feet. His world wavers—Uncle Ig's grip on his forearm stabilises his body.

"Come and sit. Lie back against the cushion; take a deep breath. Here is Manny now; he went to the dressing room to wet a towel." Drumbeats thunder behind his ear where the stolen punch struck. The cool towel against the back of his neck slowly merges two referees in the neutral corner into one figure again.

"There are eight more rounds—use the next one to clear your head. Pace yourself. You have the stamina for the full fight." A banana bunch-sized hand pulls him upright by the forearm. Roberto also works sparingly with his punches in round eight, protecting the cuts on his eyebrow and cheekbone.

On the gong, Manny pushes Uncle Ig's little suitcase through the ropes on its side.

"Eddie, he's just a man. Mock him. Lure him to you. When he storms in, cut him with your right."

"I'll bend double if he hits me in the ribs again."

"Do what I say. The title will not just come marching to you. Go take it—you can." Coming out of his corner, Gonzales glares from under the swollen mass over his left eye. Arms clasped against his ribs, Eddie dances closer to him with sprightly steps. Southpaw, forcing anticlockwise rotation; he stays in Roberto's blind spot, shooting right-hand jabs. Bull's eye left hook, as though it were Roberto's snapping legs striking the gong.

Uncle Ig, on the gong for round ten: "Keep it up—take the fight to him!"

Eddie trots out of his corner. Between his gloves, Roberto ducks and dives ever closer. Eddie fakes a step to the left and his right uppercut whips Roberto's chin upwards, as though lifting his shape out of his skin. Left uppercut to the upper stomach—solar plexus, Eddie made the discovery when he convinced Chris to invite Doctor Wilfried Bucholz to the BBA to explain the location of the body's sensitive points to his boxers. Full-weight, lateral right hook.

Roberto's head whiplashes and sends his body to the ring floor like a spinning top.

In the neutral corner, Eddie is counting along. On the count of ten, Roberto has still not moved. Uncle Ig dives through the ropes, Manny sails across with ease. Carried around in the ring on Manny's shoulders, the world champion searches for his wife in the shadowy mass. The World Boxing Association champion belt fits snugly around his body. Manny produces Elijah Ndlovo's crumpled ostrich feather headdress from his tracksuit jacket and presses it on Eddie's head, "You're the king." He bows in all four directions and freezes for Uncle Ig in his corner, cheeks glistening with tears and waving the orange, white and blue national flag.

Later in the dressing room, hands heavenwards, "Eddie, now I can go."

"Where to, Uncle Ig?"

"If the sweet Lord comes to fetch me on the way home, tell Annette, I went to heaven a happy man."

With Uncle Ig's forearms like bull's horns in his hands. "You're going nowhere, Uncle." Ig makes way for Trudy and her victory dance, excusing himself while muttering that he has packing to do.

"Troedels, we're going to live now. This title is staying mine for a long time."

An explosion of camera flashes lights up the Jan Smuts Arrivals Hall. Suzette supports Mom by the elbow. Her limp step dissolves and flows in front of his eyes. "Eduard…You're the champion," she sobs against his chest.

"Take that! Welcome to the fifty-thousand-dollar league," is Chris' only comment.

Then it's Sybrand, "Eddie, tell us everything—the country is waiting to hear all about it."

"Floyd Peterson," is Chris' answer during the press conference to Sybrand's question about who Eddie's next opponent will be, "The entire America thinks he should have gotten the first chance against Gonzales. Now he can get his hiding from Eddie on home soil."

The front page of *Beeld* on 9 April features Eddie, WBA champion belt diagonally slung over his shoulder, curled-in arms showing off muscles.

Thirty-Three
The Ranch, 1986-1989

Philly

His greatest wish is to fight Floyd Peterson in the magical Madison Square Garden Arena and make Trudy's dream of seeing New York come true. According to the American promoter, Dan Kingston, Franklin Field Stadium in Philadelphia is better suited—or Philly, as Kingston refers to Peterson's hometown.

"The golden rule of business…" Chris snorts in the downtown Johannesburg offices of Turner Brothers Promotions high up in the Carlton Centre towers, "…the man with the gold makes the rules."

Uncle Ig says, "Peterson has his home crowd in that stadium, but inside the ring, he stands alone." The main negotiator, Manfred Turner, reads aloud a fax copy of the contract.

His secretary's head appears around the office door, holding out a roll of paper to him, "Fax, from Kingston." The door shuts softly. Manfred flattens the full length of fax paper on the table in front of him—What the fuck? New venue: Trump Plaza, Atlantic City, New Jersey—prize money a six-digit number.

Eddie counts on his fingers…how much would six digits be, exactly?

The leather chair tilts backwards, and Manfred's finger opens a cupboard behind him. The World Boxing Association Rule Book bounces on the table. He pages, pages back, and pages forth, then reads. Again, the chair tilts—his hands raised in the air, "Same WBA rules apply in New Jersey as in Pennsylvania." His index finger sweeps between the two fax rolls, comparing them.

Eddie is dying to ask but waits until Manfred gets to the new prize money clause.

"Only the venue and payload changed—let's make them pay, a full hundred thousand dollars."

"I'll make Floyd pay in the ring." Eddie scribbles down a signature—his shakiness mustn't show: a hundred thousand dollars. He can't get his thoughts around the sum; it's a pile of money.

*****

He imagines seeing Floyd Peterson's face in Manny's fluttering open-handed gloves as he gets his focus in. Peterson is a one-punch artist; his bulldozer style will tap your energy—Uncle Ig after they studied films at the BBA of his last fights. Ig then arranges a few light heavyweight sparring partners for Eddie and ties the lace of a boxing boot around both his ankles—feet separated by a forearm distance: Muscle memory, Eddie, to learn to keep a featherlight balance against a steamroller boxer.

From under the boxing gown hood, only his name on Uncle Ig's tracksuit is visible. He follows up the few stairs and ducks through the opening between the ropes. Budweiser is printed diagonally across the floor canvas and on his blue corner cushion and Trump on the neutral corner cushions. Trump Plaza flickers in neon red against the wall to the far right. Peterson's golden gown darts into the ring, triggering a deafening boom from spectator pavilions.

From the neutral corner, Robert White steps forward. White Bob, as he is nicknamed in America, respected as a boxing referee and for his black belt in karate. His shoulder-length grey hair gleams under the spotlights.

Presentations by the announcer follow and in conclusion: Ten-point scoring system—ten for the winner and nine for the runner-up in a round, eight count knockdown rule. The bell saves a boxer, except in the last round, which ends the fight. "Ladies and gentlemen, welcome to the WBA championship boxing-g-g."

As though slamming shut a giant book with both hands, White Bob gestures the boxers towards the middle of the ring. Floyd is in his face; Eddie stares him down and vaguely hears the referee's rhetoric, "Protect yourself at all times...let's have a clean fight...Fighter, are you ready?"

Eddie nods in agreement, looking confidently into Bob's blue eyes. Peterson's answer to the same question: Yes. "Touch gloves...back to your corners."

A karate chop cleaves the air as the gong sounds: Let's get it on.

Eddie after round three, "Peterson smuggles in the ring as well. He's a real cheat." Since the demonstrations in front of Madison Square Garden, Peterson was caught with cocaine in his possession and spent six months behind bars, reported *Ring* magazine. "When he comes within reach, do like we trained: sidestep far to the right and when he turns, swipe a right into him and chopping left punch." A light left air punch flies down past Eddie; another wipe of the sponge before round four.

Peterson rolls forward like an armoured vehicle. Push, press, wrestle—pitch-black eyes lurking right behind his defensive gloves. Sidestep to the right—Floyd follows as if on tow. Dance away, "Com'on, Floyd, burn me." Sidestep to the right and swipe left hammer chop.

Lighting right punch in the mouth. Peterson steps this way and that, arms loosely crossed. Gong. He heads clumsily for a Trump corner and then for his little red chair.

"Bull's eye, Eddie." A shower of drops from the sponge. "Manny, wet it again." Crouching on one knee, "Floyd will expect the same tactics. Surprise him and sidestep to the left." Peterson's style of blocking hampers Eddie from scoring points with clean punches to the face, the sides of his head, against his chest or in his stomach. Frustration mustn't get the better of him now. The crowd wants more from their man. They were brought here in busloads from Philly: Your boxing ticket doubles as a return bus ticket the banners of The Philadelphia Inquirer were blazing forth the entire week. Their Young Hopeful from the Strawberry Mansion neighbourhood is now being whistled at. Shame Floyd. Boo. Gong. End of round eleven.

"My legs can't take anymore. My calves are cramping."

"Don't show it, Eddie. Any sign of fatigue and Peterson will let you have it." Ro-o-und number twelve. Floyd probably feels that Eddie's counter push is not as firm anymore, because punches are raining on him from all sides. Then Boo from the crowd again, as Floyd fortifies his defences and pushes a head of frizzy hair into Eddie's face. It stinks. When was the last time the man showered? Probably before he went to jail, or is it deliberately part of his strategy?

"Three more rounds, Eddie. We must win each of them. Manny, rub the knots out of Eddie's calves."

Deep Heat athlete cream aroma fills the air in his corner, standing up in between rounds, he feels Manny's thumbs working deep into his calve muscles.

The crowd sounds their discontent by the result, a draw. Uncle Ig as well, because according to his scorecard, Eddie wins easily on points.

The next morning at the airport, he has still not cooled down, "I should have given my damn glasses to that third judge. He missed a bloody good fight. You and Trudy must enjoy New York."

Thirty-Four

Photo Portfolio

Ring baptises him Eddie the Eliminator on the cover page of their November 1987 edition—his trademark in the run-up to The Desert Duel, promoter Dan Kingston's brainchild to combine two world titles between Eddie and Victor DiCavalli, the World Boxing Council champion. International sport boycotts against South Africa trip up the Turner Brothers, who hoped to arrange for the fight to take place in Johannesburg, but Caesars Palace Casino Hotel in Las Vegas plays host.

He drives into Randgate on his way back from the BBA, fingers tapping on the steering wheel along with the Eagles' Hotel California. Shortly after fighting in Las Vegas, the two of them will go there. Trudy has been dreaming of a Californian holiday for a long time. At last, he can make her wish come true.

A cloud bank with a silver lining crowns the horizon. Is it raining on The Ranch? Are the horses safely in the stables?

Their decisions over the past two years have been good ones, he reckons to himself. His townhouse sells for a hefty profit and the vacant land in the Dwarskloof district, west of Randfontein, was just waiting for them. They build their house and soon after moving in, daily driving to the Barclays Bank branch in town becomes too much for Trudy.

"I'll buy you too a nice BMW, my love."

"OK, fine."

Shortly afterwards, she is sulky again. "My work here is not like in Randburg. One after the other day, there's a poor white miner's mug in front of me, drowned in debt and with a record at the credit bureau. Another piece of white trash wanting to trade in a souped-up Ford for a new car."

But these are his people she's looking down on? His suggestion that she could stop working unleashes a fountain of tears: she wants to contribute financially to their life as a couple. Jointly, they take the decision to invest in racehorses. Deep dimples formed when four thoroughbred yearlings were delivered on The Ranch.

He drives into Randgate under the black granite cloud bank. A stop sign brightens up in die headlights. He glances quickly at Charlene's old house. The latest news via Suzette is that Charlene and her husband live somewhere in Pretoria. Her parents have gone to a retirement village in Warmbaths, the hot springs resort town.

He turns left and drives past Uncle Ig's house. Nowadays, he is at the BBA one or two days a week. The other days, Manny replaces him as assistant coach. The Meat Cauldron has a new, young owner—with royalties from Eddie's prize money, Uncle Ig is now a retired blockman. Outside town, lightning bolts crack the heavens into pieces. Drops thud against the windscreen. Left turn into a turf brown whirlwind rushing across the road. Thank goodness, the horse camps are empty.

Lightning colours the world silver-white. Hurriedly, he passes under the signboard of The Ranch, bobbing on the crossbar above the entrance. He parks his next to Trudy's BMW. Long strides in the direction of the veranda. His lips press on hers even before she can say hello.

"Hi, sweetheart, how was your training?"

"Tough. Fifteen rounds against three different sparring partners to counter all tactics that Mister DiCavalli can come up with. Your day?"

"Great, thanks. The horses are fun. Oh, their big, soft eyes. Can't imagine, for the life of me, a jockey sitting on their back with a whip—it feels terrible."

"I'm talking to a jockey at Gert's practice track. Jerry says he doesn't whip his horse during a race. During practice runs, he lightly touches his horse with the whip and in the race, it's enough to just show the whip to the horse and give it free rein. His philosophy: racehorses are born to run and that is all they want to do—no punishment is necessary."

"That's the jockey for our horses. Will you see him again?"

"Oh, yes. Little Jerry is doing his apprenticeship with Gert at Randjesfontein."

"Come, sit down—I suppose you're hungry?"

The last spaghetti rolls around his fork and mops up Trudy's carbonara sauce. The telephone rings and the little ball of pasta slips back into the soup plate. He leans over sideways to reach the telephone, "Oh, hello, Chris, this is a surprise. I was at the BBA this afternoon and wondered where you were?"

"Lunched with advertisement agents. Wheel-and-dealers—as we know."

"What's news?"

"Good news. Is Trudy home?"

"You can talk. We don't have secrets in our house."

"OK, but can I speak to Trudy?"

"Uhm…yes." Head tilted, eyebrows lifted, jaw hanging somewhat askew, the receiver swinging from his relaxed wrist, "Chris wants to talk to you."

"Hello, Chris."

He licks the last of the sauce out of his plate—over its edge he sees her face beaming with happiness. "Chris, that's wonderful news. When do they want to see me?" Fingers slap across her mouth. "OK, I'll come to the gym with Eddie tomorrow." The receiver sinks back onto the stand.

"What was that about?"

She lays her hand on his. "An advertising company is offering me a contract—ice cream or fruit juice. Chris showed them my photo portfolio. There's an appointment organised for lunch tomorrow. We'll drive there together from the BBA."

"That's fantastic, Troedels."

But when did she give her photo portfolio to Chris?

Thirty-Five

Alone

He dries himself, dresses and puts his training clothes in the sports bag. Chris and Trudy are back, hopefully—he wants to be on his way to Randfontein before afternoon peak traffic starts out of Johannesburg.

Her arms wave from the other side of the ring ropes.

"What is it, Trudy, ice cream or fruit juice?"

Cinnabar tickles his nose. A hand comes resting softly on his kidneys, "Come, my love. I'll tell you all about it in the car."

Behind her Chris gives a complacent nod, still wearing teardrop sunglasses under his Beatles-cut black hair.

"It's a two-year contract for fruit juice," she enthuses from the passenger seat. "Fruit Dew's new range. The contract was all drawn up, just ready to sign."

One gear down to take the Crown Mines onramp to the highway, pick up speed and he gears one up, "And?"

"And so, I signed."

"Fantastic. Congratulations."

"Eddie," her tone softens, "Fruit Dew wants to boost sales this summer already. The first shoot is between Christmas and the New Year."

"We're in America then, Troedels."

"I had to think and decide fast. The agent hinted at another model in case I was not available. He was just ready to get up and leave. It was really a scary moment."

"Our tickets for Vegas are booked for 20 December. My fight is on the first of January and then we are going to California…Malibu Beach, Troedels. Remember?"

"You'll have to go without me. Sorry, hubby."

The steering wheel quivers as he slams it with the palm of his hand. If he speaks now, it will hurt. He is not going to spoil her moment.

Her hand caresses his leg, "This is my big chance now, isn't it?"

Is he going crazy? Or has he become punch-drunk? Their previous conversations feel like pieces of a puzzle that don't fit anymore. What did he not understand? And when? The only thing she ever wanted was horses—that's what he had heard not so long ago. She would give an arm and a leg to visit Universal Studios in Hollywood—where the movie Jaws was filmed, she thought aloud while paging through the popular pony magazine Huisgenoot the other day. "Are you cross with me?" She breaks the silence in Randfontein.

Maybe it is not so bad. "No. Just need a mind shift to realise that I can go to America alone and win. But yes, Troedels, this is your big chance."

Thirty-Six

Vegas

Amongst the crowd behind the departures lounge glass wall, his own people are also present, Leon and Jeanette with his godchild, Leon Junior, on her arm. Suzette and Ollie and Trudy, next to Mom. Further off in the sea of faces, Chris grins. This time, Eddie successfully managed to oppose his claims for so-called new, unforeseen expenses and, again, an extra slice of his prize money. His respect for that man Rossouw has gone. He just takes all that he can from the boxers under his management; Eddie grinds the thought one more time.

He feels Uncle Ig tapping him on the shoulder. "Are you coming, or should Manny go fight DiCavalli?"

He tries to smile and blows a kiss to Trudy. All around her, women are blowing back kisses. He turns around decisively—if he looks back now, he will crack. He so much looked forward to exploring California with her and especially, to have her next to the ring when he faced DiCavalli.

*****

From his plush velvet seat in the back of their limousine, Caesars Palace comes into view. A flickering neon billboard announces their fight: Desert Duel at the top and lower down: The Stallion vs. The Eliminator. DiCavalli's face is pictured opposite his own.

The chauffeur shoots a two-finger salute off the rim of his cap to the official next to the pedestal-mounted gold-plated VIP sign and drives in, stopping beneath the porte-cochère. Reception staff swarms closer. Tailcoats with top hats. White gloves eagerly unload luggage and divert signature hunters. With Uncle Ig and Manny on either side of him, he enters the glittering reception hall.

From distant twilight shadows, the jingle-jangle of slot machines washes closer across thick red carpets.

On the reception counter, three envelopes await them. Golden ribbon tied in a bow around each. One is presented his way. The blond receptionist's mention that the double suite is for the Blignaut couple strikes like the scratch of a nail on a wet scab: What the hell's been gnawing at Trudy lately?

Next to Eddie, Uncle Ig paws his envelope suspiciously. A handful of roulette chips appear, "Manny, you're not gambling a single dollar until after Eddie's fight." He appears hypnotised and deafened by the cleft in the full bosom in front of him.

"Warm welcome, gentlemen. Anything you might need, please let us know. For entertainment from outside our hotel, the concierge is over there." Centimetre-long, blood-red nails point at a counter opposite where an equally busty brunette is smiling, lips as red as the blond's nails. Click-clicking on the keyboard, she glances briefly at her computer screen. "Your luggage just arrived in your rooms. You have complimentary access to our Panorama Bar on the upper level. Enjoy your stay. Elevators are to your right." Uncle Ig heads in that direction.

"Good luck with your fight, Mister Blignaut," wafts across the counter in a whisper, accompanied by a coaxing smile and fluttering lashes, as if it were a sin to say such a thing aloud here.

He manages a *Thank you*.

On New Year's Eve, Uncle Ig wants to inspect the ring: measure the sides, test the tension in all four ropes and feel the texture of the floor canvas. The ring measures eighteen feet; his request for a twenty-foot ring to give Eddie more room to move is ignored. His insistence that the slack top rope be tightened is adhered to—ropes are part of Eddie's agility and when attacking Victor, he must not be able to lean back over a slack rope to escape Eddie's punches. For a firm foothold, Eddie wears boots with a fine texture sole, the same grain as the canvas. Ig finds Caesars Arena surprisingly small, maybe four thousand seats? The first spectators' row, only a few metres away from the ring, is the bottom rim of the ascending wall of seats which dams up all the way to the ceiling. Apparently, big basketball games are often played here. How is that possible, because from here inside the ring the place feels terribly confined?

During contract negotiations, Eddie's camp understood that Caesars' profits emanate from sales of television rights for the live broadcast of Desert Duel on

New Year's afternoon from 3 pm Pacific Daylight Time. Turner Brothers first wants the fight to take place in Eddie's home country, but Kingston retorts with Apartheid politics. Chris demands increased prize money to fight in Vegas. Granted. An afternoon fight is the Turners' last trump card for the sake of Eddie's supporters back home, where it will be midnight.

His fight only a few hours after lunch is not the only novelty today; it is also his first opponent with identically the same physique and style as him: flitting slender legs like pendulums working upwards through his hips for shoulder swings which extend his long arms even more, distributing explosive jabs from the front or back foot in masterly body balance and distance control with trained intuitive anticipation which costs opponents dearly when they try to come within their own reach. The only difference between us being Blignaut's will to survive.

Intimacy with the crowd is palpable—jeering from backbenchers has never been so clearly audible. "You're both champions," the referee tells them. "You know the rules. Touch gloves. Back to your corners." They were given a talking to in the dressing room by a Nevada State boxing official: the ten-point rule applies—ten to the winner of a round, nine to the loser; a fighter, knocked down three times in the same round, loses; the count out continues after the ringing of the gong, except at the end of the last round when the gong ends the fight; gloves are received from the referee and fitted on in the ring. Hands are bandaged in the cloakrooms, under the supervision of both the WBA and WBC officials and a delegate from the opposition camp—Manny proudly took care of that.

Gong. He and DiCavalli measure one another punch for punch—his camp has clearly studied Eddie's style in detail.

"Eddie, our plan is that you take the fight to Victor, but he sees you coming and counters you. Box more static, like standing in front of a punchbag. Let him come towards you and punish him with counter punches…" the gong interrupts Uncle Ig's advice.

Eddie settles round two in his favour with more clean punches than DiCavalli.

"Turn southpaw—Well done, get him against the ropes like that again and throw right-left combinations. Target his heart area with right hooks, DiCavalli is getting slow to retract his left arm after a punch," Uncle Ig advises in Eddie's corner between the next rounds.

Before round ten. "Right hooks in his ribs are your best gap, and a bit lower in the liver area. You must win this round, Eddie, after that I score you five rounds each."

According to the crowd, their darling is winning—he acknowledges their cheering and dances out of his corner, arms victoriously above his head. Eddie jog-trots nimbly out of his—I'll break you in, little stallion.

Uncle Ig's advice gets Eddie to score points until Victor's cannonball hooked right strikes him on the chin. The ring keels over and bobs around. Uncle Ig shoots past, and the canvas pulls him like a magnet—the face of the main adjudicator flashes between the ropes followed by DiCavalli's glove brushing past his head. Stay on your feet, block, clinch. Gong. Phew. He stumbles left—No, there is Uncle Ig to his right. The flung sponge of cold drops brings some clarity to Eddie's head. His buttocks hit the three-legged stool.

"It's your round. Your glove did not touch the canvas. You saved a knocked-down eight count with a few inches; would have cost you the round. He thinks he's got you. That'll be the bloody day."

Relief comes when Uncle Ig relaxes the elastic of his boxing shorts. "Breathe in deeply, out slowly. Eddie, my boy, our game plan is now like you trained: Let him attack and you throw right jabs on his left glove. Crack open his defences and shoot straight lefts to his chin. The bastard has to drop."

Manny's ice pack lifts from behind Eddie's neck when the main adjudicator crackles barely audibly over the loudspeaker: "Seconds out. Rou-u-und eleven."

Victor is on him like a shot. Eddie defends as best he can. In between, he jabs and jabs on Victor's left glove—he shows uncertainty about Eddie's new tactic. "Ten seconds left, Eddie," comes from his corner when DiCavalli moves in again and staggers backwards with big, expressionless eyes after a right jab on his glove and a direct left hit in the mouth. "Victor's round, like the tenth was yours. Now, you had the sting in the last few seconds. He's tired and more shaken than you were. Right jab and straight left. Keep it up like that." After round thirteen. "Eddie, the entire country is watching, and they believe in you like I do. We have two rounds left and a plan. Go do it. You can."

Is that a crack in Uncle Ig's voice? His usual tap on the shoulder is now a firm body hug as Eddie gets up. He bites his mouthpiece out of Uncle Ig's hand and looks him squarely in the eyes. "I will. Talk to me, don't stop—I want to hear that I'm not alone." Trudy, why are you not here? Are you even watching on television?

He crushes open a right jab path through the round, hips swinging through behind explosive straight lefts over and over. Victor has his breath back and also shows a will of steel to become a double world champion. Uncle Ig at the end of round fourteen, "You're that close to flooring him."

Eddie follows the referee's gesture of curling index fingers, moves to the middle of the ring and touches gloves with Victor. Under a fluttering orange-white-and-blue South African flag, a duet is sounding from Eddie's corner: "Go, Eddie, go Eddie." Another flashing right jab—the follow-up straight left jerks Victor's jaw askew and drops him. Eddie's straight right flies afterwards through fresh air as though he wants to bash him through the canvas, and the momentum in his legs carries him to the neutral corner. Victor is counted out as the gong jingles.

Stretched out on the hotel bed, he waits for a reasonable time to phone South Africa—it's four o'clock in the morning there. He switches on the television: What is the press' reaction to his victory? The evening television news channel is dominated by coverage of a charge of rape brought by a hotel cleaner in Las Vegas. While taking a Coke from the mini bar fridge, he hears the judge's decision: Rape, because against her will or without her consent is a sexual violation and against the law. Then the face of the American president appears on the screen across from a man with a stain on his forehead. It is reported that President Reagan and Soviet leader Mikhail Gorbachev exchanged optimistic New Year's greetings, expressing mutual hope that they would reach a nuclear arms control treaty.

At last, he is screened on Manny's shoulders in the ring with a protesting DiCavalli coach in the background. According to reporting, the DiCavalli camp appealed against the match result—their man was ostensibly counted out after the gong rang for the end of the fight.

Synchronised slow motion on a split viewing screen shows how the referee shoots out a tenth finger over Victor, and on the other half of the screen, the gong starts ringing immediately afterwards.

Little pony, you are definitely counted out before the gong started ringing—hometown advantage doesn't change a single rule in your favour.

The State of Nevada Court dismisses DiCavalli camp's appeal.

Dan Kingston capitalises on the contested result and contracts a return bout at Sun City casino resort in Bophuthatswana tribal homeland—the new playground of South Africa's wealthy citizens. The perspective of fighting in front of his South African supporters is priceless to Eddie. Apart from this being his highest prize money yet, he believes that his supporters who carried him through his boxing career deserve to see their hero in action. He will give them his all in Jungle Law, as Kingston baptised the rematch.

Thirty-Seven

Klaas

After the press conference at Jan Smuts Airport, Eddie is in a hurry to get home. In the back of Leon's Volkswagen Microbus, Trudy's sensuality is irresistible.

On The Ranch, Leon takes the luggage out of the microbus while Trudy and Eddie dash for the front door as lightning bolts turn the night sky into pale white. "Thanks, pal, just leave the suitcases here in the entry hall. I'll phone you sometime this week."

Thunder rumbles across the skies while her breath pants in his neck—his own racing like the gusts outside, subsiding after the first drops. Dissolved into one another they drift off to dreamland.

"You feel like coffee?" She whispers as he wriggles out of her embrace and slides open the patio doors.

"And a beskuit, please."

"I'll quickly go check how our horses are doing while waiting for the kettle to boil. It's almost ten o'clock."

"The horses can wait a bit. Klaas knows what to do, doesn't he?"

"You should hear the hooves beating and the neighing when I walk into the stables in the morning. I don't see them doing that for Klaas."

"Okay, I'll wait for you."

"Wake up," he senses her breath in his ear. How long did he sleep?

She makes herself at home next to him and flattens the bedclothes with the tray.

"You know, Troedels, I'm starting to feel excited about becoming a dad. What do you think of a little bambino?"

Her back stiffens under his hand.

"You mean…a child?"

"Yes, starting a fam—"

"Up to now, your boxing career has been our priority. I have my first model contract and Chris says another agency is interested in me. A model's career doesn't last forever, you know. No, oh no, I don't feel up to a child. Anyway…people must be sure of their feelings for each other if they want to have children."

You are sure of your feelings for your partner when you get married—she did say yes when he proposed; and then why not have a family? Is he now imagining things? Maybe jetlag is playing up on him. His eyes follow her leaving the room, in silence.

He must have dozed off again. Blinding sunlight shines through the patio door. He hops out of bed.

From behind a magazine in the living room, "I went to buy a Huisgenoot—look." Pages flap above the sofa.

"Cool. You look beautiful surrounded by those piles of fruit and that waterfall. Where did the shoot take place?"

"Witwatersrand Botanical Gardens." Her legs swing off the sofa, "You hungry?"

"Bacon and eggs with baked beans, please. The next few days, I eat what I like."

"Thirsty?" A carton of Fruit Dew wiggles in the air. The salmon pink Miss Cassidy trouser suit is an elegant fit. While he was working in Las Vegas, her wardrobe was being filled with new outfits.

"Can't wait to taste it."

A toasted bread crust wipes the last baked bean sauce from his plate. "Thanks, after the junk food the Americans eat this was genuinely nice. Excuse me for a few minutes." The stables smelled of dung and straw. A horse snorts. His hand rummages into the hessian bag for a sugar lump.

"Hello, Klaas."

He stops grooming Sea Breeze, "Hello, baas Eddie."

After his neighbour's passing away, he took on Klaas and Mpho; their other option being to go back jobless to Ga-Rankuwa tribal homeland.

"The horses, they missed you."

The mare lifts an upper lip for the lump of sugar in the palm of his hand. "In a few weeks, they'll train on Gert's course at Randjesfontein."

"They stay there?"

"Yes, horses have to be trained every day."

"I go too. Other men not looking after my horses."

"I'll ask if there's a room for you."

"Okay. I take my lunchtime now."

"Sea Breeze, you're going to kick dust in everyone's eyes." Sundance, Lightfoot and Gullwing each get a lump of sugar and a rub between the ears. "Look after Sea Breeze, you guys. She's our lady."

Trudy is back on the sofa with her Huisgenoot when he enters the living room again.

"It's nice of Leon to always play taxi for us. Shall we invite them over for a barbecue this weekend?"

Eyebrows lift over the edge of the magazine. "Are you ready for their two spoilt brats?"

"How can we invite them and say the kids are not welcome…"

"Invite them, on condition that you clean up after the hurricane had passed through our house and they've ransacked my cosmetics drawer."

"Gee, Troedels. There was only that one time when little Sanet painted your dressing table with nail polish."

"Okay, but remember my condition."

Halfway to the telephone, it starts ringing. "Eddie Blignaut."

"My-my-my, the champ himself. You're talking to Timothy Larney…is my model home?" The charming voice with the slight English accent tilts him into a bad mood.

"Timothy who?" In the corner of his eye, the Huisgenoot shakes. The voice from the receiver sings a few bars from a local hit song: "I love you, Timothy, I love you, Timothy, and you're just the guy for me…Timothy, from Stars-up! I see my beauty queen eventually made it into the mags."

"Look, mate, my private telephone is not your chat line. My wife's not available."

"Well, well, tell her that her prince will soon catch up, mwa, mwa, and her kisses might just turn me back into a frog, ha-ha-ha …"

The receiver is rammed onto the stand. "It's your prince, Timothy. Do you want to tell me about him?" He stops, facing the trembling magazine pages. "Or, are there secrets in our house?"

"Timothy is the boss of Stars-up! Model agency."

"Your prince?"

"He groomed me for the Miss South Africa competition."

"Does that make him your prince? I've never even heard you mention his name."

Quietly evasive eyes, "Timothy was very possessive about me."

"You're mine now. If I get my hands on him, I'll bash him up so well, he'll look like a frog without you having to kiss him. When was the last time you saw him?"

"He phoned a few times when I was living with Petrus and them. One afternoon, he turned up at Barclays Bank. I asked Marleen to say that I was busy with clients."

"And since we've been married? The boytjie sounds pretty horny."

"No, that day in the bank was the last time."

"You sure, Troedels?"

"Yes, my love. Can we leave it at that?"

"Okay. I'll phone Leon."

Who else didn't she mention? He never heard this Timothy guy's name before today, yet she knows him well—maybe even intimately.

Should he ever show up near Trudy, he'll get a thrashing.

Thirty-Eight

Raging Bull

The winning spirit of the horse-racing business fascinates him. Both he and Trudy become well-known faces at the Gosforth Park and Turffontein racecourses. They recently graced the cover of Huisgenoot. Eddie frequents Gert's training track at Randjesfontein where young Jerry Simpson is getting his horses fit for their first race meetings.

In preparation for DiCavalli, Eddie and Trudy find themselves together at the BBA more often than on The Ranch. Chris, now also her manager, clinches a second advertising contract—this time, diet cereal. A photo session takes her to the wheat fields of the Western Cape.

He is grooming Rostrum—his new yearling. Outside the stable a vehicle engine switches off. It's hopefully Trudy. She did not phone him once. Before she left for the Western Cape, an argument started about some or other trifle, something that has happened often since Las Vegas. Jokes from the beginning of their relationship about different dispositions and backgrounds have become the stuff that her insults are made of. Brushing his teeth before bedtime suddenly becomes a precondition for intimacy. Also, his efforts to try and understand her detachment trigger a biting reaction.

An orange Ford Big Six—spoiler on the tail and chromed rims—freezes him in the stable door. Who is this?

Bertus, hanging halfway out of the car window, "Howdy, neighbour." The door swings open.

"Hello, Bertus. What a surprise."

"Well, what do you know? Looks like you breed horses?" With his right hand fingers deep in his flame-red fringe, he turns around in a circle. Elbow askew in the air and hand behind his head on eye contact, "Nice camps too."

Klaas comes to the fence with a foal. "Baas Eddie, the little stallion he's like your child: he sees you, he goes to you." His khaki floppy hat lifts in Bertus' direction, "Afternoon, baas."

Eddie moves closer, "Klaas, this is Bertus. We were at school together."

"Jo, you know him from l-o-n-g time."

"What brings you here, Bertus? Not my horses, I figure."

"No, but it's nice to see everything you have, just the same."

"It took blood, sweat and tears, all the same."

"Yup, no pain, no gain."

Eddie feels annoyed anew: Bertus must not be here when Trudy comes back. Annoyances from way back towards the freckled-faced redhead are crawling back under his skin. Streaks of grey show in Bertus' hair. "Almost ready to mount. Can I give a hand with breaking them in?" The foal gets a scratch between the ears.

"Chum, these are not those donkeys you broke in at the Gerbers, back in the day. For you to know, I don't breed. I race. These are thoroughbred racehorses. They are broken in at the Randjesfontein training track and coached by Gert van der Linde." With an open hand towards the high white columns at the entrance of his estate, "By the way, I'm expecting guests any minute."

"Eddie, I've come to tell you that my mom died yesterday of lung cancer."

"Oh no, Bertus. Sorry to hear that. My condolences." Aunt Willemien? He feels too embarrassed now to ask what her name was. The quiet woman in the house across from Mom's, Sergeant Bert's wife with the flame-red beehive hairstyle, apricot powdered cheeks, pencilled eyebrows, and menthol cigarette between her two fingers—always. Bertus suddenly appears defenceless with his short pants pulled up high, short-sleeved shirt tucked in deep, and socks pulled up almost to his knees. Shiny, military red Grasshopper shoes. Not much has changed since schooldays, although with his budding potbelly, he resembles Sergeant Bert more and more

"The funeral is tomorrow. Dutch Reformed Church in Randgate."

"I spar every day this week in Booysens; not sure I'll make it. Want to express my sympathy to your dad, too. Hmm, tonight or tomorrow evening?" Time with Trudy is his first priority.

"Any evening. Our whole family is with him." Across his shoulder on the way to the Big Six, "You have it good, neighbour. What about a loan—a thousand bucks or so?"

"What do you mean by have it good? It was one helluva battle to get here. Cheers, chum." The dust has not even settled on The Ranch when an engine roars closer along the dirt road skirting the horse camps. At last. With arms wide open, he awaits her outside the stables, "Beloved little stranger, welcome home."

"Hello, Eddie, can we talk?"

"Oh, now that sounds serious." Where does such abruptness come from? "Come, I'll make us coffee."

"Don't know if I have time to sit down."

"Troedels, just…a…minute. You've been away for a few days, and you don't know whether you have time to sit down with me?"

"Eddie, feelings have developed."

"What feelings?"

"Between me and Chris."

"What are you talking about?"

"I don't know how, but I have feelings for him."

"Does he know it?"

"Says he's in love with me."

His head is a pressure cooker, "Trudy, you are my wife. He keeps his filthy paws off you. I'm going to bash that bantam cockerel's face up, break his slender little nose, right there in his BBA from where he thinks he can rule everyone. Get in, we're driving straight to Booysens."

"Chris stayed behind in the Cape. I just came to collect my clothes."

"Clothes?"

"I'm flying back to Cape Town tonight."

One swift step and the key is pulled out of her BMW's ignition. His fingers gently encircle her upper arm, "You are going nowhere, Trudy Blignaut. You are staying right here."

"Imagine a photo like that in *Beeld*?" With contemptuous dimples, she flips her thumb to and fro, "The wife of our country's boxing hero hitches a ride next to the road, carrying only her suitcase of clothes?"

"Trudy, please, don't threaten me."

Her index finger waves under his nose. "And you don't dominate me any longer."

"Troedels, is this really happening? What will I do without you?"

"What you have always done: live for yourself. Dominate and rule—exactly what I wanted to escape from at my father's, and now with you, I've walked straight into the same chauvinistic shit."

How can she feel that way when he is trying his best to ensure their financial future?

The suitcase in her hand by the front door, minutes later, strikes like a low blow, "Should you want to come back—"

"Goodbye, Eddie."

Horses neigh nervously in the camp as the boot slams down like a cannon shot.

Nauseous, as though he swallowed a balloon but can't bring it up, he stares at the back of the BMW disappearing between the high white columns of The Ranch, down the dirt road along the horse camps, until it becomes enfolded by a cloud of peat brown dust. His feet carry him to the stables, back to the house, to the stables again. On the way to the stables, hope flickers in his mind that he will see Trudy's BMW driving back along the dirt road. No, Eduard Blignaut, your imagination is playing tricks on your brain: your opponent has already left the ring in triumph.

He finishes grooming Rostrum. His estate feels drab and quiet. Inwardly, he is a raging bull.

After a shower, he drives to Randgate in the late afternoon.

Uncle Ig will have advice.

Thirty-Nine

Terminate

"You look like death warmed up. A double world champ shouldn't look like that. Come in."

"Afternoon, Uncle Ig—I'm shattered."

"You need a good night's sleep. Tomorrow, three tough sparring partners will be waiting at the BBA."

"I'm sparring at your gym tomorrow."

"It's already arranged at the BBA, Eddie."

"Can you phone my sparring partners?"

"Of course, but it's been years since you—"

"Phone them—please."

"Why?"

"Because Trudy's gone."

"Gone? Where?"

His tongue feels like a lump of lead, "To Chris Rossouw."

"Oh, yes, he manages showbiz contracts as well, nowadays."

"She left me, Uncle Ig. For him."

"Come and sit down, I can't make head or tail." A knob switches off the television. The cap on the J&B bottle slowly turns, "Whisky?"

"No, thanks."

"And that's why you're not going to the BBA tomorrow?"

"I'm never going to goddamn BBA again. I terminate my contract with Chris."

"You can't. DiCavalli is in the country and in two weeks' time the two of you are climbing through the ropes."

"On 9 April, I'm climbing through the ropes without Chris Rossouw. I'm seeing my lawyer tomorrow afternoon. Will you go with me?"

"Of course, where did things go wrong between you and Trudy, if I may ask?"

"Wish I knew. She says I live only for myself. I know I put a lot of time into my boxing, to ensure that we live well. She, especially."

"It takes two people to form a relationship, that's true, and only one to end it…But perhaps it's not just her doing, Eddie, my boy." Whiskey is mixed with tap water from a jug. "Chris has a reputation for being a womaniser—was married twice before. Okay, a man has to do what a man has to do: you decide about your contract with Chris, and I'll make sure you're in shape against Victor. You want to sleep over?"

His gaze lifts from the teak block flooring to where the reading lamp throws a whiskey reflection against the wall. Then to Uncle Ig, "No thanks, Uncle. There are two foals worth forty thousand rand each on The Ranch."

On his way out of town, he pulls off the road. With Mom, it will be more difficult than with Uncle Ig. He makes a U-turn, to Van Deventer Street.

He stops in the driveway behind her new, shiny little car—his recent gift for her forty-seventh birthday. Deep breath. Get out. Blessing in disguise that Dad is in rehab again. The kitchen door is ajar. His hand slips through the security gate lattice and knocks.

She appears out of the passage.

"Hello, Mom, is this a good time?" Recently, he heard from Suzette that she's working the night shift again to have time for gardening during the day.

"Hello, Eddie. What a nice surprise."

"Your garden looks lovely. I've come for a quick coffee."

"Thanks, I've rediscovered my floral heaven."

A bunch of keys appears from her gown pocket. She switches the kettle on in passing. The security gate opens with a jingling and a peck on her forehead. She makes tea and coffee for him.

He sits down opposite her on the couch and starts telling her. The palm of her hand wipes away a tear and, trembling, scrapes the lemon wedge from the bottom of the cup. "Eduard, one must pray that it all comes right again…"

Is her face distorting because of sadness or the lemon? "Will you do it, please, Mom? You are better at praying than I am."

"I will."

"Thanks, I'm leaving again. You should come over and look at the new foals." He puts their cups in the sink, "And the spare room, now that there isn't a woman in my house on The Ranch anymore." She gets a kiss on the forehead.

"Eduard, it wasn't about Trudy in person, but two women in one house doesn't work." Keys jingle as the security gate is locked.

He stops halfway to the car. "News about Dad?"

"Had a call from Swartfontein Rehabilitation Centre. They want to see me. No idea about what, nor how to get there—somewhere near White River. Could you drive me there?"

"Of course, after DiCavalli we'll talk about it. Okay?"

Through the lattice of the security door, the outside light illuminates her smile, "Thanks. Are you ready for Victor?"

He gives a thumbs-up over the roof of his car, "That's not my greatest worry. Bye, Mom." Now, Mom knows and Uncle Ig as well. But he needs buddy comfort to speak his heart. Back home he phones Leon's number for some man talk. "I want to talk privately, pal."

The voice from the receiver drops to a softer tone, "That's a coincidence, me too. How are you placed this weekend—Saturday morning?"

"Hunky-dory! Coffee here on The Ranch."

Forty

Star

How does he get Trudy to change her mind? Petrus—she will have a sympathetic ear for her chaperone brother.

The telephone rings and rings, "Good evening, Petrus Potgieter."

"Evening bro-in-law, is this a bad time?"

"No, was busy with the kids—bedtime stories and stuff. Almost showtime for you. How are the things?"

"Shitty."

"How so?"

He swallows a sob, "Trudy left home. Left me, I mean."

"What…when?"

"Today, this afternoon. She's gone to the Cape."

"What new Trudy bullshit is this, again? We'll go and fetch her."

"Petrus, you can go. Maybe, you'll convince her otherwise. If I go to the Cape, I'll rearrange Chris Rossouw's face."

"Chris who? You sure she hasn't gone back to Timothy?"

"Chris Rossouw, her manager—my previous manager. What do you know about Timothy?"

"At the end of her standard nine, she went to the Cape with that Timothy guy—told my parents she was going to the seaside with a girlfriend of hers. The girlfriend's appendix burst and her mother phoned to tell Trudy. My dad answered the phone and by the skin of our teeth, we prevented Sergeant Major Potgieter from starting a third world war. Dutch Reformed Church council disciplinary committee met to devise appropriate discipline for her shit. Trudy had been catechised a few weeks earlier, confirmed, first communion—the whole caboodle. Her school principal is on the church council, and when she is summoned before the disciplinary committee of the Eldoraigne congregation, she wants to leave school by any means possible. That's when she came to live with us to finish her matric at Hoërskool Randburg."

"Okay, bro, now we both know more. Please share the news with your parents, depending on what you accomplish in the Cape."

"It was easy for me to talk, Eddie. It's my little sister, but it's your wife. You decide."

"I can only think of one thing: Victor DiCavalli. I'm not getting a hiding in front of my own people. We'll talk again after my fight. Cheers, bro."

"Bye, Eddie. I'll talk to my parents."

A few days later, the ringing telephone strikes a flickering of hope: It's Trudy, hopefully?

Deep breath. Pick up, "Eddie Blignaut."

"You're treading on thin ice, old bull. If you think a contract is that easy to breach, you should think again."

"Chris fucking Rossouw. You're breaking up a friendship and a marriage."

"You're missing the mark, chum. I'm your manager, not your buddy. You climb through the ropes under my management against DiCavalli, or I'll sue you."

"You want to see me spraining a finger while handling my horses? Then the fight is off. Think again. I don't need the two hundred thousand dollars in prize money. I'm climbing into the ring for my supporters."

The telephone is hung up on the other side. Pensively, he stares at the floor. Luckily, he had already spoken to his lawyer. On The Ranch, the receiver sinks back onto the stand.

"Why didn't you tell me?" Suzette shoots from the hip, walking across the front porch of The Ranch. "I must get it second-hand from someone at work who happens to read *Star* newspaper."

"What are you talking about, Sis?"

She pulls her chin in askew, rolls her eyes and scratches inverted commas in the air with her index fingers, "That you and Trudy are separating."

"Nothing is final. It may all be okay—I hope. That's why I'm not saying anything."

"So, why are you saying something to the newspaper?" Her handbag zips open and a crumpled newspaper page lands on the coffee table, "There: Blignaut couple separates shortly before world title defence."

"I didn't talk to *Star*."

"Who did, then? Trudy has a lot of tricks up her sleeve, but she would not have gone that far. Who else knows?"

"Mom, Uncle Ig, and…now you too, and the entire bloody world. It's Rossouw, I tell you."

Elbows on the table, her freckled face framed by wide-open hands, "So, big brother. Tell me more."

"I wish I knew, Suzette. But I'm not thinking about that now. I eat, sleep and live DiCavalli."

"How do you feel about the fight?"

"Better than before our fight in America. For the first time in my career, I have a home crowd advantage. They have carried me all along, but now more than ever, I need their support—close to me in the seats around the ring, and I will give it my best shot, for them."

"Okay, I must go. My lunchtime is one short hour and it's a ten-minute drive back to town." He walks her to her car.

Small fists drum on his chest, making big eyes at him, "Don't ever let me hear from the newspapers what's up with my big brother again."

He waves her red Volkswagen Golf goodbye. He will phone her more regularly—even if it is at her work. If he phones her at home, he might just have to talk to Krisjan—which will probably mean another argument.

During the first years of Suzette's marriage, he actually got along with his brother-in-law, Krisjan. After he became boxing champion and Krisjan's first high school rugby team mostly lost, his judgements became more vicious—like one day on The Ranch: Box is a barbaric sport, because the intention is to eliminate your opponent, not just to win.

"Krisjan, what do you mean boxing is barbaric? Look at that Joggie Jansen tackle on the All Black, Cottrell, in the 1970 rugby test at Loftus Versveld Stadium?"

"That was a very good tackle and within the rules."

"Granted. But the SA Mirror sport highlights film shows many good tackles in that test, screened at drive-in theatres all over the country. Why did our country get hysterically excited about that one tackle especially?"

Standing squarely in front of his swaer, Krisjan in the thick atmosphere hanging over The Ranch patio, "Let me tell you: because Cottrell didn't get up—eliminated after he had been shouldered on his solar plexus. When a boxer gets knocked out, he is not allowed to box for three months afterwards. Cottrell was revived and kept on playing."

Neck extended, his blood-red face right in Eddie's. "You do that for your people and for your country's honour."

"Like old Frik du Preez punching Chris Laidlaw behind his ear in the same game? Laidlaw suffers a concussion and keeps on playing. Frik becomes a folk hero because of public assault. In boxing, a sucker punch is considered a cheap shot."

"Who wants malva pudding?" Mom intervenes elegantly.

At about the same time that Eddie invests in racehorses, Krisjan becomes an elder in the Dutch Reformed Church. His judgement, one Sunday during lunch at his and Suzette's house, is the last straw, "Careful, Swaer. Racehorses lead people astray, to gambling, and that is a sin." He wanted to remind Krisjan of his suspended sentence for culpable homicide after the car accident with the train in which his first wife died but kept quiet for Suzette's sake.

Should Krisjan make even one rude comment about the Eddie-and-Trudy affair, he will definitely not keep quiet again.

Forty-One

Fifty-Fifty

"Howzit, pal? Morning, big boy," he greets Leon and his godchild the following Saturday on The Ranch.

"How's the champ?" comes with a pincer-like handshake.

Leon Junior, head tilted sideways and one eye screwed up against the sun, "Can I go look at the horses, Uncle Eddie?"

"Klaas," Eddie calls in the direction of the stables.

He motions Leon to go into the house. Klaas, with Leon Junior's hand in his, is on his way to the stables.

Stuttering, Eddie begins, "I can't tell you anything more than what is in the newspapers."

"A kick in the balls. Everything seemed to be running smoothly. What flew into Trudy?"

"My manager, Chris Rossouw. Thinks he owns you when he manages you."

"The fucker. What are you going to do?"

"Manage myself. You feel like a game of snooker?"

"Would be nice." He rummages in his wallet for a coin, "Heads or tails?"

"Tails."

The coin spirals into the air. Leon catches it in both hands, "You sure you can manage yourself?"

"For sure, I can manage myself. If I don't know the ropes in the boxing game by now, I won't ever."

The coin is slapped down on the snooker table. "It's tails, you open, pal."

Clack-clack the white ball cracks apart the triangle of reds.

"Don't you want to manage a business, too?"

Eddie, taken aback, "How do you mean? I am a business," his open hand waves from his chest to the memorabilia on the walls, lowers and aims to strike a red ball.

"We have a first option on a house in Randfontein Central. Park Street. Business rights. If I move Leon's Tuning & Styling there and you increase your ten per cent to fifty per cent, I can use your share as a deposit on the house. How does that sound?"

His easy shot is completely off the mark, distracted and surprised by Leon's directness. Then, quite business-like, "How much is fifty per cent?"

Leon aims, sinks a red ball, "Thirteen thousand rand, half the price of the property."

"I don't want to own half of your house."

"What I mean, Eddie, is that you invest thirteen thousand rand, and we share fifty-fifty in the profits of my business."

Isn't his life damn complicated enough? "We can do it, on condition that my lawyer draws up a contract." Money changes people, he has come to know that much and doesn't want misunderstandings or differing expectations to ruin his friendship with Leon—even though his craftsmanship is most sought after and he shows some business acumen.

"Deal, champ," Leon gives a high-five.

Pussyfoot now, until he has spoken to Lukas about a contract.

Forty-Two

Forever

He hardly hears the gong above the din in a Sun City Super Bowl filled to capacity. He starts his first-round southpaw to destabilise Victor—Uncle Ig's instruction.

Talking, cursing, insulting, DiCavalli comes for him.

Uncle Ig after round five. "I score you three rounds and two for Victor. He leaves his ribs and sides open. Work him with body hooks," Uncle Ig translates the advice of Doctor Wilfried Bucholz in the BBA: repeated punches in the sides cause fibre spasms in the hip muscles and delayed mobility.

All through round eight, every hook triggers an imperceptible pull in the corners of Victor's mouth—and another as the gong rings. "Four rounds each. He feels your hooks, Eddie. Move upstairs—attack the head. Body shot-uppercut-body shot-uppercut," Ig demonstrates, looking himself ready to face Victor.

By round nine, Victor only clinches and growls in Eddie's ear, "Where's your slutty wife tonight, racist?" He wrenches himself free and his flashing right rips Victor's jaw askew, wavering like a reed in the wind. The whoosh of the follow-up left snaps him backwards. A limp figure rises from the canvas, teeters as hears the mandatory eight counts and takes cover behind folded arms until the gong brings escape.

Manny's wet, cold sponge behind his neck opens up his nose—in the opposite corner, DiCavalli is helped to his chair. In between squirts from Manny's water bottle, Eddie utters, "Victor is made of rubber."

"He's just human. The entire country is behind you—go finish him." Uncle Ig's double pat on his shoulder blade propels him to the middle of the ring. Chaotic screaming is going on in Victor's corner. The referee starts counting out DiCavalli sitting on his little three-legged chair. A white towel is flung into the ring and a man from Victor's camp leans over the ropes, arms crossed: Victor won't be carrying on the fight.

Arms in the air amidst the milling about in the ring, Sybrand Goosen's flash captures Eddie's joy on film. And now, what does he say in front of the television camera? "Thanks to everyone here tonight and to everyone at home, for your support during my boxing journey. I got here tonight only with your support."

Beeld's front page on 9 April 1988: Eddie forever!

Forty-Three

Your Half

The next two weeks are reserved for holidays and family time—he answers journalists' questions about future plans after his fight against DiCavalli.

He suggests to Mom they make a long weekend out of their visit to Dawid in rehab.

"White River, 10 km," she reads the road sign aloud.

"It's beautiful here. All the valleys and pine tree plantations. Boxing took me to so many places in the world, but I have never been to the Eastern Transvaal."

At the four-way stop in the centre of White River, her index finger lifts towards a road sign, "That says Swartfontein Rehabilitation Centre," then dropped open hands to carefully smooth down her skirt, before touching up the beehive hairstyle here and there.

He turns left and, just outside of town, right into the entrance.

Between two dabs of lipstick, "It looks more like a village than a rehab—all the cute little houses."

He stops. Hand-painted, against the wall of a building under a green corrugated iron roof: Reception.

The receptionist adjusts her spectacles, "Good afternoon."

"Afternoon. Blignaut."

A visitors' book opens with a crack. She phones while they sign in and asks somebody to inform Mister Blignaut that his visitors have arrived.

A side door opens. "Morning, Dad."

Dawid shakes his hand without a word. Elusive gaze. Absent eyes. Does he even know his son is a double world boxing champion?

"You can use the room next door," the receptionist indicates, "For privacy."

"I'll wait for you outside, Mom," Eddie winks.

The land starts sloping down steeply from the reception veranda. Far below, a wisp of mist drifts up the valley.

He changes from one buttock to another on the steel-and-meshed-wire garden chair. It's been more than an hour now, he estimates. What is being discussed in that room next door? He asks the receptionist about a toilet.

"Is Mister Blignaut your daddy?" She whispers.

"I am his son, Eddie." At the same time, he looks at her name pin on the white overcoat, "Pleased to meet you, m-i-i-ss Naude." She is not wearing a wedding ring.

"It's not my job to tell you this, but Mister Blignaut is quite a handful for our small group of staff." Her index finger pushes up the gold-rimmed glasses and she rubs the side of her neck somewhat self-consciously.

Eddie leans closer, "How do you mean?"

"He is a lovely man—rather, person, I mean actually. He is making such progress that we ask him to drive the refuse removal tractor—Swartfontein uses White River's municipal refuse dump. Our maintenance foreman is going on pension soon and we want to offer your daddy the position. But oh, dear—I am not allowed to tell you this—when he came back from the dumping site recently, he was completely wasted. We could smell his brandy breath when the tractor was still a long way off."

Oh no, damn, still the same addiction. "The toilet, please?"

Dad's goodbye greeting is to quietly just glance past him.

They have hardly left the centre when Mom bursts into tears.

Eddie wants to lighten her load, "Never mind, I heard everything from the receptionist already."

"For Dawid to stay here for longer, it will cost two hundred rand per month. He insists that we sell the house. I will certainly not see a cent of that money and then I will lose my garden as well."

"The house won't sell overnight, Mom. I'll pay the two hundred rand every month; Dad doesn't need to know."

"Thank you, Eduard. But he is going to insist on selling—you know Dawid."

Back from their long weekend in Londolozi Game Reserve, he collects his mail and frowns at the post office note between the letters. He enters the building and joins the queue for registered letters and parcels.

Back in his car, the words swim in front of his eyes. He folds the subpoena back into the envelope. A divorce? Trudy is out of her mind. He must speak to someone now or his head will burst.

Mom listens over her cup of tea, "Oh, Eduard. I am very sad for you. What are you going to do?"

"I'll phone my lawyer today. Lukas must give me some advice."

"I dreamt of a Blignaut grandchild. Suzette and Krisjan's two little ones are beautiful, and I love them very much, but they are little Olwagens and when they marry one day, they will get a different surname."

"A son is my dream as well, Mom." He sips the remaining coffee, "I've got to go."

His arm wraps tenderly around her shoulder when they reach the security gate, "Mom, I'll buy the house. Then you can stay here and there won't be problems for you getting your half."

"Eduard…" she shakes, sobbing, against his chest, "It sounds too good for words."

Forty-Four

Undefeated

He once saw the pink palace in Huisgenoot, in an article about the royals of Monaco. Now the palace towers into the air right here in front of him. He has made a small fortune from boxing and horse-racing, but the wealth here is in another league.

His fight against Richie Leonard takes place in the nearby Monte Carlo Casino complex. The Englishman is the first contender for his WBA world title; bookies give him a three-to-one chance against Eddie.

It's as though Leonard comes from a new boxing generation: his agility surprises Eddie and overwhelms him during the first few rounds: is he getting slow? Only in the second half, he gets a grip on the fight. A split decision after fifteen gruelling rounds allows him to retain his title.

Maybe the toughest fight of his career, he reflects the next morning, pacing his broken body to the shower. Is age catching up with him, after thirteen years in the ring, he ponders under a steaming hot shower.

"We have to talk," Mom whispers when he arrives at Jan Smuts Airport.

"Eduard, when you bought the house, I thought your father was going to take it easy," her words pour over the rim of a teacup on her sitting room couch. "Now there's something new." A paper tissue rolls out of her dress sleeve. "He wants to divorce me, and I don't even understand why, except if there's someone el—" The tissue muffles her words in the palm of her hand.

He has never seen Mom so hunched up by sorrow and finds nothing to console her with in her search for a reason, "Can I make you more tea, Mom?"

"Please." More restrained. "We had many issues, but he is still my first love. He can move back tomorrow, but now there is someone else—that's all it can be."

He pauses reflectively in the kitchen until the kettle boils. He's lived with their conflict for years—but why divorce after more than thirty years?

"There you go, Mom. Slice of lemon and all."

Her trembling hand spills tea from the cup.

The tissue blots the drops up from the opened family album at a photograph of Dawid, all spruced up, next to a cream-coloured A30 Austin. "The weekend on Uncle Andries's farm was nice, but too short to be called a real honeymoon."

"What are you going to do, Mom?"

"What can I do?" Words hang suspended in an uneasy silence.

"Maybe talk to my lawyer?" He hears himself saying.

"If it becomes necessary." A trembling teaspoon scoops the slice of lemon from the bottom of her cup. "First want to pray about the whole thing."

"OK, Mom, let me know."

There's light in Uncle Ig's living room.

He buttons up his jacket—this winter of '89 is severe. Eddie knocks.

The handshake feels limp. Weak, watery eyes sunk deep in their sockets. "Evening, Eddie."

"Evening, have you got a moment for me, Uncle?"

"Come in. You know I always have." His head motions towards the kitchen, "Annette is watching Dallas in the living room."

Elbow on the kitchen table, chin in the palm of his hand, "My motivation for the ring isn't there anymore. All ten contenders are hungry for my titles. I want to retire undefeated, but how do I explain that to my supporters?"

"Boxing has been good to you, Eddie, and you've been good to boxing. But, you're also a person in your own right. You sure you want to retire?"

"I am. I owe nobody anything and my horses win regularly."

"Talk to the South African Boxing Council and then to the WBA and the WBC. Afterwards, you organise a press conference and announce your retirement."

"You'll sit next to me when I face the press. Okay?"

A hearty laugh from Ig's stomach, accompanied by an alteration to the thick-rimmed glasses and a rub across his bald head. "Okay, but I'm going make their lenses crack."

"Thanks, Uncle. I'll phone the council tomorrow." He pushes himself up from the table in relief.

Softly, under his breath, "Is there a new love in your life, Eddie?"

"Not really, dating different girls, trying my luck. I'll let you know if I ever fall in love again."

A hand rests comforting on his shoulder blade as they walk to the door.

In the sports pages on 3 September 1989 edition of *Beeld*: Eddie hangs up his gloves.

Forty-Five
Randjesfontein, 1990-1991

Most Fundamental Law

Beyond the plain of golden-brown winter grass, Rostrum's gleaming; black buttocks are bouncing up and down in a gallop. Eddie focuses the binoculars properly: Jerry comes into sight, his riding whip swaying next to the horse's head. A wide-open foamy mouth bursts out of the turn and flashes past under a thundering of hooves.

He walks to where Klaas is waiting for Jerry. With a swing of his leg, he slips out of the saddle, "You're looking at the 1991 Turffontein Spring Cup Champ."

Eddie holds up an open hand to Rostrum, a sugar cube balanced in his palm.

Klaas, with a roguish laugh, "Check his lips, like saying thanks for the lump of sugar." In his mind's eye, Eddie leads Rostrum to the podium, in the same way as Klaas is now cooling down the horse—saltpetre showing white all over the stallion's buttocks.

"Jerry, could you take Rostrum over the finishing line first in the Spring Cup?"

"For sure, Eddie. Best four-year-old stallion in the country. We have only six more weeks until the Cup. Randjesfontein training course is too flat."

"What do you mean, Jerry?"

"We must go practise on Turffontein race course so he can get fit for the uphill in the back straight. Could you organise that?"

"I'll do it today. And Ruby? Do I enrol her for another race on Cup Day?"

"Yes. We back them as a couple and on Rostrum alone a few weeks before the race already, when nobody expects him to win. Then we make the bookmakers poor on top of two hundred-thousand-rand first prize in the main race." Under his jockey cap, he is beaming with self-confidence, rubbing his thumb and index finger together in the air, "Big bucks."

Eddie lifts his binoculars: in the distance, Klaas is performing a tribal jive in front of Rostrum—knees lifting high, feet landing on pointed toes and his other hand swaying a piece of wood like it is a spear—steam rising from the horse's back under the early morning golden glow.

In the run-up to the Cup, Eddie is at Randjesfontein training course before seven in the morning. Rostrum and Ruby are loaded into Gert's low-bed truck under his own supervision, after which he drives ahead to Johannesburg's Turffontein racecourse for breakfast in the Owners and Trainers Enclosure—the OTE, as they call it amongst them. Here, he learns how other owners manage their horses and gets tips about placing bets.

Before daybreak when he leaves The Ranch, Mpho is already busy around the kitchen. In front of the stove, beaming face, round cheeks, pearly white teeth, "Goomornin, Baas." Mischievous eyes peer into the warming drawer—mimicking surprise about his previous night's dinner still in there, complaining about how alone she feels now that Klaas stays in Randjesfontein. Soon Eddie's cup of milky coffee is placed on the kitchen table like clockwork—again this morning.

The bell of The Ranch's security gate tinkles in the entrance hall.

The mug of coffee stabilised in one hand, he lifts the receiver with the other, "Hallo?"

"Morning, neighbour."

This time of day? He presses the Open button and walks outside. The sliding gate reveals the orange Ford Cortina Big Six. Chromed mag rims roll closer, glittering in the first-morning sun rays.

From the open car window, "You heard about old Sammy Naidoo?" Still a self-appointed broadcaster, you are, "What about Sammy?"

"Shot and killed in the backyard of his shop for his Mercedes. This morning, coming back from the night shift, I stopped by the Corner Lounge to pick up a newspaper. Christos showed me the article."

"Why Sammy?"

"You know the answer; nobody is safe in this country anymore." He gets out, *Beeld* in his hand. The paper spreads open across the hood, pages turning, then one page back, his index finger searching, then tapping, "Here it is." Randfontein businessman shot in cold blood.

"And Rashida?"

"Was in the car apparently. If she didn't get out to help Sammy, she would have gotten a bullet as well. The second thief jumped in behind the wheel and they chased away as if Sammy had unlocked the gate for them."

Under Bertus's left hand, the August wind plucks at the newspaper, his shoulder lifting in phase with his chin and eyebrows, "How about a little tip there, Richie Rich? Something like a thousand bucks, or even better, three?"

"You carry on as though I owe you something?"

"Eddie Blignaut, you owe me big time." A few pages flap over and Bertus' right hand presses down on a loose page to not blow away, "What do you say about his?"

Eddie strains his neck across the hood at what appears to be a photocopy of a page torn out of a school exercise book.

"What's this?"

"Read."

South African Police 28 December 1976 stamped at the top of the page. Moving closer to see more clearly, Bertus backs away from the car, the page stuck under his stretched-out white fingertips.

Eddie focuses: I, Stephina Tokwane, declare that Mister Eddie Blignaut sexually violated me at 67 Van Deventer Street, Randgate. I lay a charge against Mister Blignaut, as it had led to—His right hand shoots out and Bertus jerks back. Half a page flutters in Eddie's fingers. On faint blue lines on the bottom half of the page:

Signed: Stephina Tokwane.

Group: Sotho. Tribe: Bafokeng. Pass number: 010633.

Witness: Lethabo Matsamela.

Group: Choana. Tribe: Kgatla. Pass number: 004238.

"What shit is this?"

A nimble step forward makes Bertus jump into his car. His head of carrot-red hair leaning out from the window, "From my father's old work briefcase, where he stacked it in his garage after retirement. Go check the Immorality Act 21 of 1950, dear neighbour: you get caught screwing across the colour line, and they put you in the slammer."

V6-engine vibrations throb under Eddie's hands. Dust swirls up into his face and gravel spatters against his legs. "Make those five thousand bucks, fat cat from Randgate—don't forget where you come from."

"I wouldn't blackmail anyone if my father had murdered a man." Moreover, with his bare hands.

A dust cloud follows the roaring Big Six as it speeds away between the white pillars. Damn, he should have closed the security gate after Bertus had come onto his property. The mug of coffee quivers ripples under the milk skin when he picks it up from the yellowwood table in the entrance hall—welcome relief for his bone-dry mouth. In his hotel room, that night, after his fight in Las Vegas, he hardly paid attention to the television newsreader reporting something about a judge ruling sexual violation, on a charge brought by a hotel cleaner. Meanwhile, it had already been written down, about him.

Nightmare thoughts run away with him then ram to a standstill, and repeat on his way to Randgate. A shiver rattles down his spine. Shame surges through his veins—Sergeant Bert ripped the page out of the Randfontein Police Station charges book, but didn't breathe a word about it through all these years. His hand slaps over his mouth in disbelief. "Thank you, Lord."

On the veranda outside Naidoo General Dealer, little has changed. The nylon string that used to tie the fat tyre Humber bicycles together on the porch is now a steel chain with a lock. Inside her shop, Alisha's silver-grey hair contrasts with the darkness over her face. A sombre soul in a purple sari.

"Alisha…I am very, very sorry."

"Oh, Mister Eddie." The delicate, gold-framed spectacles are removed, and her one hand keeps on touching the bun behind her head. "I am broken. Why him? My dear Sammy never did anyone any harm."

He reaches across rolls of material on the counter, "I am not sure that I can help in any way, but here is my telephone number." He feels in a hurry, not only to get out of this woman's place, but Alisha's sadness is just too much for him, "Call me if there is anything I can do for you."

Small semi-detached houses flash by down Lazar Avenue. Should he go and thank Sergeant Bert for having kept him out of jail after his intercourse with a black woman? No, he might just run into Bertus at Sergeant Bert's. With the original of Stephina's charge, Bertus can destroy everything Eddie Blignaut ever fought for. Loss of esteem amongst his supporters, South Africa's whites, will be the most devastating knockout. He won't be able to get up again from that one. He'd rather telephone Sergeant Bert—as soon as he has the courage.

That's going to be a difficult task because interracial incest is a transgression of South Africa's most fundamental law.

Forty-Six

Out of Control

Jerry brings Rostrum into the home straight on the Turffontein race track. Horse and jockey shoot across the finish line. In the OTE, Eddie lowers his pair of binoculars and purses his lips contentedly, thinking *Hello pension cheque*.

"Your horse looks like the Spring Cup champ."

Eddie turns around. "Oh, hello, Charles. Congrats, I hear your last album went gold."

"Yeah, thanks. The year in America taught me so much more about singing Country and Western and my fans appreciate it."

"Same thing with horses—we learn something new every day. Walk with me to the stables. I want to talk to Jerry before he takes Ruby out on the track. You racing in the Cup?"

"I've entered Country Girl."

Eddie pushes the OTE door open. The Cowboy hat lifts in acknowledgement. No wonder he has the nickname of Charming Charles.

Jerry hands the reins over to Klaas.

"Excuse me, Eddie, I'm just going to say hi to Country Girl."

"What you're feeling about Rostrum, Jerry?"

He peers around the horse, waiting until Charles disappears behind the stables, "I'm reining him in a little. Saturday, the two of us come into that straight alone."

"That's what I want to hear. Go out and see how Ruby does."

Saturday morning, the boom to the OTE parking lifts and the gate guard gets a ten-rand note held out the window.

He drives inside and stops beneath the Eddie Blignaut signboard, gets out, adjusts his tie in the reflection in the window, unhooks his jacket from the hanger in the back of his BMW, slips it on and leans inside for his Panama hat and binoculars.

"Hi, Eddie." John Watkins waves across the car roofs. "You look fit for race day."

"Hi, John, how're you doing? Saw you on TV the other day. Pity about that last putting shot at Sun City."

"Yeah, damn well cost me the title and a million dollars. See if I can recover some of that today."

In the OTE, Eddie shakes hands, exchanges a few words here and there and makes his choice from the breakfast buffet. There's an open seat at a table next to the window. Predictions zoom through the air. He makes discrete notes in his pocketbook. The winners' ring outside feels closer than ever. Maybe he should bet a few more rands on Rostrum and Ruby?

He gets up, "Excuse me, friends."

"Now don't go break the bank," someone jokingly remarks.

Outside, he takes a deep breath: spring is in the air. This day is his.

"Mister Blignaut." Erika, the barmaid, stands framed in the OTE doorway. "Telephone for you."

He jogs back up the steps and shuffles past her with dance-like sideways steps.

"It's right behind the counter, Mister Blignaut."

"Hello. Eddie Blignaut."

"Morning, Mister Blignaut. Sergeant Bruwer here, Halfway House police station."

"Yes, Sergeant, how can I help? I'm in a hurry—"

"Mister Blignaut, are you transporting horses today?"

"Yes, I'm expecting the truck here at Turffontein Racecourse any moment now."

"Mister Blignaut, is a certain Klaas Mokgatle working for you?"

"Yes, why?"

"There was an accident. It seems the vehicle went out of control, left the road and overturned. Mokgatle didn't look good when the ambulance took him away."

"Where to, Sergeant?"

"Baragwanath Hospital."

He steps around almost imperceptibly. His legs are still there—no, he is not dreaming. The OTE suddenly appears sombre—the people seem strangers and far off. "Baragwanath? That's in Soweto, isn't it, or—"

"Yes, in Soweto."

"And, Sergeant, my horses?"

"I had to shoot both. My constable is putting everything on file for you."

"I'll come read it later. Goodbye, Sergeant."

Is Klaas alive? The idea of a heap of mutilated horse meat pushes his breakfast up his throat. He turns the dial.

"Jeanette Griesel speaking."

"Hi, Jeanette. Is Leon around?"

"He and little Leon are having their hair cut. You sound stressed?"

"Problems with my horses. I'll phone again later. Bye, Jeanette."

Forty-Seven

Soweto

The half-mast parking area boom brushes over the BMW roof. How does one get to Baragwanath Hospital? The BBA flashing past helps to recall. Onramp to the highway at Crown Mines and soon afterwards, he takes the Soweto exit. And now? He weaves his way between jam-packed microbus taxis.

A colossal building comes into view on the left; the signboard at the entrance reads Baragwanath Hospital. The BMW shoots in the direction of Emergencies. He parks and rushes inside—a woman is seated behind a counter.

Both hands on the counter, panting, "Hello, I'm looking for Klaas Mokgatle."

"I beg your pardon?"

"Klaas Mokgatle, where is he?"

Leisurely, the admissions register turns back one page. Her finger scans line entry by line entry.

Then she decides to phone.

The receiver sinks down slowly back onto the stand, "He came in this morning."

"Yes, I know. Where is he now?" Please don't say the morgue.

"Ward H, sir. Go down this passage, then take the lift to the third floor."

Already halfway down the passage, "Thanks."

He worms himself out when the lift door is still only slightly ajar and jogs along the directions indicating Ward H.

At last. "Where's Klaas Mokgatle?" He asks a nurse pushing a patient in a wheelchair.

"I'll have to look in the register, sir. Please wait here." Ages later, she comes back with an empty wheelchair. He tries to read upside down in the book she opens meticulously, "He's still under surgery."

Klaas is alive. "What's wrong with him?"

"We will know when he comes out of the theatre."

"Can I use your phone, please?"

"Visitors are not allowed to. There is a public telephone on ground level, next to the kiosk." He swears under his breath. He has to phone quickly because Mpho only works mornings on Saturdays and usually goes to visit the neighbouring plots in the afternoons.

Claustrophobia grips him and he pushes open a window but recoils from the sour smell of coal gas. The brown-grey landscape of Soweto shacks stretches out all the way to the horizon. Smoke is drifting everywhere as if the hazy air were sucking it out of the chimneys. He jogs to the lift.

The kiosk is a hole in a wall, "Coffee, please."

The woman scoops instant coffee powder out of a tin and pours water out of an urn, "Milk and sugar, sir?"

"Yes, please."

"Fifteen cents." His polystyrene cup comes pushed through the opening under the iron bars, followed by a plastic spoon.

Deja vu from his army basics training flashes through his mind: the queue at the public telephone is metres long. Only, in Bloemfontein, the coin-operated telephone was inside a booth, granting some privacy. Here, it is simply bolted to the wall. He slurps his coffee, while the morning's events race through his thoughts. He has heard some chilling stories from the horse-racing industry, but what is happening now feels unreal. Horrific.

It's his turn to phone. The kiosk paper serviette wraps carefully around the receiver. He turns the dial with his pinkie. How many sick people have already stuck their fingers into these holes?

"Hello, Leon speaking."

"Hi, pal."

"Jeanette says you phoned earlier. You're racing today. How're the odds?"

My horse trailer overturned sounds ominous.

"Where? When?"

"I'll tell you later. Please, go and fetch Mpho on The Ranch and bring her to the hospital."

"Sure. Robinson Hospital?"

"Baragwanath."

"Fuck't, pal. You in Soweto?"

"I am. You'll find me in Ward H, third floor." What does he tell Mpho? How does he explain?

The clock on the wall shows midnight when he, Leon and Mpho walk out of Ward H towards the lift. He wanted to wait until Klaas was completely awake after his anaesthesia. While the surgeon explains to Klaas that he is permanently paralysed, Mpho's body shakes uncontrollably. Eddie is speechless—never again a tribal jive.

"Mpho, are you sure you want to stay here tonight?"

"Tonight, I sleep in the reception, baas Eddie. Tomorrow, I see Klaas and then I take the taxi to your house."

"Okay. Have this."

Her hands cup to receive the twenty rand note.

Leon is already waiting outside, "We've got to get out of here—a white oke will be skinned alive around this place."

He's had enough of skinning for one day, "Thanks for today, Leon. You can go back to Jeanette. I'm going to stop at the Halfway House police station to read the accident report and get a case number for my insurance."

"Constable, what caused the accident?"

A brown cardboard ledger opens. "Front tyre burst."

He takes down the case number in his notebook and draws a thick line through this morning's Rostrum 2:1; Ruby 8:1. On Monday, he'll phone Gerbrand—thanks to his insurance broker's advice, his horses are well insured. Third-party insurance covers Klaas' medical costs.

An eery solitude greets him under a full moon. Tonight, there is not even a horse's breath on The Ranch. He parks at the front door, gets out and stands motionless. Here Klaas walked, but now he is confined to a hospital bed, and when he gets out of there, to a wheelchair. Eddie shudders.

Forty-Eight

Comeback

Late October, in the Randfontein branch office of Anchor Insurance, cold sweat trickles down his spine. "Gerbrand, you know that I am well insured. Rostrum and Ruby cost me a fortune."

"Eddie, here, read the assessor's report yourself." Gerbrand's swivel chair wheels closer to the curved inlet of his desk—specially cut out for his potbelly. "The horse box was on the road illegally. No third-party insurance or licence disks on the windscreen. What's more, the vehicle was badly maintained—how else could it lose a front wheel? According to the assessor, the cause of the accident is the vehicle owner's negligence. Sue him for your losses." Eddie does not recognise the smiling smooth talker, who sold him his insurance, in the emotionless beady eyes between drooping cheeks with their mutton chop side whiskers, flowing down into a fat neck and onto his shoulders.

Over the past weeks, during the investigation into the horse box accident, Eddie felt himself a stranger amid laws and insurance conditions, at times even a suspect. "Look, Gerbrand, Gert van der Linde is my friend. I'm not claiming even a cent from him." The Anchor file shoots across the table.

Roly-poly fingers catch it and wave warningly, "Your choice, Eddie. It's either you or Gert—whoever's going bankrupt."

"Gerbrand, I'll phone you when I've decided on the road ahead."

On the way home, he takes stock: The Ranch is paid off. His BMW as well. He pays Klaas a pension but Mpho's salary is minimal. Mom has been okay, financially, since he bought the house. His share in Leon's Tuning & Styling is a drop in his bucket. He has no debts, but no pension reserves either.

Coffee at Mom's or with Uncle Ig? With Uncle Ig, he must have a plan to discuss, at least. For now, he just wants to chat, get things off his chest and test a few thoughts. Yes, just put his heart on the table, unfiltered also, to talk in confidence to a woman—the big longing in his life. He enters her driveway.

Approaching with a limp, a contagious smile, and the scar above her eye almost invisible amongst the wrinkles, she comes out of her garden. Sunlight shines on her grey hair, "Do you have news?"

"If Mom has coffee, I'll tell you."

They wait in the kitchen for the kettle to boil. Mom prepares a pot of tea.

In the sitting room, she lowers a lemon wedge into her cup, "And...?"

"Gert's truck was on the road illegally. Because of that, Anchor Insurance and third-party insurance refuse any payouts. Klaas' medical accounts run into thousands of rands. There's not much of my money left."

"You can be a motor mechanic again. You've your papers..."

"There's no way I'll work for a boss again, even less so as a grease monkey."

"But what are you going to do?"

"Back to the boxing ring, make some money to buy young horses for training and then race." He will manage himself—same way he won against DiCavalli.

"Eduard, it's been almost three years since your retirement. Look at that tummy over the belt of your pants."

"I'm a comeback champ, promise."

"I was so relieved when you hung up your gloves."

"No choice, Mom." He rubs over his midriff. "May I ask how things are between you and Dad?"

"I received a summons to divorce on his behalf. Never thought he would use his share from the sale of the house for that." Eyes shut, chin on her chest, "Meanwhile, I am still praying that he comes back." She takes a sip of tea and rubs over the soft leather of the new sofa with an open hand. "This is my way of spoiling myself a little. It is so nice to sit on."

If he had a better relationship with Dawid, he could have convinced him differently; but alas. A relationship with your son starts in his childhood, doesn't it, Eddie argues with himself. He recalls only his father's brutality as far back as he can remember. One thing led to the next, ending in today's animosity.

On his comeback road to boxing, he'll be relying more upon himself than when first turning professional, when his iron will to survive drove him. Then, he had Uncle Ig believing in him—and why not now again?

Forty-Nine

Ga-Rankuwa

He stares at the memorabilia in his snooker room: trophies from his amateur days, framed newspaper pages—John Roberts, Hitboy Malinga, Jerry McIntosh, from whom he took the South African middleweight title, and Elijah Ndlovo, his last opponent as the South African champion. His international glory graces the opposite wall: Luis Mendez, Rudolph Schmidt and a bleeding Jeff Porter. WBA champion belt around his waist with Elijah's headdress after he had dethroned Roberto Gonzales in Buenos Aires. A present from Doctor Wilfried Bucholz, the framed *Ring* front page: Eddie the Eliminator. His favourite, he and Victor DiCavalli squaring up one another in front of Caesars Palace in Las Vegas, bare-fisted. A close second is one of himself in front of the Pink Palace in Monaco.

Eddie Blignaut is a household name; his signature is still in demand. From boxer to businessman, Sybrand wrote about him in *Beeld* recently. The idea of a lower standard of living is a terrifying thought. He's going back into the ring and will come out on top, again.

"Afternoon," Mpho's voice comes from the kitchen. "I make the coffee?"

"Please, Mpho."

She lingers at the sink and wipes her hands on her apron.

He slurps contentedly, "Thanks, Mpho."

She clutches a handful of the apron and positions herself in the middle of the kitchen floor, "Klaas asks for a little talk, please."

"What about?"

"He will say for himself, but I think he wants to go home."

Eddie finds him in the last rays of the sun, on the western side of their room, "Klaas."

His head whips up from his chest in a snore. A rub of his hand shifts the khaki floppy hat from his eyes, "Afternoon, baas Eddie."

"Looks as though you can drive that wheelchair with your eyes closed now?"

"Eish, it's difficult, this thing."

"What is difficult?"

"My bum will break on this thing because I sleep so easy."

"One sleeps at night, doesn't one?"

"I don't sleep at night, Baas. That dream troubles me a lot. Just when I sleep, that thing happens again."

"What thing, Klaas?"

He props himself up with his elbows and gazes into empty space: "Eish, that day. I take my horses from the stables, I load them in the lorry with baas Bertus, the one who goes to school with you. The other man, he washes the window; he polishes the wheels; he fastens the nuts. Then I dream, over and over: I look in the back of the lorry, my horses lie dead inside. Then I am awake, the w-h-o-l-e night. I don't sleep again. I will sleep better thereby Ga-Rankuwa, I think."

"Bertus wasn't at Randjesfontein that day?"

"That day he was. He helped me very nice."

"And what other man are you talking about, Klaas?"

"Don't know him. And Jissis, baas Eddie, I dream of the accident also. Eish, we drive and then he pushes in before us, that bloody white car with a roof like chocolate and brake lights come in almost under the lorry. The driver swerves and everything they swerve for me too. Next, I see the ambulance and lots of cars. I ask to go to Ga-Rankuwa, baas Eddie."

Does this mean he's losing his domestic help too? "You want to take Mpho with you?"

"Who will look after me? Our children work every day at Marble Hall."

"When do you want to go?"

"The children must first build the other room. Their one room for them and three children, it is full."

"Okay, Klaas. We'll talk again."

Walking back to the house, feelings of betrayal overwhelm him: Bertus, you lowdown shit. Back in his kitchen, "Mpho, how much work is it to build your room in Ga-Rankuwa?" The mop sweeps once or twice over the kitchen floor, "The walls they are." Only walls? He will give money to finish the house. It can't be too much.

"Okay, Mpho—me, you and Klaas will talk about this soon. Make me some more coffee, please."

On the patio, he gets his emotions under control. Was it a mistake to entrust the loading of his horses to Gert so that he could be at the OTE earlier on Cup Day? How did Bertus get onto the Randjesfontein training circuit? Who was with him that morning?

He needs to soundboard with someone he can trust.

"Ig Bester," answers a hoarse voice.

It's not a time to bother him if he has a cold. "Evening, Uncle. I wanted to come over for coffee?"

"Annette baked beskuit. How does tomorrow eight o'clock sound to you?"

"Tomorrow at eight. See you then, Uncle Ig."

He lets the pages of the West Rand phone directory fan out under his thumb to D and makes a note in his pocketbook: Du Plessis, Bertus, Squirrel Avenue 47, Greenhills, Randfontein, telephone number 763 5024.

Bertus, I'm going to make you pay—Klaas could have been killed.

Fifty

Afrikaners

As though Uncle Ig was already waiting for him, the front door swings open even before he knocks. The tracksuit hanging like a grain bag on the emaciated body is shocking.

"Uncle Ig. Good morning." The hand without the grip of steel feels strange.

"Good day, Eddie. Come in."

The embroidered letters spelling Eddie Blignaut hang baggy over Uncle Ig's back.

On the kitchen table, two mugs and a plate of traditional rusks are waiting.

"I suppose Uncle heard my news from the gossip?"

"Eddie, I talk to people, not about people. Pass the coffee."

He puts the cream-coloured enamel pot of groundnut coffee on a hot pad of woven grass and sits down across from the old man. A shaky stream fills the first mug.

"Uncle Ig, I'm going to box again."

A splash of coffee lands on the table. "Make a comeback, you mean?"

"Yes."

"Why? It's bloody hard work coming back—boxing fans quickly forget yesterday's hero; they're always looking for a new one."

"I need money."

His head notches forward an inch, pulling the sinewy strings of his neck out of the tracksuit collar, "How much?"

"I had more than a million rands' damages in the accident."

"For that, you need to fight internationally—you know that. What happened?"

He tells him, the palms of his palms turned upwards towards Uncle Ig, "... all that time I assumed that Gert was doing things according to the book."

"But for heaven's sake, sue the bloody guy."

"What I know about racehorses, I learnt from Gert. I will not crucify him because of one mistake."

"True friendship doesn't have a price tag."

Dare he burden Uncle Ig with his own suspicions? But if not, who else can he trust? He hears himself telling Klaas' story. An unpleasant feeling washes over him to cast suspicion on Bertus for sabotage.

The thick-rimmed glasses are placed next to the coffee pot on the plastic tablecloth in a calculating gesture, "The man gives me the creeps, from his boyhood, but I never thought he would be capable of such a thing. The son of a policeman, I mean."

Another coffee is poured for each of them. "Eddie, you're learning what life's all about. I haven't seen one of us Afrikaners who doesn't begrudge another the air that he breathes. We climb on one another, pull one another down, gossip and slander. Make sure of your facts if you want to haul Bertus over the coals and don't fall into those same bad habits. So, now you want to box again?"

"I've come to ask if you will train me?" He snatches a quick bite before the soaked tip of the rusk breaks off.

"If you haven't heard it from the townspeople, they've discovered I've got throat cancer. The treatment makes me as sick as a dog—miserable and nauseous. I want to say yes, but I can genuinely not."

"Hell, I'm sorry to hear that." His hand stops halfway across the table—real men don't touch one another. "Can I use your gym?"

"My doors are open for you. You can dust off the punchbag and speedball while you're at it."

There is a tenderness he has not noticed before in the defenceless, watery eyes; under the thin skin, death is lurking. "Is it sore?" He manages in a strangled voice.

"Terribly, when I swallow. I get soup only; can't get anything else in."

"What can I do for you?"

"Come for coffee and rusks in the morning after your training. Just say hi when you arrive—the throat already has me up at the crack of dawn."

"Deal." From now on, he is really alone. Should he draw a last bit of wisdom from the moment?

"What would you say if I asked Manny to train me?"

"Manny is your best bet—you know one another. Training is firstly a game of trust and respect between two men—after that, it becomes a physical game."

The limp handshake brings helpless sorrow.

"I'm also climbing through the ropes again for you."

"Do it firstly for yourself. A boxer who feels satisfied about who he is gives his best performance."

On his way to The Ranch, sorrow keeps gnawing deeper. A sob tears through him, "Lord, is it necessary? How can you take Uncle Ig and allow Dawid Blignaut to live?" Life without Uncle Ig—unthinkable. His BMW hits the strip of dirt next to the tarred road in a cloud of dust. He shoves the door with his shoulder and roars towards the ground—bits of rusk vomit cling to the inside of the door. Having wept his fill, he lifts his head from the steering wheel. If Mom already knew, she would surely have talked about Uncle Ig's illness when he told her of his decision to make a comeback. He's going to tell her.

"Hello, Eduard. You're a godsend." The bunch of keys jingle around and around in the security gate. "Come in, I'm making coffee. You have to sit when I tell you." She switches on the kettle.

The bile still burning his throat, "No thanks, no coffee today." Does she perhaps have news about her and Dawid? Hopefully, his parents are not divorcing anymore. His innermost darkness lights up somewhat.

She sits back comfortably and strokes her leather sofa. "There you have it." Another little sip of tea, "So, Annette, old blabbermouth she is, gets what she's always wanted, at last. First, she stole Ig from his first wife, then she caught him by getting pregnant with little Sandra—the entire Randgate knows about her cunning. After that, the parasite just lived for Ig's money—she didn't position herself at his butchery cash register for nothing. She doesn't regret the poor old man's cancer one bit."

Mom already knows everything. He'll keep his own sorrow to himself. On the way to Greenhills, he gathers fragments of his mixed emotions and tries to focus.

First thing, he must get a grip on Bertus and who helped him that morning of the Spring Cup.

Fifty-One

Civil Case

Entering Greenhills brings back memories from his amateur boxing days—doing roadwork with his club mates through these streets named after animals. After driving hither and thither, he finds Squirrel Avenue and parks in front of a townhouse with 47 on the garden gate. He rams it open with his hip.

He's going to choke the truth out of Bertus right now.

The front door is ajar. The ringing of the doorbell echoes from the inside. Somewhere a chair clatters across the floor. Spectacles reflect in the dusk, "Can I help you? Oh, Eddie." The high-pitched feeble male voice sounds somehow familiar. Then Eddie figures it out: Wessel Vermeulen, the Apostolic Faith Mission apprentice pastor who sexually molested Peet in his standard seven school year. Now after poor Peet is long dead comes his chance to eventually punch up this queer for that? A limp wrist ventures out between the security gate bars.

"Hello, Wessel. Sorry, I thought Bertus du Plessis stayed here?"

"Bertus also stays here."

"Is he at home, please?"

"No, he's doing a double shift. The morning shift skip man didn't pitch at the mining shaft."

"Okay. Goodbye."

Exiting the garden gate, "Whose car is parked in the street?"

"Which car?"

"This white Ford with the brown vinyl top?"

"Mine. Why?"

He closes the gate behind him and darts a last look at the reflecting spectacles, framed like a still photograph in the front door—fucking paedophile. Perspective rises within him as he drives downhill through Greenhills. It was destiny that Bertus wasn't home. He would have rubbed the thing with Stephina under Eddie's nose and humiliated him in front of Wessel, for sure.

Now for Lukas—he has to talk to his lawyer about the accident report.

Back at The Ranch, he phones Smit and Kruger Attorneys.

"Hello, Elsie, it's Eddie. Is Lukas available?"

"Hello, Mister Blignaut. I'm putting you through."

"Lukas Kruger."

"Hi, Lukas. Eddie here. I'm opening the accident case again; I have new suspicions about what happened."

"Hello, Eddie. New facts, you mean?"

"A new witness. I want to have the wreckage inspected again."

"The case was closed. It takes a while to re-open the whole thing."

"It's important that it's done thoroughly, this time, rather than quickly."

"Who's your new witness?"

"Klaas, my stableman."

"The assessor and the police heard his testimony."

"About the accident, but not about what happened earlier that morning."

"Then we're talking about a civil case, it seems to me. Not the third-party case again. Eddie, I'm on my way to court. I'm putting you through back to Elsie again. Make an hour appointment. Is that okay?"

"That's fine. Goodbye, Lukas."

That's one more thing he can tick off. Now the question being: would Manny be prepared to train him for his comeback?

He phones.

Fifty-Two

Why Now?

"Come on, champ, straight lefts, right hook," Manny's voice resounds a week later through Uncle Ig's gym. Eddie makes dust whirl out of the punchbag.

A month later, he receives a letter by registered mail—his licence from the South African National Boxing Board of Control. He phones immediately.

"Beeld, Sybrand Goosen speaking."

"Sybrand, I'm back."

"Eddie, what a surprise to hear from you. Where are you back from?"

"I'm challenging for Sugarboy Matlala's title. Can we talk?"

"Of course, where and when?"

"The Ranch, tomorrow morning around ten?"

In the sports column of *Beeld*, two days later: *South Africa's boxing golden boy, Eddie Blignaut, is making a comeback to the ring, almost three years after retirement. 'I still have a lot of boxing in me', he said yesterday on his country estate outside Randfontein. He is training extremely hard under the watchful eye of Manny Perreira, his new trainer. Eddie is managing his own comeback career. He wants to sign a contract soon for a chance against South Africa's middleweight champion, Sugarboy Matlala.—Sybrand Goosen, Sports Editorial.*

Turner Brothers Promotions cut the knot for a fight in December 1991. An unprecedented amount of prize money is the deciding factor for Matlala to agree to the fight because according to the board's conditions, he had already defended his title for the required number of times in the past year since he won it.

"You still carry a kilogram over the middleweight limit. Your hand speed is good, Eddie; your leg stamina is not. We've got work ahead. In two weeks, you face Mister Sugarboy in the Super Bowl," Manny gives it to him one morning in the gym. Eddie finds his training approach confusing: ideas tip over to those of Uncle Ig and then tumble towards Manny's new ones—especially some technicalities in the physical fitness part of training. He doesn't offer much emotional intuition, but Eddie feels he can manage that on his own. Whatever is lacking in his mental preparations, he gets from Uncle Ig during their morning coffee together after training.

Gasping for breath, "Manny, I've already done five kilometres more this morning." But he snacks the entire day. The investigation into the truck accident, still dragging on, chafes his nerves. It is emotionally draining for him to convince Klaas repeatedly to go to Lukas' law practice for more declarations and cross-examinations.

Manny, after a session of shadowboxing against his fluttering hands, "Eddie, my man, you're flat-footed. Have you forgotten Uncle Ig's basics?" He jumps out of the ring. Comes back up the steps with a boxing bootlace in his hand and ties it around Eddie's right ankle—measures an arm's length towards his front foot—and knots it around the left ankle. "That's the gap between your feet to keep the bounce in your legs for a tight two-step shuffle." More shadowboxing follows.

After rope skipping, six rounds against the speedball and the punchbag, it's time at last for a nice shower. Every practice session is a conscious mission for Eddie nowadays—how could he have done it so effortlessly before? Once out from the shower, he takes a shortcut through the backyard to Uncle Ig's kitchen door, knocks and walks in as has become a habit over recent weeks.

On the woven grass coaster, steam rises from the pot spout. The coffee aroma fills the air.

"Gee, your timing is perfect, Uncle Ig." Eddie lightly touches the side of the pot. Deep breath, "Smells nice. Damn, I'm dog-tired."

"It's my timing," Annette's voice comes from the pantry. "Uncle Ig keeps on peeping into the gym. As soon as you go and shower, I've got to rush to make the coffee so it can brew before you come in."

"Oops, I take back my words. Hello, Annette. Thanks."

"You men must excuse me; I've got ironing to do."

In passing, she lovingly caresses Uncle Ig's cheek. He gets a warm kiss on his bald head, "Annette, easy does it."

He pours and pushes the mug and rusks across the table.

"Thanks, but no thanks. Manny moans about my weight every day."

"Of course, your weight is important. Try one." Eddie tucks in.

While getting up to say goodbye, "…I'm seeing Sybrand for brunch on The Ranch just now."

I feel stronger than ever. The few years outside the ring have improved my idea of what happens inside. Before, I tried to focus on too many things. Matlala must prepare himself to get the essentials from me. 20 December is my gateway back to the international boxing arena, Sybrand quotes after his interview with Eddie, a week before the fight.

Another look into his sports bag: boots, socks, shorts, protective cup for his genitals, underpants and boxing gown. It's all in there. He hesitates between bed and wardrobe but makes no progress with his suitcase. What must he wear at Sun City? Trudy always packs his clothes. He looks over his shoulder at the empty suitcase, throws in a few pieces of clothing, zips it up and undresses to take a warm shower. The ringing of the telephone stops him at the bathroom door.

"Eddie Blignaut."

Hello, Eddie makes him sink down on the bed, his tongue as weak as his knees, "Hello…"

"It's Charlene speaking."

"I hear that. I mean, I know…How are you?"

"I'm just phoning to say good luck for Saturday evening."

Why is she phoning him now, before an easy fight? Why now? So many times, he longed for her support—just one word. Now he's getting a whole mouthful—or that's what it feels like. "Thanks."

"Wish I could be there to cheer you on."

Unbelievable. "I'm sure you could still get two tickets for the Super Bowl?"

"Eddie, I thought Suzette would have told you?"

"What, Charlene?"

"I'm a widow. Jurgens was diagnosed with a brain tumour two years ago. In March, it will be a year since he died."

"Oh, no, Charlene. I am so sorry to hear that." Overwhelmed by feelings of guilt that his emotions could get the better of him despite thinking she was married, "I appreciate your call. Do you really want to come and watch?"

"Can't arrive as a woman on her own. I'll follow you on television."

"Charlene, where do you live? If it's not too far, then…"

She lives in Eldoraigne where she is a teacher at the high school. Will he be taking advantage of her call if he invites her for coffee? He does it anyway. She suggests the Wimpy fast-food restaurant in Verwoerdburg.

He sits glued to the edge of his bed. Numb. A long while later he phones.

"Manny Perreira."

"Hi, Manny, listen …"

"What's up, Eddie? It's almost midnight. Did a Sugarboy nightmare wake you up?"

"I have stuff to do tomorrow. I'll drive to Sun City on my own."

"You should only have Sugarboy stuff on your mind. Don't be late, we face the press tomorrow evening at seven. That's where you fire your first shots at Matlala. Cheers, Eddie."

"Don't you worry. Good night."

He simply has to get Charlene beside the ring on Saturday evening—his one unfulfilled boxing dream.

Fifty-Three

Wimpy

Mommies and children stream into Wimpy Restaurant. He takes cover behind his Ray-Ban sunglasses at a window table—today is not the time for handing out autographs. A head of blond hair bobs past on the sidewalk. He finds himself at the entrance when she comes inside. "Charlene."

"Hi, Eddie." Tiny wrinkles around the eyes appear when she removes her sunglasses. He gets a peck on his mouth.

"We have a table next to the window over there. How are you?"

"Exhausted. Children tire me out. Colleagues even more." Her handbag plops down on the chair next to her. "You look well. How are you feeling?"

"Ready for Sugarboy."

An open hand, palm upwards, points in his direction. "You've done everything a man could dream about."

"You went on and studied, Charlene—that's fantastic. We all take the road we were supposed to."

Her gaze drops, "With surprises. Some quite rough."

The waiter places a menu in front of each of them. "Coffee for me. You hungry?"

Her gaze brightens somewhat, "Tea please, and a toasted cheese sandwich. Aren't you eating anything?"

He can't help giggling, "I'm watching my diet till after the weigh-in tomorrow morning." He tells her why he's boxing again. Where he lives. Makes a detour around his failed marriage. Her fingers zigzag through her hair, pushing it backwards, "It's nice to see you before the fight. Wishing you all the best."

"Thanks. How did you know I'm boxing on Saturday?"

Toast crunches. A paper serviette picks crumbs from the corners of her mouth. Her face brightens again, "The entire country is talking about it. I read in *Beeld* that you've got a new coach?"

"Manny Perreira, he was Uncle Ig's second in command all those years."

"Why not Uncle Ig anymore?"

"He's dying, Charlene. Throat cancer." The coffee relieves his hoarse vocal cords.

Hand over her mouth, it comes softly between her fingers, "Cancer is a monster."

She tells him how her Jurgens suffered. Hopeful times after his operation and during the chemotherapeutic treatment. Hair loss. Brain tumours always growing. Increasing memory loss. Cortisone injections. Puffy face later unrecognisably deformed. Declining bodily functions. Painful last days—for him and for her. "But life goes on."

If only she knew how pleased he was to see her now, "I tell you, pleasant surprises happen." Her chair pushes back again. Is it a nervous twitch?

Handbag hooked over her arm, "Tomorrow night, your life will reach new heights."

He pays on their way out.

"Come and tell me about your fight. Then I'll talk to the new SA champ."

He's going to risk it, "Last night, you wished you could attend my fight?"

"Was just dreaming aloud."

"Suzette is going to Sun City. Ollie as well, only to please her. Please phone Suzette. Tell her I'm asking that you go instead of Ollie?"

"I can't just join out of the blue. No, I'll see you on television. Promise."

Her goodbye kiss is longer than the first, or is his imagination playing tricks on him?

Fifty-Four

A Thrill

On Saturday morning, Manny walks in front of Eddie entering the weigh-in venue. Voices are buzzing. "Check it. Richman-Poorman, arriving," someone mutters from Sugarboy's camp. He is flexing muscles on the scale.

Eddie's turn comes. He stares Sugarboy down.

The doctor's words sound unreal: *Seventy-two, comma seven kilograms. You have until noon to come within the middleweight limit.*

Disappointment becomes frustration. He was so bloody convinced to be inside the weight limit.

"Let's move, Eddie. We must get you down to fighting weight." Dammit explodes behind Manny's hasty heels.

Eddie walks out from under the shower to his third sauna session. Maybe it's a good thing if tonight he climbs through the ropes in a foul mood. Anything to boost his performance.

Some members of Sugarboy's entourage are still hanging around in the weigh-in venue when he briskly walks in. Bulging around the gut, a voice comments from somewhere. Shut up, you shithouse you—Manny fires back.

"Seventy-two, comma five kilograms," the tournament doctor reads the scale.

"My bum is lame after all the saunas."

"Better knock Sugarboy out tonight. Not sure you have stamina left to go the full distance."

"Let's go and grab brunch. And find my people."

Perhaps Suzette is agreeable to exchanging Swaer Ollie's seat for Charlene?

*****

On the way to the ring, Manny leads the way. Eddie's thoughts are all focussed on Sugarboy—his first challenge back to pro-boxing. From under his boxing gown hood, Klaas' wheelchair protrudes halfway into the aisle. On passing, he exchanges light punches against Eddie's gloves. His people are seated behind the front row of journalists. Next to Charlene, a vacant seat—one more Ollie no-show—probably a migraine headache, again. Tonight, Charlene is watching on television. Uncle Ig as well, for sure. A spurt of adrenaline rushes from his solar plexus.

Manny stretches open the ropes. With hands up above his head, Eddie acknowledges the crowd's applause in all four directions. In the opposite corner, Chris Rossouw leans over the ropes and talks to Sugarboy behind a cupped hand.

He is an easy target during the first few rounds though Eddie finds himself slower than Sugarboy. The result of three sauna sessions or age? He nevertheless outwits Sugarboy with nimble experienced footwork, use of the entire ring as well as the ropes, and prevents the champion from earning points with his rock-solid defence.

Manny, after round five, "I score three rounds to you, one drawn, one to Sugarboy. He absorbs your punches. Pace yourself. Just jab him with straight lefts."

On the gong, Sugarboy appears in front of him firing a whirlwind of punches. A blinding overhand punch on his eye makes Eddie grit his teeth on the mouthguard. His weary arms instinctively throw counterpunches. He has got to get out from under Sugarboy's fists. Blood is blinding his eyes. The gong brings relief.

"You gave him that round." Manny works Uncle Ig's little iron over his left eye, "Damn, your eye looks a mess. Turn southpaw."

Little shit, he puffs through his mouthguard when Sugarboy also dances southpaw out of his corner.

"C'mon, kid, you can do bet—" A direct hit jerks his neck backwards. Dance back—another direct strike. Has-been, Sugarboy throws a verbal parting shot after the gong has gone. "That's his round. Three each, one draw. Keep at his body: when he drops his hands, then knock him out. You can do it, man."

Rounds eight and nine show gaps in Sugarboy's defence, but his sneering smile carries a bitter message: Eddie's fists make no impact. Blood streams over his left eye. The bell of mercy rings.

"You're too equal for comfort; go for the knockout." Cold spray from Manny's sponge brings clarity. The referee nods—gloves touch, last round.

"Box."

His punches make Sugarboy's head tremble and shake. He receives a few punches himself. Grit. Ouch.

"Break." The referee motions Sugarboy to the neutral corner and nods to someone outside the ring.

The tournament doctor leans in.

Oh, shit, please don't stop the fight.

"High cut, no danger to his sight." In the neutral corner, Sugarboy impatiently knocks his gloves together.

"Box."

"One minute," Manny's anxious voice pitches above the crowd. Sugarboy mercilessly rams forward. The feeling of ropes chafing against his back fires Eddie up instinctively. New rhythm—full weight behind a bull's eye straight right punch. Sugarboy staggers. Clin-n-g. Eddie's arms shoot up.

Behind the journalists, his people hug one another. Klaas half lifts himself at a slant out of his wheelchair and swings a clenched fist.

"I believe you've done enough to become champ." Manny unlaces the gloves.

"Ladies and gentlemen: Judge Malingwe scores it ninety-nine to ninety-seven for Matlala, Judge…" With his head to one side, he hears the scores of all three umpires, "…we have a draw…" Damn. "…and still reigning middleweight champion of South Africa, sweet Sugarboy Matl-a-l-a."

He aims for his corner and slips through the gap between the ropes Manny pulls open.

Down the steps, colliding with Suzette.

She rubs over his eye, "They all love you. Listen to them chanting your name. You are their darling."

"Give me a minute."

He's back up through the ropes. Bows and waves in all four directions to the beat of applause, Ed-die, Ed-die rising up from the crowd.

Sybrand sits right in front when Eddie leads Manny into the press conference venue. Suzette, Leon and Jeanette take their places behind the journalists.

*****

Jubilation bursts out from his room telephone, "Wow, what a thrill. You are just as impressive in front of journalists as inside the ring. Are you really going to start a boxing club for boys?"

"For sure. I'm going to teach youngsters to box, so they keep off the streets and rather put South Africa on the world boxing stage." He plucks up courage, "Charlene, have you got holiday plans for December?"

"Over Christmas with Gerda and them at Warmbaths. Since my mother died, my father has been staying there in an old-age home. The hot mineral spring water helps with his back pain."

"I'll phone you sometime in the week. Okay?"

"Okay, Eddie."

He feels the thumping of a super heartbeat, like a few evenings ago when she called him out of the blue on The Ranch.

She is okay with a phone call sometime in the week, but it feels as though she is saying yes to a lot more than a conversation by telephone, or is his imagination running away with him?

Fifty-Five
Eldoraigne, 1992

Powder Blue

Charlene is a stalwart in the lawsuit through his weekly appointments with Lukas. He drives to Eldoraigne two or three times a week and is often only back on his estate by midnight.

He tries to make up for lost time, but something seems to be holding her back. One afternoon at the Monavoni Highway exit to Verwoerdburg, he gets it. It's logical, her husband's illness and passing. But he feels it is not so much that she is in mourning but rather that she is somewhere avoiding him. Dismissive avoidance or fearful avoidance? He cannot quite figure that one out, while he again feels so secure with her although sensing that they both have evolved into somewhat different persons from their school days.

The car hardly comes to a standstill when the school bell rings. Her blond head bobs closer amid the stream of children. A boy carries the apple box which she uses for books. Eddie gets out and leans against the car, "Afternoon, Miss."

Her lashes flutter, "Good afternoon, Mister. Jasper, you can put those books on the rear seat. Thanks."

Eddie drives straight past her townhouse. "Where are you going?"

"Inviting you for a treat. Coffee and a bit of fresh air."

"Okay, but not too long. You see that box full of books? It must all still be marked."

"Fine. You're awesome, teaching Afrikaans to matrics. I never even got that far." He presses her leg, softly. They climb the stairs to the terrace cafeteria at the Voortrekker Monument. "You're serious about fresh air," she pants.

He heads for a secluded table in the shade, "How was your day at school?"

"Teaching scholars brings me joy. Wish it could end there. So many hidden agendas between colleagues. Sometimes, I think about other options. But Eldoraigne is home to me—work, church and friends."

"Was there anyone in your life after your husband's death?"

"Oh no. I was not going to expose myself again to the unknown. And you? A girl called Trudy if I understood the magazines and newspapers correctly?"

He begins to tell her. About Trudy and Chris as well. Waves of humiliation wash over him.

Is he blushing? "People see love in so many different shades: money, self-interest, opportunities…"

The arrival of the waiter is his chance to change the subject. They each order a milkshake and share a toasted ham-and-cheese sandwich.

His hand hesitates across the table towards hers: "Charlene, I…I never stopped loving you." Her smile becomes an exuberant laugh. Her eyes have a moist sparkle.

"Eddie, there is something like true love. You can believe it." She folds her hands over his, "I also have feelings for you…old feelings and new ones."

He must get it right now, "I couldn't understand your indifference, before."

"You became a popular public figure. Never contacted me again."

"I wanted to. Spoke to your parents once, while you were studying at college…"

"Those were different times. I wanted to free myself while they tried to protect me for my own good." Perhaps rediscovering their broken-up past is what she is avoiding?

The evening TV series about Boer War prisoners on Saint Helena, Arende, is on. He lies stretched out across the sofa. How can she do the marking and still follow what is happening on the screen?

Finally, the last book lands with a bang on the pile in the apple box. "Feel like a drink?"

"I would like to say whiskey, but I still have to drive home."

Fingers tickle him under his chin and down his neck, "Only if you want to."

Her lips press down on his. The linen skirt tightens. He feels his way to the zip and it pulls down easily.

*****

The theme from Arende is playing in the background.

"That was awesome." His tongue plays with hers. "So deeply satisfying."

She giggles and slides out from under him. "Whiskey?"

"Let me pour. What are you drinking?"

"Sherry, thanks."

He puts the tray with drinks on the coffee table and snuggles up against her on the sofa. "Cheers," her glass tinkles against his.

"Cheers," then nodding his head at the shoe box next to the tray, "New shoes?"

She sips at the sherry and closes her eyes. "My mother died suddenly, three years ago of a heart attack. My father is totally lost and asks me to sort out her wardrobe. That's how I discovered this under her winter things." The box's lid lifts, "Letters, birthday cards…"

Ice cubes jingle as he puts down his glass and takes the top envelope, recognising his own handwriting.

Her voice trembles, "It's your letter with the dates for your army seven days. I only got to read it three years ago."

He opens the letter. Past and present flow into one another and start whirling, sending his head reeling. How is it even possible? Old Bettie, now dead and buried, actually intercepted his letter.

"I believe she thought she was doing it for my own good, Eddie."

He strokes her temples and moist cheeks.

"You driving home tonight?"

"I'm going nowhere."

She jumps up and runs to the bedroom, "Catch me if you can."

Lately, his routine takes the opposite sense: in the morning from Eldoraigne to The Ranch and back at the end of the day.

One March evening in her little garden, "Charlene, will you be my wife, I mean, will you marry me?"

"But?"

He lifts her up, kisses her, and rubs his nose on her neck. "But what?"

"Yes, for sure. But how and when I don't know—too many things in my head. You must decide."

"The only thing I know for sure is that I'm living a new life with you."

They drive out of Eldoraigne. "We should enjoy the weekend. If I listen to the ANC, Van Riebeeck Day will be abolished when they come into power."

"My boxing career and the horse-racing industry have made me insensitive to public holidays. On one New Year's Day afternoon, I fought in Las Vegas. Boxing Day Handicap is on the Turffontein Racecourse calendar."

"The world is really your playground."

"It's all starting anew. I've been speaking to Uncle Ig about taking over his gym. After the April school holidays, Young Hopefuls Boxing Academy will open in Randgate."

"The Randfontein boys are fortunate."

"Fifteen boxers from across the entire West Rand want to join. From novices to South African champs who want to turn pro. Will you help me dust down the gym? It's been closed since Uncle Ig's illness."

"Of course, I'd like to say hi to Uncle Ig as well."

"He's just skin and bone nowadays." His heart lights up. "I…would like him to see we're together again. Perhaps tomorrow, because now I head straight to The Ranch."

*****

He lets her walk ahead of him and puts their drinks on the patio table. She moves their chairs a bit, facing north, "Good heavens, how beautiful the flat old Western Transvaal becomes before it meets the rolling foothills of the Magaliesberg mountains." Her fingers feel their way across his hand. Knuckle by knuckle, finger for finger and softly enclose his wrist. "The life inside of you, your warmth, your heartbeat, are wonderful."

What course would his love life have taken if Charlene had received his letter with the dates for his seven days? He takes her hand and slips the engagement ring on her finger.

"It's so beautiful."

"I love you more than ever." Her eyes are powder blue in the evening glow.

Fifty-Six

True Essence

They decide to alternate—one weekend in Eldoraigne and one on The Ranch.

"Orange juice for me please, without Campari," she replies and turns the patio chairs towards the Magaliesberg range. "Please bring me a jersey before you pour the drinks. It's Easter weekend and winter is already upon us."

Her voice—is she nervous or excited? Maybe she just feels really cold.

"Eddie, my angel," when he puts down their drinks, "I think I'm pregnant."

"Think or know?"

"I think so."

"Because if you know, we celebrate. If you think so, we find out. What do we do next?"

"I'll be seeing my gynaecologist sometime this week. Was so scared, you'd be angry. People will think I've trapped you. Imagine the gossip. I'm not made for the spotlight."

He kisses away a tear, "I dream of being a dad. Can't wait to hear what your gynae says."

On Wednesday afternoon, he answers his telephone in the stables: "Eddie Blignaut."

"Hi, angel—"

He speaks louder to cover a horse's snorting, "What's the news from your gynae?"

"She's on holiday this week. Have you heard from the guy who wants to hire your stables?"

"Yes, Gerald has confirmed. From the end of May, we'll have six foals here."

"Oh, cute. News from Lukas about the truck accident?"

"He phoned earlier today. The investigation has been completed. He is finalising documents for the court hearing."

"I'll be so glad when it's all over, sounds as if you're busy. I have some marking to do. Love you."

"Me too, bye."

Whatever Charlene's gynae says, finally, his life is settling outside of the spotlights of glamour, like rediscovering his true essence.

Fifty-Seven
The Ranch, 1992

The Confession

He walks through the stables one last time. What would Klaas say about his former kingdom, should he see it today being prepared for someone else's horses? His voice echoes across The Ranch when his letters to Eddie talk about the house they are building, assuring him that they are not wasting his money. But it's been more than a month since he had news from Ga-Rankuwa. A car comes rumbling closer along the dirt road.

Eddie leans out over the stable door, hand shielding his eyes against the sunlight. With the remote control, he slides open the security gate and a 404 Peugeot station wagon appears. The bottle-green jalopy comes to a standstill in front of the house and the passenger heads towards the front door. The driver's golden-yellow hair surfaces above the roof of the car.

"Can I help you? Are you lost?"

The long, black habit turns around. A swaying wooden cross on a string of beads around the man's neck follows the movement and comes to rest outside the stable door, "Mister Blignaut?"

"That's me. Are you lost?"

The snow-white cropped head inclines imperceptibly over the black clerical collar showing a white strip under the chin. A sinewy neck fits loosely inside. Patches of unshaven beard cling to the hollow cheeks. Eddie shakes the bony hand.

"We're not lost. I'm Father Patrick from the Roman Catholic Church." His other hand gestures towards his driver. "Do you have time for me and Lethabo?"

"Maybe a few minutes, I'm expecting a visitor."

The robe takes a firm stance. "Some time ago, a member of my congregation passed away. She died of pneumonia, after having contracted AIDS."

"So what? I don't know anybody in your church."

"Stephina left behind a son who turns sixteen this December. Being old enough to work legally then, he must leave the Roman Catholic orphanage. Mister Blignaut, I have reason to believe that the boy is not an orphan."

Why is the albino guy nodding his head? "Bullshit, reverend. Sorry for my words, but I don't know anything about a woman with AIDS or her kid."

"I could understand that you do not know her child. However, I believe you knew his mother?"

Bullshit, man—just another person wanting to exploit him. "Reverend, don't tell me stupid stuff."

The albino takes a step closer, "We've got evidence, Mister Blignaut."

Eddie grabs and lifts him halfway across the stable door. A button jingles on the floor. The priest's hand gently on his forearm prompts Eddie to let go.

"Mister Blignaut, allow me to explain."

"Explain what? Nobody talks nonsense to me on my own property. You guys see the gate where you came in? That's your way out."

He rams the stable door open with his hip. Trespassers. His widespread arms herd them towards the car. The driver gets pushed into his seat and the door slams shut. Now, for the preacher man.

The eyes speak from deep within their sockets, "Mister Blignaut, allow me one remark, please?"

"Only one."

"In the Roman Catholic Church, we do confessions…"

"What?" After catechism, he kept well away from church polemics about baptising children or adults, receiving communion from a chalice or a glass and whether strong liquor and dancing were one-way tickets to hell. He never heard anything about confessions.

"That is when people tell me, in confidence and anonymously, about things that happened in their lives, to forgive or obtain forgiveness. Stephina wrote a confession about the two of you."

"What did she write?"

"Just before passing away, she wrote about when you two were together. Afterwards, she found herself pregnant."

"That's bull…I mean, I don't believe you. Come inside the stable—the sun is very hot." The blotchy rash over his cropped head must be sensitive and inside the stable, they will be out of earshot of his driver.

"Mister Blignaut, confession is a holy act. As a practising Christian, Stephina understood that. I believe her son is related to you."

"Anybody can write anything. How do I know that Stephina wrote…whatever you call it?"

"If you don't believe the confession, my doctor-friend had your blood on Sugarboy Matlala's gloves analysed at Baragwanath Hospital. You're the father."

"I'm going to beat you up good." Lethabo makes a beeline for the Peugeot with Eddie in tow.

He tries to wrench the door open, but Lethabo locks it in a flash.

Things are getting out of hand now.

Father Patrick, framed by the stable door, his hands folded around the wooden cross, "Sorry, if I upset you, Mister Blignaut. After Ruben's birth, I found Stephina at my church service one Sunday, Ruben wrapped in a blanket to her back. The Mohlakeng black township residents expelled her because Ruben was brown. They took her as just another prostitute for white men from Randfontein. We helped her until she found a job…Looks like your visitor has arrived, Mister Blignaut."

Gerald's Mitsubishi Pajero enters the security gate. He wants to inspect the stables today before the arrival of his foals.

"Goodbye, reverend."

"I'll contact you again in the days to come, Mister Blignaut."

"Would prefer not to see you ever again, Dominee."

Fifty-Eight

Five Weeks

His thoughts keep going in circles after the priest's visit. He sifts through vague memories of his seven days. Does he really want to remember or rather to forget? Wouldn't Stephina have told him if she was pregnant? Maybe not, after Dawid chased her off his property.

This is a nonsense story—it could be any man's child. In his mind's eye, he sees the priest with the cross clasped in his hands. The man is holy. He will not lie. Neither would Stephina. But Lethabo? What does a driver know about blood tests?

His hands fidget here and there, but he gets nothing done on The Ranch. Each day lasts an eternity. If news gets out that he has a child with a black woman, the country will be abuzz. The possibility of losing his supporters triggers feelings of abandonment and rejection in him. Their loyalty is the greatest asset of his boxing career. Who could he speak to? Ideas flare up and fizzle out. No longer to Uncle Ig; he could barely utter a word when he and Charlene went to clean his boxing gym. But Charlene? He will have to tell her about him and Stephina sometime or other. For that, he'll definitely need more proof from the Catholic dominee. Yes, he'll ask him for a photo of the boy. That could just become his way out of this fix.

With Gerald's foals eventually here now, he spends more nights on The Ranch.

The pendulum clock strikes three o'clock, like last night.

And the night before last.

And the night before that.

Was he dreaming, or was his imagination playing tricks on him? He offers the dominee money to keep the child out of his life—half of what he kept as a nest egg in case Mom became incapacitated. But how can he think about money when the acknowledgement of another person's existence is at stake? Eduard, you Judas.

At six o'clock, he is out of bed. The indictment of his conscience hits him on the way to the stables. If Father Patrick's story is true, there is a boy who does not know who his father is. That faceless man who left him drifting through life. Anchorless. Terrible.

What did he want to do here in the stables again? His feet carry him back to the kitchen for another cup of milk coffee.

This afternoon, he leaves for Eldoraigne earlier than usual; his mind is a mixture of longing, anguish and uncertain hopes. How will she react when he reveals his missteps of the past?

On his usual parking under the thorn tree in front of her school, he rolls down the window.

He twitches from the caress across his cheek, "My angel, having such a nice snooze. Someone will carry you off, and then what happens to me?" He is still awakening when Charlene is already next to him in the car.

"Have you got marking to do?"

"I do, but it's only for Wednesday. Will do it Monday afternoon. The weekend is ours."

"I need it," he gives a waggish laugh. "Let's go pick up your suitcase."

She sighs delightfully, "I've been thinking about so many things during the week. If I am pregnant, then my date is late December or early January. I'll see Cindy on Wednesday. It's good if I can work till the end of the school year. I'd like to see my matrics through. I'm thinking about a spring wedding so that our child can be born within wedlock." She giggles. "Even though we have overstepped."

His head is spinning. The flush in his face feels like boiling water about the thoughts he harboured over recent days. He wants to be honest with Charlene, but her feelings are more important to him than his spilling his beans. He will keep the news about him and Stephina for later.

Her enthusiasm takes over their weekend. The spare room becomes a baby room. They measure for curtains, a cradle, and a set of drawers. A boy will be baptised Eben—a little girl, Isabel. She is overprotective, in a motherly way, of anything small on The Ranch: chicks, foals and rabbits.

On Sunday afternoon, they talk about their wedding. It will be on The Ranch.

With his head tilted, "Charlene, you are pregnant, aren't you?"

"Two miscarriages make me doubtful."

"This time it's for real. Feel like a sundowner?"

"Orange juice, please."

Wednesday afternoon in Cindy's room, he listens attentively. Charlene is seven weeks pregnant. In five weeks, the foetus will attach to the uterus. "Everything looks normal. Just like your previous pregnancies," Cindy assures.

"We know the end result of my two previous pregnancies, Cindy."

Eddie folds his hand over hers. It is trembling.

Better he keeps his shocking news for five weeks longer.

Fifty-Nine

Relief

He says goodbye to Gerald in a hurry after their barbecue lunch and runs inside the house. If it is Charlene phoning at this hour, something is wrong.

"Hello…"

"Hello, Eddie, Annette speaking." Sniffs, "Ig left us this afternoon."

He stomps around unsteadily, pulls up a kitchen chair and sinks into it.

"No, Annette, so sorry to hear it." He still wanted to stop by, but litigation about the truck accident, the dominee's story and Charlene's pregnancy have been taking up all his time. "My sincere condolences. It's my loss as well. Are you home?"

"Yes. Yesterday, Ig insisted on coming home. So, they discharged him from Robinson Hospital."

"I'm coming immediately."

There is no answer at Charlene's.

White pillars swim and dissolve in his sight as he drives out of The Ranch.

Antie Annette appears at the front door. Hunched up older.

Choked sobs against his chest through the hands covering her face, "Twenty-five beautiful years gone by so quickly. He was glad that you and Charlene were back together. You are again the boy who grew up in front of him, he said. Last night, he still asked to phone you, but I was so busy nursing my old hubby that I clean forgot."

"Did Uncle Ig feel any pain?" The man who taught him to ignore pain by consciously taking mental control of one's own body.

"I don't believe so. He was full of morphine."

"Tell me if there is something I can do. I'm just a few minutes away."

"Thanks. Sandra and her husband are on their way from their farm near Koster. You taking over the gym is already a big help." He doesn't feel like running into Sandra now and is in a hurry when his coffee cup is just empty. He has enough on his mind.

"Bye, Annette. I'll phone tomorrow for further arrangements." He cannot imagine the words Uncle Ig and funeral in one sentence.

The BMW crawls into The Ranch. He phones immediately.

"Hallo, Charlene speaking."

"You okay?"

"Perfectly fine. You sound down?"

"Uncle Ig is dead."

"Oh, no-o-o-o," it quivers out of the receiver. "When?"

"This morning at their home."

"I'm phoning my head of department—taking a few days' leave to be with you."

"I'll come and fetch you this afternoon."

"The funeral?"

"I'll ask Annette tomorrow."

"Okay, I'll pack in my funeral clothes as well."

Annette's tragic news earlier today gets another hammer stroke: Uncle Ig and the funeral in one conversation deeply drives home reality to Eddie. People say death is a part of life, and it is, but the day you feel it close, the finality is shattering. The end of life. A great life. You, Ignasius Bester.

He pulls a tissue from the Kleenex carton next to the telephone. His thumb and index finger press it in the corners of his eyes.

*****

The last time he was in this NG church, the congregation said goodbye to their doctor reverend. He is called up to a higher service as a National Party candidate in a political election, as he phrased it in his farewell speech at the time. Till today, Eddie could not picture politics of more importance than people's souls.

In the entrance hall, Eddie hesitates. There are seats open in one of the side pews, almost right in front. Charlene's hand tightens around his. They proceed down the aisle and then shuffle past knees—faces around him like a showcase of memorabilia.

A rustling noise becomes audible from the rear of the church. They also stand up and look backwards. Sybrand greets with a nod. In the back row, Chris Rossouw stands alone. The coffin rolls noiselessly down the aisle. In the first row, Annette and Sandra are wiping their tears.

With both eyes fixed on the coffin, Eddie's thoughts wander out of context with the reverend's meditation. Live forever, Uncle Ig. After the meditation, he and five other pallbearers go forward.

Uncle Ig's wish is to be cremated.

Coffee is served in the church hall. He swells with pride next to Charlene while he and Sybrand relive his boxing career with the late Uncle Ig when someone approaches.

"Morning, will you introduce me?"

"Hallo, Chris. Meet Charlene, my fiancée. How are you?"

"I am well. Congratulations to both of you. Hello and goodbye, actually— still have a few things to do today."

Like stealing someone else's wife? Eddie feels Charlene's arm softly around his waist, "We had better leave too, so the family could have some intimate time together."

"Life is so precious. You realise it intensely when you see how easily it comes to an end. Everything feels possible while the person is still alive," she chats on the way back to The Ranch, "then, all of a sudden, nothing…"

He feels her fingers around his wrist. What a relief not having to face the road back to The Ranch alone today.

Sixty

DNA

Monday morning, on his way back from Eldoraigne, the bottle-green 404 Peugeot station wagon awaits, parked in front of The Ranch entrance. He presses the remote-control button and drives inside, the Peugeot as if in tow.

Wooden cross and string of beads swaying, the lithe figure ambles towards him. The right hand lifts in a greeting as Eddie leaves his garage. Should he chase him off his property straight away? It's unlawful entry. Trespassing; but then again, he did open the security gate, albeit for himself.

Shoulders pulled back. A deep breath. He takes a determined first step towards the priest. "Peace be with you, Mister Blignaut." The hand moves from the forehead to the solar plexus, to his heart, and then to the right. From behind the car, Lethabo lifts a hand on the driver's side, "Good morning."

"Do you have a moment, Mister Blignaut?"

"Only for you, reverend. Come in." His glare convinces Lethabo back into the car.

In the entrance hall, "I stand in the service of God and His church. Before Him, we're all equal, and He loves all of us equally."

"Why are you preaching to me? I'm not in your church?"

"Sir, you fathered a son, who is becoming a man. It is only fair that he meets his father, don't you think?"

"How do I know that he is not another guy's son?"

"Here, take this." An envelope emerges from the inside pocket of his robe. "You asked for photographs. It took a while to receive it from Holy Cross Sisters Orphanage in Parow Valley."

Eddie takes the envelope. Does the reverend see his hand trembling? Now he must gain ground, "What's this Lethabo fellow's thing about blood tests? If you plan to blackmail me, think twice. I'll sue you both."

"After Stephina's death, Baragwanath Hospital called me to have her belongings collected. She gave my name as next of kin upon admission. Lethabo went to collect at the hospital and came upon Stephina's written confession, folded into her Bible. Unfortunately, he first spoke to his doctor-friend who visits patients at the sanatorium, where I serve Mass on Sundays. Afterwards, he shared Stephina's confession with me as well. I apologise on behalf of the Roman Catholic Church."

Eddie takes a photograph from the envelope. Anxiety overwhelms him, "Excuse me, reverend Patrick."

The fresh air outside on the patio brings no relief.

Another photograph. Oh, you bastard, no—broad chin, high cheekbones, nose flatter than his own, protruding ears like seashells; even though today Eddie's own right ear is a cauliflower intergrowth compared to when he was a teenager. Copper-coloured skin, Stephina's big, soft eyes. Brown frizzy hair; the colour of ripe wheat.

He rushes past the priest, "Excuse me, again." In the snooker room, he holds up the photograph next to photographs of himself from his amateur boxing days. Holds his hand over the top part of the photograph. Does the same with one of his own. Cold sweat trickles down between his shoulder blades. The priest's voice jerks him back to the present moment, "There are more photographs, Mister Blignaut."

"I don't need more photos. Can I keep this?"

"It's yours."

"I need time, reverend. What's your telephone number, please?" A pen comes from inside the robe and Eddie holds out the envelope with photos.

"7-6-3-1-9-8-4, my home number where you can reach me in the evenings."

"Thank you, dominee. Goodbye for now."

He can't put off telling Charlene any longer. His heart misses a beat at the realisation as if his blood pressure were spiralling downwards. They have moved so much closer to one another over the last few months and up to now, the small challenges on their life path have come from outside their relationship. This time, it's right in between them, originating from his DNA which now is also inside her.

His next Rubicon feels daunting. How could he do this to her?

Sixty-One

Brown

It is still morning darkness. Last night, he didn't sleep for a second. Every time he closes his eyes, images of the boy fill his mind. On his toes, he slips out to the snooker room. The pregnancy tires Charlene out—she needs sleep.

In the drawer, under some newspaper clippings of his boxing career, he feels the thickish envelope. In every photo of the boy, he finds a feature shared with himself. Memories slowly surface about the day he arrived at his parents' house on a seven-day army pass. Damn, how could his sex drive overwhelm him like that?

"Morning, my angel," triggers a lightning bolt in his chest; the envelope dropping on the snooker table, spilling photographs out like playing cards—but, not a good hand. He turns to Charlene.

"What are you looking at? Photos of the lorry accident?"

It's now or never. "Come, I'll make us coffee and tell you." Their eyes meet. Her lips feel soft on his; the taste of sleep still lingering in her mouth. A warmth welcomes his hand under her gown, where their new life is starting.

He takes two cups out of the cupboard. The kettle whistles and he pours.

"Oops no," she holds a hand over her nose. "The smell makes me feel nauseous. Just a glass of water for me."

"Fine, then it's two coffees for me for my long story about my child."

"Remember, only in three weeks' time I'll be pregnant three months. After that, we can talk with certainty about our child."

"Charlene, I have a child."

"I believe everything will turn out well. Oh, I'm starting to get really broody. Daddy-champ, just think."

"My love, I am already a dad."

"What do you mean?"

"Father of a child. Like that."

"A child?" Without make-up, her complexion is very light. Now, she turns almost transparent.

"Yes, a child."

"Why didn't you tell me?" She prepares to get up. The last few weeks, she's been telling how well her husband's life had been insured. Financially, she can survive very well on her own and care for a child too.

"I only recently found out myself."

Her chair is shoved in under the kitchen table. He tries to come closer to her, but icy blue eyes nail him to the spot. "Eddie, how long have we been dating one another? Five months, going for six. Now I want to know all about the skeletons from your past."

"Well, the child—"

"Not the child, Eddie. Who's the mother?"

"She's dead."

"And now her baby is on its way to us? I thought you were talking about our child—look where we're going now. No, please no. Wake me up when this nightmare is over."

"It's not a baby, Charlene. He's almost sixteen."

Gown sleeves blot away her tears, forehead frowning, deep groove between her eyebrows, "How could you not have known?"

"His mother didn't tell me."

"Didn't you see her again, after…you were together?"

"Never again."

"So, a one-night stand?"

Words choke out like giving birth, "The child is brown."

In a panic, as though caught in a snare, she pulls at the panels of the gown, "So, the child's mother is—"

"Stephina. Our previous housemaid Mabel's daughter."

Arms drop next to her sides, dejected, "How? When?"

"When I had my seven days…"

Charlene, cowering in the gown, reduces him to silence.

Their eyes meet, and then he loses her…rosy, pink blushing cheeks when she looks up again, "The week when I wasn't home for you?"

"It's what I did then—it's not what you didn't do."

Through an empty stare. "Who else knows?"

"The dominee from the Roman Church. Oh yes, and his sidekick."

"This is too much for me. Who can we talk to?"

"I thought of talking to you."

"Can't handle it alone. I'm already intimidated by all the attention from being with you. Your mother?"

"No. She's got enough shit with my dad."

"Suzette?"

"Definitely not. Krisjan will know immediately."

"Please, just for my sake?"

Charlene hasn't broken their engagement. If that's what she needs, he'll phone his sister.

"Okay. Krisjan is going to gloat over it. First, boxing was a sport for savages. Then horse-racing tempted people to gamble. In my imagination I already heard the NG church elder with his suspended sentence for manslaughter: Sexual intercourse across the colour line is against the Immorality Act."

Sixty-Two

Human Self

Late that afternoon, Suzette's red Volkswagen Golf draws a dusty line on the other side of the horse camps. He presses the security gate remote control and senses Charlene's fingers weaving into his own.

Around the coffee table, he reveals this morning's story to his sister as well.

Her index finger points to the television, "Everyone saw how the Super Bowl almost worships Eddie Blignaut. It's a disaster. What got into you? Okay, Stephina practically grew up with us, but couldn't you keep your hands off her? This story is not going to blow over anytime soon."

"Don't play the prude. Remember high school. Are you and Krisjan lily-white by any chance?" Is she blushing or seething?

"Listen, big brother, a child is going to appear on the scene. Either we face your issue, or we dig up years of family shit, pronto."

Charlene's pinch of his hand stings like a bee. "Okay, we face my issue."

"Are you sure, it's your child? Nowadays, one can determine with blood tests—"

"I have no doubt."

"What are you going to do?"

He motions in the direction of Randfontein. "Enrol him for a trade apprenticeship—at the Technical College next to Jan Viljoen High School."

Charlene suddenly sounds distant, "Non-whites can enrol anywhere nowadays."

In his mind's eye, appears the priest's eyes…It would only be fair that he meets his father, don't you think?

"Maybe, he can stay here—to get to know one another?"

"Where? That spare room is for our baby—" Charlene gestures down the passage.

"He was abandoned once in his life; not again." Eddie finds his back grown tall.

"Klaas and Mpho's room is empty," Charlene's open hand now gestures towards the servants' quarters behind the stables.

How can he blame her? "The Roman Church dominee wants the child to come to Randfontein for the coming winter school holiday."

Her jaw drops, "In a week's time?"

"Why did you ask me to come?" Suzette's attempt at being a lightning rod.

"Suzette, around here I can handle it." Open hands cover Charlene's face. "It's how South Africa will react to the news that scares me. I want to run away."

Her moving up closer to him in a cuddly way gives him courage, "Ladies, can we decide about the next step?"

"For me, there is no decision to be taken. You don't know the child. He's made it up to here on his own—he can also go it alone for the rest of his life. At sixteen the law allows people to work. He can as well."

His eardrums are abuzz; Suzette's salvo brings déjà vu from his own vulnerable exposure to life as a teenager. Trying to compensate the boy for his father's dereliction of duty, alas, it is too late to make reparations. Now, he wants to be there when the challenges of adult life stare his son in the face.

"Here you are, you and Charlene," Suzette interrupts his train of thought. "You are starting your own family and don't need such shit. I must go. Krisjan was already suspicious because you wanted to see me alone. When I get home, he's bound to interrogate me."

Charlene appears overwhelmed by dread—waxen as she leans forward awkwardly. "And if the news leaks out?"

"My love, the world does not own me. They supported me. I entertained them. Now, I am my own, human self: Eddie Blignaut."

When they get to the car, Suzette hugs Charlene against her, "In a few months' time, you'll be a mommy. I'll phone you soon and then we'll organise your stork tea."

She pulls away—and then the red Golf stops again. Leaning out from the window, "Maybe you should tell Mom before she hears it from someone else in town."

Heaven forbid, Randgate chatterboxes will love this one, most of all, Bertus du Plessis.

Sixty-Three

Segregation

He conducted interviews with the world press about his boxing career, answered thorny questions about his private life and gave his view about the South African domestic political aberration. Now his tongue bobs up and down like a cork on water while he recites aloud how to communicate the news about his child, himself, and Stephina to his mom.

It feels like self-arrest when he gets out in her driveway, the revisiting of his own crime scene.

In the sitting room, he chooses the chair in front of the window where the lace curtain billows in the breeze. Through the security gate, he catches a glimpse of fern shoots on the front veranda, swaying like giant fingers.

"Mom, I have something to tell you. It's that I have a child."

"How wonderful that our little Charlene's pregnancy is going well." She spoons the lemon wedge out of her tea, sucks on it and smiles with eyes closed, her mouth skew as though from pure enjoyment.

"Mom, it's a son."

"Wonderful." She gets up from the sofa and limps to her trousseau chest, "Here are a few sets of blue baby clothes I knitted for neighbour Amelia's pregnancy—and then she miscarried. The yellow sets, I gave to our housemaid, a long time ago, when little Stephina told me she was pregnant. Blacks don't worry about colour, you know." Bent halfway over the open chest, she rummages for something almost right at the bottom.

"Mommy, listen to me."

Dusk falls over the sitting room. "Babsie l-o-v-e, hello, my love-bug," a voice singsongs.

Mom freezes above the chest. Her eyes wildly opened and stared across her shoulder at the front door, the small lemon rind like a limp cigarette between her lips.

He reclines at an angle in his chair to get a better view of the front door. A potbelly presses against the bars of the security gate.

"Afternoon, Sergeant."

"Crikey, Eddie, what a surprise. Didn't see you were here."

As if in a trance, lemon rind between her lips, Mom moves to the gate. The bunch of keys comes out of her skirt pocket, "Afternoon, Albertus, come in."

"Don't want to disturb."

To Eddie, his confession feels easier—Sergeant knows about his shame, after all.

He enters, puts a small cage with two white fantail pigeons on the coffee table and aims for the sofa. He seems very much at home next to Mom with his legs crossed and hands comfortably folded over his stomach.

Wind rustles through the lace curtain, "I'm just telling Mom that I have a child."

"A boy." She enjoys a sip of tea, her eyes shining and humid across the rim of the cup, "A little boy."

"Mommy, what I'm trying to say is my child is sixteen years old."

Tea splashes on her skirt. She motions to wipe it off but stares petrified at the small wet stain.

"U-hum," a throat is cleared next to her.

"It's a brown child, Mom." He feels dizzy, half-winded, "Stephina's child."

Confused eyes look at him, turn to Sergeant and back to him, her mouth moving without a sound.

How could he have deceived his mother?

"It's okay, Babs," Sergeant Bert's tone of voice sounds like that of a movie hero telling the heroine that he loves her.

"But, Eduard…oh dear, why didn't you ever tell me?"

"If I had known, I would have told you, Mom. Promise."

"How could you not know?"

"She never told me."

"So, how did you find out now?" Perplexed, she nibbles away on the lemon rind.

Bert lifts himself up, his head somewhat askance.

Everything Eddie says now, Bertus knows by this afternoon. "The dominee of the Roman Church told me. The child turns sixteen soon and then he can't stay in the church orphanage anymore."

"But can't we go and visit the boy there?"

"It's down in the Cape Province, Ma."

"Stephina will surely—"

"Ma, she's dead."

"Oh, dear oh dear. The poor child."

The man next to Mom speaks softly, "So, what are you going to do with the piccaninny?"

"The Roman Catholic guy is organising for me to meet him."

"Surely not to stay with you?" The last of the lemon rind disappears in her mouth.

"I'm still deciding. I mean, we're still deciding."

"You and the pastor?"

"Me and Charlene. I'll keep Mom posted."

He's suddenly in a hurry to leave—the retired sergeant certainly did not come over to see him. He says goodbye, somewhat consoled by the fact that he's not leaving Mom behind alone to deal with his load of emotional baggage.

It's hallucinating, all the thoughts churning in his pressure cooker head: Sergeant Bert knew about him and Stephina all along, and now Mom as well, and he himself knows about her and the sergeant. Damn, he must give vent to his emotions or blood will spurt out of his ears.

On his way to The Ranch, he picks up mail at the post office. Eagerly, he opens the envelope with Klaas' handwriting: His and Mpho's room is finished in Ga-Rankuwa. With Eddie's financial support, they even managed a bathroom with a ride-in shower for the wheelchair and in their room a ramp next to the bed. He can almost hear Klaas' voice, reading the last sentence: I sleep well now.

Amongst the other envelopes, also one with the Smit & Kruger emblem. He quickly reads it. As he drives past, his eye catches the For Sale sign on the wrought iron garden gate of Annette's house.

He feels sadly relieved: he doesn't have to reveal the news to Uncle Ig about his brown son out of wedlock, making him a criminal under his split country's racial segregation laws.

Sixty-Four

Acquittal

On arrival at The Ranch, he jumps out of the car, in a hurry to tell Charlene about his visit. She is nowhere to be found—sitting room, baby room, kitchen? He sneaks into the bedroom on his toes. Her breathing has a peaceful rhythm, arms are folded tightly around a pillow.

The anxiety about whether her pregnancy will be successful this time tires her out emotionally; she told him when their weekend started. Still, she supports him heart and soul during his litigation on the cause of the truck accident. That must burden her even more. He tiptoes back to the kitchen. Sifts through the mail.

Lukas' invoice is accompanied by a note: The summonses of Mister Bertus du Plessis and Mister Wessel Vermeulen are ready and waiting. Eddie, please come and see me. Regards. Lukas. He phones and is put through to his lawyer. "Hello, Eddie, everything is ready and waiting. That little du Plessis and his Vermeulen boyfriend are going straight to jail for malicious damage to private property with the intention of inflicting serious injuries. Every piece of evidence fits: they signed in at access control to the Randjesfontein training course, the registration number of Vermeulen's Ford Granada and his false statement as Dr Vermeulen, vet. From the register, it is evident that they were there a few times before—always in the early morning. Come and see me. If you're okay with the contents, I'll instruct the messenger of the court to deliver the summons at their little nest in Squirrel Avenue."

"Lukas, drop the case."

"What? I mean, excuse me?"

"Drop...the...case."

"Eddie, what's eating you? Our case is watertight. Detailed forensic investigation shows that the nuts on the wheels had been loosened halfway and third-party insurance and licence disks had been scratched off the windshield. They're ipso facto turning Eddie the millionaire into Dick, Tom or Harry. Listen to what I'm saying, they're going to jail. The judge might even rule it as attempted murder because of what happened to Klaas. It is dolus eventualis—they knew well enough what could be the outcome of their acts."

"It's over. I'm sending you a cheque for your last invoice. Close my file. Thank you for your service, this time. Goodbye, Lukas." The receiver clicks as it is put down.

Her voice sounds sleepy behind him, "What's wrong?"

"Oh, nothing."

"Doesn't sound like nothing. You're upset?"

"I'm terminating litigation about the truck accident. I'm certainly not going to spoil my mother's pleasure in life."

Deep grooves form between her eyebrows, "What do you mean? What does your mother's pleasure in life have to do with the accident?"

"It's very simple…" One step and he is next to her, the delicate tenderness of her shoulders under his hands, "…and very complex." He didn't want to burden her with his issues, but Charlene was his only confidante. His revelation about Bertus' complicity in the sabotage of Gert's lorry makes her back away in horror. "But, he grew up with us?"

With his hand gently around her upper arm, he talks about Sergeant Bert's visit to his mother. His grip tightens somewhat when she pulls back, shaking her head. "What does your mother see in him?"

"It's her choice…she deserves some pleasure in life after the hell she had to go through with my father."

"So, are you single-handedly trading your mother's pleasure for Bertus' acquittal as a criminal?"

"Yes. But, there is more to it than what Bertus did—"

"What else is there?"

"In 1976, Sergeant Bert tore a page out of the police office charge book and hid it in his briefcase. Hadn't he done it, I would have been a criminal today; my life ruined under the Immorality Act 21 of 1950."

Seconds drag past. As if, at last, she has made her decision, an arm nuzzles around the lower part of his body. The bump around her navel presses against his own. "I understand. Come, you deserve an afternoon nap."

Sixty-Five
Ruben, 1992

Ruben

The priest's tale has his mood swinging pendulum between heart and head. How is he going to solve this thorny problem? Tonight, rational thoughts get the upper hand: new information will come to the attention of the Roman Catholic Church. Something factual, which will unequivocally indicate that the boy in the Cape is the child of another white man. Certainly not of Eddie Blignaut. He phones.

"Fitzgerald speaking,"

"Hello, Father Patrick. Eddie Blignaut here. Do you have news?"

"How are you, Mister Blignaut? I was wondering whether I should maybe call you. Ruben will arrive at my house in a few days' time."

"I want to meet him, please. Where can we do it?"

"Here, at my house?"

"No, I don't agree." People gossip even more in church congregations than they do in Randgate. "Can you suggest another place? Somewhere out of public sight?"

"I visit members of my congregation at the sanatorium twice a week. There is a small chapel where you and Ruben can meet."

The thought of that place gives him the creeps. Though, the priest is right. Nobody from town ever goes there. He'll look past the surroundings and all the sick people. "Okay, that's good. Please call me for a time when you are ready."

"I'll talk to Ruben first. When he's ready, I'll call you. Keep well, Mister Blignaut."

"Goodbye, Dominee."

At the kitchen table, Charlene pages through a baby magazine. He pulls out the chair next to her. "Sorry that I am putting you through all this mess."

"I understand better now, my love. Everything happened long ago, more than sixteen years. Sometimes, we want to turn back time, but life happens now. We're living in the moment and for our future."

"My feeling is that I first see the boy on my own. Then we'll decide where to from there. What do you think?"

"I agree. Look at this pretty baby room. The cradle is like a nest. Just imagine a little face on that small cushion. Come and look at the curtains I have been making this morning. You can help me to hang them."

*****

A strange excitement fills him on the way to his garage. Back, at the front door, Charlene's face is screwed up against the morning winter sun. He blows a kiss. She makes a heart shape with her hands in front of her stomach. His gives a churn; unknown territory awaits at the sanatorium.

Just before nine, he switches off his car next to the bottle-green 404 Peugeot, his stomach muscles feeling tied in a knot. He gets out of the car, leather jacket zipped up high. In the gaping entrance, his breath forms a misty cloud as he hesitates for a moment and looks around; doesn't want to explain to anyone what he is doing here.

Father Patrick appears under the Mother Mary statuette. Eddie walks towards him with determined strides, while trying to focus on the interior behind the priest, but the robe blocks his sight. A bony hand takes his own, "Greetings, in the name of God."

Adrenaline pumps, his head throbbing. A mere whisper, "Morning, Father. Is he here?"

"Ruben is waiting for you in the chapel."

Even softer, "Did you tell him who I am?"

"He knows you're Mister Blignaut and you want to talk to him about his future. It's the premise for his trip to the Transvaal, I told the orphanage in Parow Valley."

The robe and the cross sway compellingly into the dusk where candle flames light up bronze work at the little altar. Eddie follows with calculated steps, navigating between free-standing chairs.

A ray of sunshine from the rose window in the roof ridge of the chapel reddens the head of frizzy brown hair, the colour of ripe wheat, in the front row. Last steps.

The cross is enfolded between Patrick's hands, "Ruben, Mister Blignaut is here."

The head of the hair rustles and a cheek becomes visible. A lash slowly blinks.

Last hope melts away in the heat of his emotions—the dominee certainly did not tell a tall tale. He puts out a hand. Fingers lock firmly around his own.

"I'm Eddie Blignaut."

"Morning Master, my name is Ruben."

"Hello, Ruben." Is the chapel resonating, or is his head making noises? His son's name over his own lips for the first time brings a flurry in his stomach. A hand comes to rest on his shoulder blade—the other one on Ruben's shoulder, "I'll leave you gentlemen alone. God bless."

The robe departs, floating noiselessly between the chairs, fills the door frame and disappears outside. Eyes flash over Eddie: up and down, to his left and then right. Mistrust or interest? Something in the boy's glance speaks of greater powers of observation than what Eddie would give a teenager credit for.

"How are you, Ruben?"

He wants to step back, but his hand is clutching Ruben's. Eddie lets go and sits down on one chair further away. The boy has one bent leg curled onto the chair, the foot hooked into the hollow of the other leg and hands open on his thighs. His Adam's apple glides up and down. "I am doing well, and the master?"

The Cape Afrikaans accent is a reminder of the SABC evening news every year when, for the Second New Year, there are reports about the Cape Minstrel Carnival and people like Ruben get the chance to say why the carnival is so important in their culture. That is all he knows about Ruben's world.

Embarrassment overwhelms him, "Call me Eddie."

"Okay, Master Eddie."

"Where do you go to school?"

"In the Cape."

"Where in the Cape?"

"Elsies, Master. I mean: Master Eddie."

"And where do you live?"

"Holy Cross Orphanage."

"I've never been to the Cape. What does it look like there?"

"Pretty. There's a mountain." Big hands move horizontally in front of him, then arms stretch out and fingers spread. "And the sea Everything in the Cape is beautiful."

"What is it like in the orphanage?"

"I've got my bed, my cupboard, my locker, my desk in the hall where we do our homework—the same place where I sit when we eat and where I stand when we pray."

"What does your room look like?"

"Nah, Master Eddie, I don't have a room." A broad smile spreads across his face. "We're about ten guys together in a big room."

"Sounds like my barracks in the army. Thirty packed like sardines next to one another."

"We're packed one on top of the other. I've got a bed on top—'cos I'm a boeta. Laaities sleep on the bottom bed, 'cos some still piss in bed, then it drips through the mattress."

"What do you mean by boeta?"

"We fight it out amongst us men, Master Eddie. You can challenge a boeta if you want his bed."

"Fight it out?"

"You challenge him with a smack to the forehead. Then he knows and everyone goes behind the lavvies to form a circle. The challenger must get the boeta on his back for three counts to also become a boeta and get his bed."

"Knock him out?"

"Na-a-h, Master, we ain't so brutal. We wrestle one another. With a fist, you can really hurt a man, like Moses did to that Egyptian." His thumbnail pulls across his throat. "I defend my bed on top until Christmas when I leave."

"Where to?"

"To catch snoek." He bends down from his chair, as though his hands were pulling a fishing line from the chapel floor, "David's uncle has a boat. He says the two of us can get a job with his uncle."

All finfeet, people from the Cape. "Who's David?'

"My chommie." He rubs over the scar on his left hand, "He got other siblings too, but they're from another mother. So, we mixed our blood. Now we're blood brothers."

"So, David is not in the orphanage?"

"He is, Master…Eddie. After David's mom died, his dad got married again to a dakskroef, a real witch Antie. So, he ran away from home a few times and ended up in the Holy Cross. I'm hungry now."

"There's a roadhouse in town. You feel like a hamburger?"

"Lekka. What for a thing is a roadhouse?"

"Come, I'll show you."

In the courtyard, they run into Father Patrick. "Reverend, can I bring you a burger?"

"Yes, please, and may I have a Coke as well?"

"You've got it."

Sixty-Six

Out of Sync

Eddie follows deserted back roads between mine dumps and then takes shelter in the furthest corner, right at the back of the parking lot of Uncle Harry's Roadhouse. He flips down both sun visors and flashes his car's lights for the waiter.

Ruben makes quick work of his hamburger.

On a full stomach, the news may be better received. "Do you know who I am?"

"Nah, dunno. But can I get another milkshake, please?" He is completely out of sync with Ruben. Boxing is not popular amongst the coloured population; thus, understandably he doesn't even recognise his father's public figure, "For sure, you can get another milkshake." As soon as Ruben has quenched his thirst, he'll introduce himself. Maybe that's all he can hope for today. A draw has never looked this attractive, another toggle of the light switch. The waiter arrives at a trot and waits at his window. "Takeaway hamburger, two Cokes and another chocolate milkshake to take away, please. And the bill."

Father Patrick's robe throws a flapping shadow on the courtyard where he stands waiting. Eddie takes his own Coke out of the brown paper bag, "Can we finish our talk in the chapel, please, Father?"

"Thank you for the lunch." His other arm motions open-handed to the Mother Mary statuette, "Certainly."

A gurgling sound as Ruben's milkshake reaches the bottom of the paper goblet. Choose words wisely now. "What do you think about coming to stay with me when you finish school?"

"Where does Master Eddie stay?"

"Just outside Randfontein."

"Around here is no real mountain; just a lot of mine dumps also, no sea here. And just feel the bite of your cold." The fingers of one hand snap at the other.

"I can't stay here, ever." Ouch. What does he say after such a direct hit?

"Ruben, you can start learning a trade here next year, carpenter or mechanic. Think about it?"

"About what, Master Eddie?"

"About staying here with me."

"I can't even get that thought into my mind."

Fingers play over the scar on his hand. "The Cape is under my skin, in my blood."

Losing on points seems to be the most probable outcome now. "You still here for a few days?"

"I'm visiting Father Patrick until Friday. That same evening, I take the sleepover train to the Cape." Another broad smile breaks.

"Can we talk again before you go back?" First a council meeting with Charlene.

"We can."

Back on The Ranch, "Hell, the cocky little guy has a will of his own."

Charlene listens, eyes closed.

"In the Cape, he's got next to nothing, but he absolutely wants to go back."

"He's got David," she whispers.

Is that her alibi, maybe, to cut his son out of their lives? "Here, he has a father."

"Put yourself in his shoes. His life journey has taught him to paddle his own canoe." On Friday, he'll make his comeback. "I see him again on Friday morning. Will offer him pocket money if he does a trade here."

"Friday morning? It's my three-month appointment with Cindy. Have you forgotten?"

"Jeez, I didn't forget…didn't remember either. Friday evening, he could be gone—maybe forever?"

"I'll tell you what…" She comes a step closer, and hands gently grasp his wrists. "Your mother works the night shift, right? Let's ask her to come with me to see Cindy after she comes off duty?"

Her eyes lock with his, "You're a wife in a million."

Sixty-Seven

Liberation

The sun lights up Ruben's head of hair in a uniform crown at the entrance to the sanatorium. "Morning, Master Eddie," sounds through the chilly air.

Fatherly pride pumps water to his humid eyes. His hand lifts past Ruben's and hugs him tight. "What new, Master?" Another hug.

"Mathter Eddie?" Through lips pressed askew against his chest.

Careful now. Horrible rumours did the rounds recently about alleged sexual malpractices with boys in the Roman Catholic Church. Was Ruben spared that? He lets him go, "Morning, Ruben."

"Father Patrick asks that you and I talk in the office—he is doing Mass in the chapel for a patient who looks like she wants to go to heaven today still."

Eddie remains standing in the office. He touches nothing. Everything feels contaminated by tuberculosis.

Ruben turns a chair back to the front and sits with his chin on his arms crossed on the chair's back. Maybe he's wondering about the smile growing in the corners of Eddie's mouth. He will tell him later that his grandfather Dawid sat in the exact same way and got a kick on his shin from Grandma Babsie when he dozed off in company.

"What is your decision?"

"About what?"

Eddie tries to look relaxed and almost catches himself leaning back against the wall cupboard, "About coming to live with me."

"Not a chance. Oorlat that one I answered the other day."

"I'll give you pocket money every month if you do a trade."

A sly glance with one eyebrow and cheek lifted comes across the back of the chair, "How much?"

He has Ruben's attention. "How much do you make as a fisherman?"

"David's uncle says fifty cents for a snoek. Some days, a man can catch as many as ten. That makes five rand a day, six days a week, and four weeks a month. Easy peezy."

Eddie does mental arithmetic. "I'll give you a hundred and fifty rand a month if you do a trade. Mechanic is a good trade."

"Thanks. I take that money." Wonderful.

"But I'm going to fish snoek—in the Cape, it's a trade."

If he gives Ruben money every month, he keeps contact. Perhaps all that a cast-off dad is entitled to?

"We'll do it, Ruben. Fishing for snoek is a trade."

His son flies out of the chair with open arms. The embrace feels precious. "When is your birthday?" That a father must know, shouldn't he? "Fourteen December, every year."

A soldier never forgets his passing-out date. He was Naafi, as they said then. Sluggish and reluctant to go back to Randgate that day, while Stephina was struggling through birth pains with his child.

"So, you were thirteen when you went to the Cape?"

"You say it like it is. When I was thirteen, I came to Holy Cross Orphanage."

Sounds as though the place is his anchor in the Cape. And chommie David. He follows Ruben's eyes and hands and listens to him talking about gangs in his school who wage a reign of terror and blackmail children to steal from their parents' houses—money, watches, portable radios, tools, anything that could be of value in a pawnshop. Everyone gets a quota per week. Friday, at morning break, the gang leader takes stock. For those who are short on their quota: This agtemirrag we cut your wrists, so you die slowly. Hesitantly—from half behind Ruben's hand: Or, after school, we all screw your little sister. Eddie winces at the thought as Ruben presses his lips together decidedly, "Jassas, when the bell rings to go home, the stuff is there. Pillowcases full of it."

"Do the gangs threaten you too?"

"Already in the first week of standard six. I walk to school from the orphanage, look for the road and don't know anything about Elsies Rivier. The next moment, I'm surrounded by knives all around." He lifts himself up out of the chair, fingers on either side of his ribcages stretched out horizontally, his eyes watchful.

Eddie feels urged to intervene, "And then?"

"No-o-o fear, I keep my eyes shut, pray as loud as I can that the Djirre punish these damn shitholes, so they all get leprosy, like those ten in the Bible and that their hands and feet rot off piece by piece. I peek a bit while I pray louder and louder, but haven't gotten to my Amen yet when I stood there all by myself on the pavement."

He sinks back satisfied onto his chair. His son holds his own in challenging circumstances. "Ruben, I would like to tell you who I am," Comes across more formally than he intended.

He smiles self-contentedly, chin lifting from his crossed arms, "I know. You are my sponsor. Hundred and fifty rand every month."

"I am your father, Ruben."

The head of hair shakes in the negative, "My mother told me I don't have a father." His shoulders pull up to just under his ears, "She said we don't know him."

"Did Stephina tell you that?"

"Yes, but...how does the master know my mother's name?"

"Because I am your father—every person has a father." He finds himself with outstretched hands towards the boy.

"Not allowed, 'cos you're a whitey then?" He rubs across his cheek. "My mother couldn't have been with you—not allowed. The boere catching her with a whitey and my mother gets time behind bars."

Should he call Father Patrick for support? Ruben believes him.

No—this is a matter for a blood father.

"You know how people make babies, don't you?"

"Patla-patla?" His index finger slips in and out of his fisted hand.

"I did it with your mother."

His eyes whisk searchingly through the office, his face unpleasantly contorted. He turns away coldly and darts a disgusted glance back. "You white piece of shit, if I can take you for the truth."

Eddie zips his leather jacket open halfway. He takes out the two photographs from the inside pocket and throws his last trump cards on the table: a photo of himself in standard nine and one of Ruben.

The moment between them hangs like a brick. Will Ruben recognise the resemblances between them? He holds out Ruben's photograph to him.

"That one, I know." The corners of his mouth pull down indifferently, "Same as the one in my file at the orphanage. I see it every Sunday when it's my turn to talk to Sister Sylvia in my counselling hour. We boetas call it the weekly heart bleed." His hands look as though he were holding an open book. "Must take my Bible with and read my favourite verses to her. It's always Psalm 23, where I keep the picture of my moeks with her message on the back."

"What message?"

"My son, read Psalm 23 every day and never forget to forgive and love, Mom."

Expectantly, he holds out his own photo to Ruben, lifting it up in the ray of sunlight. "Here I am about as old as you are now."

Ruben screws up his eye against the sunlight with a contemptuous look.

He holds up Ruben's photograph in the sunlight as well. "Ruben…what is the same in these photos?"

He rubs across his cheek, "I'm fokol of yours, fucking whitey." His head shakes, his mouth, incredulous, half open. "Where were you all my years, if you are my father?"

He feared the question, "Uuh …"

Ruben's index finger points right past his nose, "We stayed just over there, in Toekomsrus. Inna outside room of the Ross family where my mother cleaned house." Again, he rubs across his cheek, "We had to leave when my mother was too sick to work…" He storms forward and his open flat hand slams well-worn words from deep inside of his chest, "… or to bring me up!"

Eddie senses the wall cupboard pressing against his back—is Ruben's next flat hand meant for him? It must have been hell to grow up as a coloured orphan in a country like South Africa, and for the first time ever the question occurs to Eddie: How different would his own life have been, was he not born white?

"I hear my mother coughing in the night, from my mattress on the ground. The albino from the church takes her to Baragwanath Hospital, again. A few days later, just the cardboard box with my Bible and her other things came back." He bites his thumb and squeezes his eyes shut. "Father Patrick was with me that day. Told me I was an orphan now. One week later, I'm inna Cape."

"After my year in the army, I came back to our house in Randgate and your mother wasn't there anymore." Has Ruben gone deaf?

Outside, Father Patrick pushes a woman in a wheelchair out of the chapel.

"I want to speak to Father." Ruben rushes out of the office. "Father Patrick!"

The two of them disappear into the dusk of the chapel.

After an eternity, the priest comes out, his cross enfolded by praying hands. Moments later he stands in the office.

Drumbeats sound in Eddie's ears. Please, Lord.

A crumpled piece of paper is pulled out of Father Patrick's bosom, "I showed this to Ruben." Eddie recognises Stephina's handwriting from the half-torn charge book page he ripped from Bertus. He reads her confession, folds it up and holds it out to the priest.

"You may keep it. Ruben forgives you—like his mom did. He is waiting for you in the chapel."

Stephina forgives him. Ruben follows his mother's example. Dizziness overwhelms Eddie and feelings of endless gratitude wells up inside him. Liberation, it rather feels like, from more than the Immorality Act.

His time is running out. He doesn't feel ready to say goodbye, "Ruben, come and celebrate your sixteenth birthday on The Ranch."

"What for a place is that?"

"It's the estate where I stay with my fiancée. You'll like my place. We'll fly you up from the Cape."

"That's a nice idea. I'll hear what David's uncle says."

"Why?"

"My birthday is a busy time for fishing snoek. It's when the Cape is full of Valies. They come to buy snoek to switch a little from boerewors. But maybe I could convince David's uncle."

Sixty-Eight

My Son

With his hand around Ruben's shoulder, they walk towards Father Patrick, standing just outside the sanatorium entrance. The robe flaps in the light breeze. His bony topography was more prominent under the winter sun.

Eddie stiffens in the entrance and pulls Ruben into his warmth. In front of his eyes, everything swims and flows together—his silver BMW, the bottle-green Peugeot and the red Volkswagen Golf. He rubs the crook of his arm over his eyes. Charlene comes into focus: one hand on her navel, the other one shows a thumbs-up.

Father Patrick's right hand moves from his forehead to the cross on the string of beads, to his heart and then to the right.

Eddie focuses on the three approaching female figures. "This is my son, Ruben." With his other arm stretched out in front of him, "Ruben, this is my fiancée Charlene, my mother Babsie and my sister Suzette."

His hand slaps over his mouth. "Good morning, but how am I going to remember the names of all the madams?"

He walks up to them and shakes the hand of each woman.

The End

Everyone that you fight is not your enemy and everyone who helps you is not your friend.
—Mike Tyson